# SILVER VAMPIRE

Book One of the Silver Vampire Series

By
Carolyn Cami-Johnson

# Prologue

Centuries ago, vampires joined the human race, and now *Homo vapirus* walk among humans. Contrary to popular legend, when bloodthirsty, vampires can subsist on human *or* animal blood. For many years, vampires lived by farming their own animals or hunting. However, others subsisted on the blood from stolen farm animals or freshly dead bodies. These bodies were drained of blood, and the empty husk was left to rot. As a result, families of the victims were often unable to identify their loved ones. It was these vampires who started a war with humans.

When wars between humans were settled, attention turned to vampires. At the close of World War II, diplomats from multiple countries offered their services to the leaders of the vampire community and a truce was signed. This truce gave vampires some rights and opened the doors for migration to North America. Human governments have been slow to grant vampire civil rights and every victory has been hard won.

One of the consequences of this uneasy truce has been a reduction in the growth of the vampire population. Today vampires are at their lowest numbers ever.

# CHAPTER 1

*She looked at her companion, "I found a couple. Down there in South America."*

*He looked thoughtfully for a moment. "No, that's a little too far. Let's try closer. What do you think of this baby?"*

*Her features softened as she gazed into the distance. "Wait, she's in labor right now!" There was a short pause. "Her mother has a strong life force and she is a witch." She smiled.*

*"Yes, the father is a good man. He will take good care of the baby. We don't have much time." A beautiful ray of sunlight reached from the clouds and touched Christine's body. No one could see it, but they would soon feel its effect.*

"Come on Christine, just breathe…"

Christine Dailage looked over at her husband, Dave, wanting to both smile and growl at him. Her dark brown eyes flashed as Dave smoothed her dark curly hair from her face. This baby was coming so much faster than her first. Kaylee really wanted out, and right now.

The doctor looked up. "We are almost there. Just give me a really good push on the next contraction." The pain and pressure flooded Christine as she pushed. Kaylee's head emerged. Just over the doctor's shoulder she could see two figures watching the baby. One looked up at her, and she was struck with the knowledge that she would never see Kaylee grow up. She looked up at her husband while trying to catch her breath. She reached up and kissed him quickly before the next contraction filled her attention. In the next breath, Christine felt Kaylee slide from her body as she felt her life slip away. Her hand fell from Dave's grip.

"Christine? Don't go!" Dave shouted, "Stay with me…please." In a heartbeat, the nurses rushed him from the room. He stood in hall, nauseous and worried.

After what seems like ages, the doctor came out.

"We did everything we could. I am sorry; your wife didn't make it. But your baby is healthy."

He just stood there in shock—how could she die so quickly when she was so healthy? "We think she might have had a brain aneurism," the doctor continued. "But we just don't know..." Dave heard the doctor speaking, but it sounded so far away. He leaned against the wall and began sobbing as the news began to sink in.

After a few moments a nurse came up to him. She noticed how his blond surfer good looks were such a contrast to his wife's dark Italian ancestry. *Their baby is going to be gorgeous*, thought the nurse. She reached out to touch his arm. *It's such a shame that the mother died and she'll never see her baby girl.*

"I'm so sorry about your wife. We have some paperwork you need to fill out for your baby girl." She paused to let him collect himself. His sea blue eyes looked at her. "Do you have a name picked out for the baby?" she inquired.

Dave and Christine hadn't agreed on a name yet, but as soon as the nurse asked he knew the perfect one. "Christine wanted to call her Kaylee."

"That's a lovely name. I will begin the forms for her birth certificate and you can sign them a bit later, Okay?"

"Yeah, that's fine," he said with tears in his eyes.

The next day, Dave headed home with Kaylee in his four-door pick up. Dave turned off from Route 20 onto a rough dirt road. The road he followed passed by Rainbow Campground and a "No Trespassing" sign. The industrial garage that housed his business was just on the right. He continued down the road, filled with bumps and ruts, until he reached his own house. It was situated on three acres of land that were so peaceful and quiet you would never know you were less than 15 minutes from the heart of a city. The white house had a large front porch and, peeking through the spaces in the tall fence, revealed a deep pool in the backyard. Dave pulled into a detached garage just off to the side. He stepped into the house and his four-year-old daughter, Grace, ran up to him.

"This is your new baby sister, Kaylee," he explained.

"Wow," Grace said, "she's so small, just like a doll."

Ann Campbell and Mary Pierce, his wife's two best friends, chuckled at Grace's comments.

"Oh, beautiful baby Kaylee," said Mary.

Ann looked at Grace. "You'll have to take care of your baby sister and be a good girl."

"Yeah, my baby sister." Grace looked around and realized that her mom wasn't there with the baby. "Where's Mom? *Mom*?"

"Honey, she is no longer with us. She is in Heaven now," he gently reminded her. "We talked about this last night, remember?"

"Why did she have to go?"

"I want you to understand: even though we'll never see Mom again here on earth, we'll see her someday in Heaven."

Grace didn't understand. "Where is *Mom*!"

"Grace, she's gone—she died giving birth to your sister."

Grace looked at the baby and then at her dad. "Kaylee took my mom. It's *her* fault! I hate her!" She ran off to her room.

Dave looked at Ann and Mary. While all three were about the same age, they couldn't have been more different. Ann was average looking, she had short brown hair and eyes, was average height, and wore glasses. Mary, in contrast, had laughing green eyes and a full figure. She wore her dirty-blonde hair in a long braid down her back.

"Oh Dave, I'm so sorry," Ann said with tears flowing down her face. "Let's get this baby to bed; she's fallen asleep in your arms." Ann gently removed Kaylee from her father's arms and bustled off with the baby. Mary pulled him into a hug.

"Should I go after Grace?" he asked. Mary let him go.

"No, she needs to process her grief right now. Ann will check on her once the baby is in her crib. You and I need to talk for a few minutes."

She sat him down and put a plate of cookies in front of him. Her sure movements in the kitchen spoke of how much time she'd spent there. She quickly put the teakettle on and got mugs at the ready. Mary sat down across from Dave. Ann walked in and wiped the tears from her face with the back of one hand, she was holding a baby monitor in the other.

"They are both asleep." She sighed as she sat down, "Grace is going to need a lot of help to get through this. Me too, I think."

The kettle started to whistle and Mary hastily pulled it from the burner. She poured three mugs of tea and brought them to the table.

"I know this is a very difficult time. Christine's death is still very fresh, but we need to discuss a few things. You know that Christine was a very powerful witch in our coven." Dave nodded, looking unsure. Mary continued, "Christine was a highly skilled herbalist and had some potentially dangerous ingredients in her stores. Unless you are planning to take her place and become an herbalist, I think we should remove them."

"Uh, okay. I am not sure what you mean though. I am sure Christine wouldn't have had anything too dangerous on her with Grace around."

Ann put her hand over Dave's. "The ingredients wouldn't have been dangerous for Grace. Grace does not have the magic that Christine had, the magic that Kaylee may have now."

"What do you mean?" asked Dave, furrowing his brow.

"Kaylee may have inherited Christine's magic," stated Mary.

"But she's just a baby—how can you tell?"

Ann took a sip of tea. "Most witches have some magic, but we use our coven and potions to help focus or increase its power. Christine didn't need any of that. She was one of the most powerful magic users I've ever seen or heard of. On top of being a powerful user of magic, she understood herbs and potions like nobody's business."

"True," Mary continued, "she was a gifted witch and generous too. Usually there is a ceremony that a witch performs to pass on her power, but it is mostly symbolic. We are each born with or without some amount of magic. You, Dave, have no magic and Grace is like you. If a person has some magic, they can always learn to focus it or add to it with potions, but if they have none then that's it."

"So," Ann added, "even if Grace played with every potion or ate every ingredient in Christine's stores, not much would happen. But if Kaylee is a witch and she gets into them, they can give her powers willy-nilly. We won't know whether Kaylee has magic or how much for a while."

"Okay," Dave said, taking a deep breath. "Can you guys lock up anything in the storeroom that might be dangerous? Would that make it safe, just in case? Who would have thought that I'd have to childproof like this?"

Ann smiled, "Once Kaylee is older we can test to see her potential. Then we can decide what to do."

Over the baby monitor they heard Kaylee begin crying. "Looks like I am going to be busy for a while," Dave said, standing up.

"Do you want help?" asked Mary.

"No, I'd better get used to being a single parent. Can you guys lock up after you leave?" They nodded and watched Dave head to the nursery alone.

Between feeding, burping, changing, dance lessons, story times, and preschool, Dave was exhausted quickly. Weeks passed without him remembering what day of the week it was. Just as Kaylee was beginning to sleep through the night, Dave started to have nightmares about his wife's death. The moment he fell asleep, he'd wake up calling Christine's name.

One night, he woke up and went to the bathroom. Just as he was returning to bed, he heard a voice call, "Dave…Dave?"

"Grace, is that you?" he called softly. He turned around and saw Christine in her hospital gown standing outside the window on their second floor balcony. "Oh, God… Is that you, Christine?"

"The spirits draw me quickly. I came back because I need to tell you about our daughter. Kaylee will be an important person in the future. It is vital that she have access to my potions and storeroom."

Dave ran his fingers through his hair. "Why? Is she a witch too?"

"Kaylee has powerful magic, more than I ever imaged. Please keep this secret. Please take care of both of our girls."

"Of course I will. Oh God, I miss you…I wish you were with me."

Christine's image began to fade. "We will get together again someday, and we will watch over our girls forever. I love you. Goodbye."

Dave had tears streaming down his face. “I love you too … goodbye.”

With that, Christine smiled and faded away.

# CHAPTER 2

"What are you going to do in school today, Grace?" Dave asked as he prepared breakfast. He put bread in the toaster and opened the fridge, pulling out jam. With one hand he started the coffeemaker and with the other he grabbed plates. He looked out the window to see the first fall leaves turning red and gold. Grace and Kaylee sat at the kitchen table with crayons and paper spread out around them. Kaylee was scribbling while her sister was neatly following the outlines on her picture.

"Girls, it's time to put away the crayons and paper," Dave chided gently, stroking Grace's hair. "Let's get ready for breakfast so Grace can get to school." He looked down at the picture she was coloring and paused. It showed Kaylee, with her long hair and blue eyes, with sparkly stars coming from her fingertips and her teddy bear flying in the air. "Great picture, Grace. What is Kaylee doing here?" he asked, pointing to the bear.

"She's got superpowers, Dad," Grace responded with exasperation that foreshadowed her teen years. Grace had mentioned something about Kaylee having superpowers before, but he'd never seen her draw them.

"Hmm, I haven't seen them yet. Let me get your backpack ready for school, Okay?" He packed a snack and lunch into Grace's backpack, then started getting breakfast ready. Dave grabbed Kaylee and put her in her high chair. He went to the fridge, got milk, and poured it into a sippy cup. When he turned he found Kaylee standing next to him. She giggled at his expression and held out her hand for the cup.

Grace was excited. "See, Dad, I *told* you. Kaylee has superpowers."

Dave stared at Kaylee while she giggled. "Kaylee, get back in your high chair." *Can she control this*? He wondered. In a shower of silver sparkles, Kaylee appeared in her chair. Dave knew she has powers, but he had never expected them to manifest this early or this strong.

"Dad, did you see that?" Grace shouted. Kaylee was smiling, clearly proud of herself.

"Girls, this is very important, we must keep this a secret in our family. Don't tell anyone, Okay?" He gave Grace a serious look. She stopped smiling and looked back at him, the wheels turning. Kaylee started to cry.

Brown leaves swirled to the ground as Dave drove up the driveway. He was returning home from a successful deer hunt with a buck strapped to the hood of his truck. The babysitter was heading to the bathroom as the engine noise alerted the girls of his arrival. They were excited that Dad was home. Grace looked out of the window to see him. Kaylee was just a bit too short to see out the window. She used her powers to float above the floor so she could see him.

"You fly? How can you do that?" Grace asked Kaylee. Kaylee waved at Dave as he walked onto the porch. When he saw her floating he panicked and ran into the house, catching her just as the babysitter came out of the bathroom.

"Dad, how can she do that?" Grace insisted.

"Shhh. Take her to your room and I will be right up in couple of minutes," Dave whispered to Grace. Grace and Kaylee headed toward to Grace's bedroom and Dave paid the baby sitter. As she left he let out a sigh. *That was close*, he thought.

He walked into Grace's bedroom. She wasted no time and began peppering him with questions. "How can she do that? Why can't I fly? Do you have powers?" The way she was standing with her hands on her hips made her seem much more grown up than her years.

"No, sweetie, I don't have any superpowers but listen carefully: don't tell anyone that she has powers. This is our family secret."

"Why don't I have powers?"

"I know you're jealous. I wish I could fly too, but that isn't the way it works. Sometimes people have these secret powers and sometimes they don't. My parents didn't have them and so I don't. Your mom had some powers, but you didn't get them. It's just like you and I having the same color blue eyes and Kaylee not. She got your mom's brown eyes. But you have hair just like your mom. Her hair used to curl up when it rained, just like yours." He hoped this explanation would be enough, at least for now.

"I wish I had powers like her and Mom," Grace said with a pout.

Dave gathered Kaylee in his arms and looked her straight in the eye. "Don't show anyone you have powers and don't let anyone see you have powers, okay? Understand?"

*What your father says is true; you need to hide your powers for now,* Kaylee heard the soft voice in her head just as she always had.

****

*You need to take karate lessons*, said the voice. Dave was tucking both girls into bed. The snow was falling heavily outside their bedroom window and he put an extra blanket over each of them. Suddenly he paused.

"Kaylee, would you like to take karate lessons?" he asked. "I saw a flier today from the studio in town. They are starting a Little Tigers program for kids three and up."

"Yeah, Dad," Kaylee replied, "I want to take karate. My angel told me to go."

"Me too," said Grace.

"Perfect, I will look into signing you both up tomorrow," Dave said as he kissed them and tucked them in. "Kaylee, who was your angel?" he asked.

"The voice in my head. It talks to me," she answered sleepily. Dave stood behind her door and wondered, *How many powers does she have? Is this new, or is it just showing now? Could this angel just be an ordinary imaginary friend, or is it something more?*

The next afternoon, Dave brought Kaylee and Grace to sign up for karate lessons with Coach Kevin Douglas. He leaned down and whispered to Kaylee, "Promise me, no powers, please." She nodded seriously in her brand new tiny white karategi and ran into the classroom.

## CHAPTER 3

Kaylee came running into the house and dropped her schoolbooks on the counter. Her grade-five math book fell to the floor. She scooped it up and dumped it on the pile. She pulled out a thin silver chain from her backpack, put it on, and ran upstairs. In her room she upended a box on her dresser. Silver spilled out: silver bracelets, buttons, charms, and trinkets.

"What are you doing with all that stuff?" her sister asked as she came into their room.

"I like it. It makes me feel like I have a shield on," said Kaylee as she picked a charm to add to the necklace.

"It looks like junk that someone threw out," sneered Grace.

"Well, I like it," said Kaylee. She turned around and headed downstairs to do her homework.

As she sat at the dining room table, she could hear the television from the next room. A voice said:

"At first, death row inmates could gain privileges by allowing their blood to be drawn for use feeding vampires. Then many vampires discovered that animals could be used to supplement the drinkable blood supply. Animals are bled before slaughter in response to many animal rights activists' charge that it is cruel to use animals for blood and then discard the body...."

Dave walked into the dining room and pulled up a chair next to Kaylee. "I got your report card from school today. You got all As, and your teacher and I have been talking. The school and I think you are ready to skip the sixth grade and start seventh in September," he said with pride as he hugged her. Grace was just coming into the dining room, but she hesitated at the doorway listening. Dave went on, "You are very intelligent and have a very powerful gift. You are also very mature for your age, and I am truly proud of you. Come with me to the basement, I have something to show you."

Grace turned around and silently stomped up the stairs, tears fell down her pretty cheeks. Kaylee and Dad headed into the basement. He unlocked a padlock on a dark wooden door. Kaylee opened the door to shelves and shelves of potions and ingredients. The labels were faded, but feminine handwriting was still readable on them. A small wooden table took up the center of the room. There were boxes under the table and along the floor. He picked one box and opened it to show her that it contained even more ingredients and tools.

"Your mother would have wanted you to have these," he said.

Kaylee was curious. "Did you ever use them? Tell me: what is this?" She held up a bottle with tiny, pale purple flowers in it.

"Ah, I don't use them and I wouldn't know where to begin. I have no special powers, like you do, and I am not a witch, like your mother was. She was gifted."

Kaylee walked around the room humming softly, touching the bottles and jars, and opening them reverently to take a small sniff or a closer look. "Dad, can I use these things?"

"I am not sure you're entirely old enough, but they are yours. Why don't you do some research and see what you can discover before you start mixing things together, okay?"

"Sure, Dad, no problem. I've got that song contest to get ready for anyway." She walked over to him and put her arm through his. "I'm really not sure where to begin with witchcraft, but I do know where to begin a song."

****

Grace stomped up the stairs with her backpack, heading to her room. The damp air was curling her shoulder-length dark brown hair. A smile played across her pretty features. It was Friday and she had plans. She rummaged through her closet and tried on a dozen different outfits before finding just the right one. In front of the large oval mirror above her dresser she put on make-up and added perfume. She heard her dad arrive home and made a face in the mirror.

"Grace, are you home?" he shouted up the stairs.

She popped her head out the door and shouted back, "Yeah, I'm here. Be down in a minute!"

"Good, you are ready," Dave said when Grace finally came downstairs. "We can head out in about 15 minutes to Kaylee's singing contest. One of the other parents took her after school. Let's just grab a bite to eat."

"No, Dad, I already have plans. I'm going to the movies with my friends."

"Grace, your plans are hereby cancelled. We have to support your sister."

"You never let me be with my friends! It's always Kaylee this and Kaylee that!" Grace shouted.

"That's enough! You will go with me now, and that is final. You have plenty of time to be with your friends at school and you can see them tomorrow—that is, if you come with me tonight."

"Fine. I'll go." Grace crossed her arms over her chest and turned away.

# CHAPTER 4

Grace walked into the kitchen and slung her backpack down on the counter. As she opened the fridge her many bracelets jingled. Dave walked in and he raised an eyebrow at the short skirt she was wearing, but he bit his tongue.

"Got much homework?" he asked.

She looked at him though long, thickly made-up eyelashes. "Nope, I am just going to grab something to drink and then head over to Janine's."

"Be home by six. We have a family dinner tonight."

"Well, I'm not going to make it. Janine and I have plans to go out to hear a new band play in town."

"Either you agree to be home by six for dinner here or don't plan to go out at all!"

"You never let me do anything! I am going tonight!"

"Go up to your room!"

"Fine! But you can't make me be a part of this family!" Grace emphasized her words with a loud slam of her door. Her heavy footsteps could be heard all over the house. Finally a loud thump could be heard, indicating she had flung herself onto her bed.

Dave and Kaylee ate in silence; the third place at the table sat empty. After cleaning up the dishes, Kaylee headed up to her room to finish her homework. As she looked out the window overlooking the yard, she saw a single figure dashing across the moonlit grass. This was not the first time Kaylee had witnessed her sister fleeing across the yard. As Grace's graduation approached, the sight of this fleeing figure had become more common.

****

Dave made an effort to heal the rift between his oldest daughter and himself. "Hey Grace?" he asked over breakfast one morning. "What do think about having a graduation party out here? We could invite your friends, swim in the pool, hire a band, have a barbeque?"

"Thanks, Dad, that's wonderful!" Grace leapt up to hug her father and Kaylee grinned.

As the party approached, the three of them begin to feel like a real family. Kaylee was even planning to sing a few songs with the local band her dad had hired.

"Nervous about tonight?" asked Grace as she and Kaylee set up tables in the yard.

"Not exactly nervous—more like excited. This will be my biggest audience; usually it's just you and Dad." She grinned and grabbed a plastic tablecloth to spread out. Grace helped hold the plastic as they taped it down in the breeze. Soon other hands arrived to help with the set up, and then Dave came with the food. Quickly the yard became populated with teenagers laughing and talking about college in the fall and summer jobs starting soon. The band arrived and Kaylee was in her element, helping them set up and doing sound checks. As the sun began to set, the music started. Kaylee and the group planned for her to sing the first few songs and then take a break.

Kaylee approached the microphone almost shyly. "Grace, I am so proud of you. You've worked really hard these last few years, and I am so excited you are starting college in the fall. This song is for you, sis!" The evening air soon reverberated with the beat of the drums and Kaylee's strong voice as she sang to her sister. The kids looked at her and began shouting and dancing. Soon a smile spread over Kaylee's face.

Grace walked up to her dad, who was watching the party from a discrete distance. He wanted to hear Kaylee sing and just keep an eye on the party. So far no one was getting out of hand or spiking the punch. He expected the party would wrap up in a couple of hours so the kids could get to town for the fireworks and an all-night locked-in party the school was hosting.

"Kaylee really has a great voice," Grace said.

"Yes, she does. I knew she was writing you a song, but this was the first time I've heard it. She's going to miss you." Dave paused and looked at Grace. She was petite, had long curly hair, and a rebellious attitude. "You remind me so much of your mother; she was beautiful and strong like you. I am going to miss you when you go to college."

"Thanks…I'm going to miss you guys too."

"Okay, before we get too mushy here, go back to your party. The school party starts in about an hour and half, so have fun!" He coughed to cover the tears starting to form in his eyes.

Grace leaned over and kissed his cheek.

Over the next 90 minutes teens sang, danced, and ate a tremendous amount of food. Grace packed into the last car heading over to the senior party. Her dad and sister, standing side-by-side, waved to her. Grace looked up and waved back, grinning. This had been the best day of her life.

Dave leaned over and put an arm around Kaylee. "What do you say to a movie and some popcorn? I think there might be a stray can of soda around here, and maybe a popcorn kernel or two." They laughed.

"Sounds like a great plan, Dad. I'll stay here and clean up before it gets completely dark."

"Great. I'll go and rent us a movie from the Redbox."

Dave grabbed a few bags of trash and hauled them over to the garage. He figured he could take them to the dump tomorrow. He tooted the horn as he drove away and waved to Kaylee, who was putting soda cans in a blue bin.

Kaylee sighed as she looked around. Her sister's friends sure could make a mess. She started with the cans, since they went in a separate bin in the garage. Next she tackled the food trash. "Dad was right; there isn't much left!" she chuckled to herself. The darkness got thicker and she realized that Dad had been gone awhile. *Must have been a line at the Redbox*, she thought. After cleaning up the dishes and putting away the chairs, she began to tie the third bag of trash when a cold chill came over her. She closed her eyes and wrapped her arms around herself. A voice in her head said, *Your dad is dead.*

Her eyes flew open. "Nooo! Dad!" she cried. As she began to run down the driveway, the flashing lights of a police car greeted her. Her father had been killed by a drunk driver.

Grace and Kaylee were completely focused on the tasks at hand over the next few days. They had to arrange a funeral for their dad, and Grace was appointed to be Kaylee's guardian. Dave had been a careful man, and his insurance paid for their house. They buried their father next to their mother Christine.

The funeral was packed because Dave had been beloved in the community. Each of the guests greeted the girls, giving them condolences and offering help. Grace looked questioningly at Kaylee when she saw two women she didn't know. One was slightly plump with a long braid down her back. Her hair was a faded blonde color and her green eyes were sad. The other woman was medium—medium height, medium weight, with medium brown hair with gray streaks. Her glasses were perched on the end of her nose. Kaylee looked up and saw who her sister was indicating. A silent question passed between them: *do you know who that was?* Kaylee responded with a shrug of her shoulders and quick shake of her head.

The two unknown women waited until the other mourners had passed before approaching the young girls. Kaylee took a step back as they approached. Grace saw this out of the corner of her eye and wondered what Kaylee was sensing.

"We are so sorry for your loss," one of them said as she reached out her hands.

"Do I know you?" Grace replied cautiously.

Ann reached out her hand, but Kaylee didn't take it. "We knew your mother more than your father. This is Mary Pierce, and I am Ann Campbell. Wow, you two are so beautiful. I haven't seen you since you were little. Kaylee, you were just a newborn the last time I saw you. Oh, you have your mother's eyes," the woman smiled, undaunted by Grace's rebuff.

"We were your mother's closest friends," Mary continued. "Your dad didn't want people around when you were little, especially people who reminded him of your mother."

"I wonder why Dad never mentioned you," Grace said, crossing her arms over her chest.

Mary and Ann looked at each other. They wanted to find out if Kaylee had any genuine powers. If she did, she would need training to properly use them. If she didn't, they wanted to remove some of the more dangerous and valuable potion ingredients they suspected were still in the house.

"Grace, Kaylee, your father was never very comfortable with your mother's…special gifts. We were more than just her best friends. We were in your mother's coven."

"Coven?" Grace sputtered. "Mom was a witch? I knew she had some magic to her, but a formal witch?"

Kaylee tried to make herself as small as possible, willing her black clothes to blend in with the grass and flowers around her.

Both Ann and Mary turned to her. Ann said, "What about you, dear? Did you know your mother was a witch? That she was truly gifted with making potions and working with herbs?"

"Why would my sister know anything about that?" Grace interrupted. "Like you said, she was a baby when Mom died."

Kaylee looked at her hands, fingers intertwined. "I know our mom was a witch," she whispered. Grace turned her head as the words had physically slapped her.

"You knew? How?"

"Grace, I don't want to talk about it now. Not in front of anyone, okay?"

"Kaylee, we can help you," Ann said. "Really, we can. Let us take a look at what your mother left you."

"Look," Kaylee said, "I am sure you mean well and were good friends to my mother, but now is just really not a good time. Give us a few months to get our lives together first." Kaylee looked at Mary and Ann with a look that belied her young age. "Grace, let's go," she added in a firm voice.

When the girls got in their car, Grace turned to her sister. "You know what they are talking about?"

"Yes, I know that Mom was a witch, and you know that I have powers too. Why I got them and not both of us is a mystery to me. Dad showed me Mom's herbs and stuff when I was younger. They are in the basement in her workroom. It's no big deal, but those women seem to want something. I don't know why, but I am pretty sure we should be careful about who knows we have any herbs or potion-making equipment."

"Well, I'm not happy that I didn't know about the workroom, but I am with you on not telling them anything."

Over the next few days the girls began to find their own rhythm as a two-person family. Slowly the realization that she couldn't go to college in the fall crept up on Grace. She couldn't just leave Kaylee, and taking her along to college wasn't going to work. She couldn't exactly keep her hidden in her dorm room. College would just have to wait until Kaylee was older.

"I decided not to go back to high school this fall," Kaylee announced one day.

"Oh, Kaylee, you have to finish school. You're only 16. What about your future?"

"I need to study witchcraft; that needs to be the school for me. I've had to keep pushing it to the back burner for too long.

"Why is this so important right now? Witchcraft can't be your future. What about a job and a salary? How will you live?"

"My angel will help me. Everything will be fine."

Grace was silent, not quite knowing what to think. Kaylee not finishing high school? The star student not graduating? After all that she'd sacrificed before her dad died, and *this* was Kaylee's decision?

Grace decided to sell their father's business. The house was paid off, but they still had the rest of the bills to worry about. The business sold quickly and next Grace decided to sell their father's tools, which were in his home workshop.

One sunny afternoon a man arrived with a small truck. "What are you doing here?" asked Kaylee.

"Oh, he's here to take Dad's tools," Grace explained. "Neither of us use them, so I thought I'd sell them."

"No, you can't do that!" shouted Kaylee. "I need them."

"What would you even use them for? We need the money."

"You didn't even ask me. I *will* use them. We've sold enough stuff of Dad's!"

"Okay, okay," said Grace. She turned to the buyer. "The tools aren't for sale after all. I'm sorry."

The buyer left disappointed, but he understood grief.

# CHAPTER 5

As the sun just began to set, Kaylee heard a car drive up. Grace came running down the stairs wearing clothes their father never would have tolerated. She glared at Kaylee who glared back. Grace was making a habit of leaving with her friends at night and was spending their father's money at an alarming rate.

Grace and her boyfriend went out to dinner together and then drove a little into the woods where they could smoke pot together inside the car. After they were done smoking, they came out and lay on the hood together. Grace smiled as he leaned down to kiss her. Suddenly they heard a noise from the woods. It sounded like both a hiss and a growl combined. They knew exactly what it meant: a vampire.

Grace's boyfriend gasped. He ran to the driver side door, got in, and closed the door fast. Grace ran to the passenger side door, but her boyfriend saw someone standing behind her. He locked her door quickly to protect himself from the vampire. Grace screamed, "Open the door!" but he started the car and drove off.

Grace was very scared. She knew that a vampire was behind her. As she turned around slowly the vampire bit her neck.

At home, Kaylee was asleep. Suddenly her angel spoke in her head saying, *Your sister is dead.*

She sat up, wide-eyed, and screamed, "Grace! No!"

The angel spoke again. *You need to be there for her tomorrow night before dawn.*

Her angel helped Kaylee prepare for the next night. She opened the boxes of her mom's potions and ingredients. She set to making a potion, guided by the voice in her head. Then she set to making a couple of silver arrows using her dad's hunting gear—silver arrows could kill a vampire. Luckily she had learned to work metal in her father's metal workshop as well as how to use a bow. She only needed one more thing.

Kaylee walked into a store and glanced at the sign that read, "No blood purchases for minors. We card." She looked at the cooler, which held single rows of "H-Blood" and "A-Blood." Unsure of which would work best, Kaylee stole a bottle of each. She left the store and hid in the woods to check out the area. Then she headed home for a few hours of sleep.

An hour before dawn, Kaylee dressed in black clothes to match the darkness around her. Her angel led her to where Grace was buried in the ground. She flew up into a tree and got comfy on a large branch. Eventually she heard a noise in the woods and saw a young vampire who looked to be in his late 20s. He stood next to where Grace's body was buried. Obviously he was the one who had marked her last night—they were out in the middle of nowhere, so why else would he be there?

Kaylee shot a silver arrow into his chest. The young vampire's groaning filled the air. He couldn't pull the arrow out because he had no leather gloves and, without anything to protect his hands, touching the silver would only injure him further. Kaylee shot a second silver arrow into his chest. The young vampire's body started smoking and with a pop he dissolved into a pile of dust. Amazed at herself, Kaylee flew down to stand by the dust and wait for Grace's rising.

Eventually Grace rose out of ground, looking weak and confused. "I'm starving," she groaned. "You…smell like good food." She looked around, confused. "Why did I come out of the ground?"

"Umm, look, you are dead and were buried."

"What?" Kaylee shook her head. "The last thing I remember…. Oh shit, I'm a vampire. No wonder I'm hungry and you smell like food."

"Yes, that's true, you are a vampire now. You need your strength, so drink this." Kaylee cautiously handed her a container of blood. Grace sensed that Kaylee would be good to eat, but she was wrong. The smells in the woods were almost overwhelming to Grace. She could smell the deer bedded down in a thicket, the fox in her den, and the squirrel in the tree behind her.

Kaylee quickly opened the second container of blood she brought. Grace took the blood in one gulp. "More blood?" Grace asked, still hungry.

"Yeah, I have some more. Here, drink until you are satisfied."

Grace was confused. Everything smelled different and her sister smelled delicious. She couldn't believe she was a vampire. She couldn't believe she was drinking blood and that it tasted good.

Kaylee said to Grace, "Don't bite me. Tell me how much you remember of the past. And don't come near me. I am the only sister you have."

Grace was confused. She has some vague memories of her past, mostly of Kaylee. "Am I dead? Do I have to learn a new life with vampires? How? Oh God, I am no longer going to see sunlight. I can't believe this! How did you know I became a vampire?"

Kaylee tried to calm her down, saying, "Don't worry, I will help you."

"Do I need to move out of the house? I'm afraid that if I am hungry or angry I will prey on you. You should move on with your life without me."

"No, you won't. I will take care of you. Trust me, please. Come on, let's go home."

"All right, " Grace agreed, because she felt she had no where else to go and she didn't want to lose the only sister she had.

As they drove home, Kaylee explained to her sister that this would mean leaving her old life behind. They would be in danger if anyone knew a vampire and a human were living together. Kaylee helped turn their father's basement workroom into a bedroom for Grace. They moved the workroom up to Kaylee's old bedroom and moved her into the master bedroom. Soon they were using Grace's old room as a training room. Kaylee made use of her martial arts training to help Grace learn to use her new powers.

# CHAPTER 6

The sun was just peeking over the horizon when Kaylee looked up. Once again, she'd lost an entire night working with some of her mother's potions and recipes. Grace walked into the basement storeroom.

"How's it going?" Grace asked sleepily.

"I'm a bit frustrated at the moment," Kaylee replied. "I really need some more ingredients and some better notes. Sometimes Mom just skips a detail or two. I guess she understood them, but it makes it hard to learn." She yawned, which made Grace yawn too.

"Guess it's bedtime for both of us." Grace smiled, her fangs showing over her smooth bottom lip. She turned and headed to her basement room, which had blacked-out windows. The girls had done some decorating to make it seem more normal, using curtains and rugs, but it was still a basement room.

*Now where to get more herbs*? thought Kaylee. An image flashed in her mind of a notebook that belonged to her mom. It was something they had kept in the drawer by the phone for all these years. She looked up at the ceiling, "Duh, of course! Thanks," she said to her guardian angel. She went to the drawer and pulled out the notebook. Underneath was a handful of business cards. Kaylee pick them up and rifled through them. "Thanks again!" she said to her guardian angel as she held one in her hand. The card was white with black and red lettering and the edges were smooth with wear from being tucked in a wallet or bag. The card was from a local herbal shop and bookstore.

After a few hours of sleep, Kaylee walked to the bookstore with her list. The sign next to the door had a vampire with a red line through it: "No Vampires." Kaylee was surprised to see her mother's friend Ann behind the counter.

"Hi, how can I help you?" Ann said pleasantly.

"I have a list of a few herbs I need. Can you help me?"

"Of course. You're Kaylee, Christine and Dave's daughter." Ann reached out and touched Kaylee's hand. Kaylee recoiled. "What can I help you find?" Ann asked.

"I'm out of Night View."

"We carry it. Let's go back to the herbal section of the store." Ann lead her to a small area of the store that looked like it once could have been a coffee bar with a tall table for customers to stand and a small bar behind that. The wall was covered with narrow shelves filled with neatly labeled jars containing all manner of plant materials. Ann positioned herself in front of the jars and stood tall. "Night View is a very powerful herb. In the wrong hands it can be deadly. What are you going to do with it?"

"I am trying to mix a potion from my mother's recipe. Maybe you can help me?" Kaylee said with hesitation.

"Only if you show me that you are powerful enough to handle such an herb. There are very few good uses for it and it can easily go wrong."

Kaylee's eyebrows rose. Ann wanted proof she was a witch, but her dad had told her not to show her power in front of people.

"Here? No…I really just need some herbs, please."

Ann stood immovable. Kaylee panicked and turned to leave, but Ann reached the door first.

"Wait here," she instructed.

Ann took care of another customer while Kaylee waited, looking at the books. After the customer left, Ann walked to the front door and flipped the "Open" sign to "Closed." As Kaylee watched her a feeling of peace flowed over her and a voice in her head said, *She has a true heart and will keep your secrets.* Kaylee's eyes opened wide.

Ann took Kaylee's arm and said, "Let's go to the back room so we have some privacy."

"All right," Kaylee agreed.

"Did your father know you have powers?"

"Yes, he did."

"Does your sister know?"

They entered the backroom and Ann pulled the curtain closed. Assured of their privacy, Kaylee floated about six inches above the floor, silver sparkles filling the air around her.

"Wow. Clearly you have power. Thank you for sharing this with me," Ann said solemnly. "Some of the herbs you will need for spells are not supposed to be sold to anyone underage. You have the power to use them correctly, do you have the judgment?"

"I just want to learn."

A few moments later, Kaylee exited the store with a large bag under one arm. Ann watched her leave and then picked up the phone. "Mary, you won't believe who was just here! Christine's daughter, Kaylee! She definitely has lot of ability and she purchased some herbs here. She surely inherited her mother's skills."

Time passed. That was not Kaylee's last visit to Ann's store. In the meanwhile, she easily passed her motorcycle driver's test. She added organ donor to the license as well as blood donor for vampires in case of death. She worked part-time at the karate studio in exchange for lessons. On warm summer evenings, Kaylee was often found on her porch singing to the sun as it dipped below the horizon. Was it the end of the day or just the start?

# CHAPTER 7

At the ripe old age of 25, Kaylee parked her Harley Davidson motorcycle in the spot farthest from the door of the small frame shop. Her well-shaped leg moved easily over the bike and her hair fell down her back as she removed her helmet. Tucking the helmet under one arm, she went into the shop.

"Can I help you?"

"I'm Kaylee. I called earlier about my photos. I understand they are ready to be picked up."

"Oh yes, of course." The clerk went through a few boxes and found the small package quickly. She unwrapped two frames and showed them to Kaylee. "They look lovely. Is that all you need?"

"Yes, that's all I need. Thank you. Can you wrap them for me?"

"Of course," the clerk said brightly, taking the two framed images and wrapping them in colored paper. "Here you go," she said, putting the frames into a bag. "Have a good day."

Kaylee strolled out to her motorcycle and pulled out the wrapped packages. She leaned back against the wall of the store. The last few years had been really hard. Kevin, her karate teacher and friend, had moved his business to the country so she had to stop working for him. He encouraged her to keep up with her singing, but she couldn't quite tell him about her new job. It was in a bar, but it wasn't singing.... She loved the money she got from stripping and, with some careful planning, she could save most of Dave's money.

Throwing her leg over her bike, she packed the frames into her backpack. Still caught in her reverie, she thought about the voice in her head telling her to wait and not get distracted by the men who were coming on to her. At the bar it was easy to say no. She wouldn't date anyone who came to a strip club.

She pulled into the parking lot next to Kevin's dojo and chose the farthest spot from the door. After more than a year, she had decided to stop by and see how Kevin is doing. She went inside, leaving her riding boots by the door. She padded through the hall and poked her head in the door of his office. An empty room greeted her. Backpack in hand, she went to one of the classrooms. She smiled, put a fist into her hand, and bowed to Kevin when she caught his eye. He smiled.

"May I interrupt?"

"Of course. Please join the class. There is space for two more students."

Kaylee found a spot on the floor next to the other students and folded her leather-clad legs into a sitting position with ease. All the students followed her every movement with their eyes. Kevin got the final match started between two students in black outfits. Their movements were fast and sure and, after a few moments, one man finally threw the other.

"Hai!" Kevin intoned sharply, indicating the end of the match. The two opponents stood and bowed—first to each other and then to Kevin. "Class, this is one of my most famous former students, Kaylee Dailage. She won nine tournaments in a row."

Kaylee stood and bowed to Kevin, who bowed back. The murmurs in the class made it clear they were skeptical that this sexy girl in leather could be a karate champion. The student who had just won the match spoke up, saying, "Master, we've never seen her here before. How could she be so good and not train here?"

"Perhaps you would like to challenge her then, John?"

John looked a bit taken aback by the suggestion. Kaylee raise an eyebrow at Kevin, who smirked.

"I will challenge her," John stated and moved to the mat. All the men in class held their breath as Kaylee slowly removed her jacket and moved to the mat facing John. They bowed and then started circling each other. Kaylee moved toward John and brought him to the floor before they could start a second circle.

"Not bad for a girl, eh?" she whispered in his ear as she held him in place for a few seconds. They stood up, stepped back to their places, and bowed. "One more round? And don't fight me like a girl," Kaylee teased, winking at John.

He bowed his consent. This time it was a better match, but it was still over very quickly. Kaylee looked down at John and held out her hand, "Much better, but still not quite good enough." She pulled him to his feet and they bowed to each other. "Next?" Kaylee asked proactively. She winked when there were no takers.

"Class." Kevin moved to face his class as they jumped to stand facing him. "I will see you on Monday." He bowed formally to them, and they returned the bow and filed out. John took one lingering look at Kaylee before leaving.

Kaylee went up to Kevin and gave him a hug as soon as the door closed. Kevin led her to his office and closed the door. "I haven't seen you for about over a year. I often wonder where you have been."

"You know me, I'm always busy. And it's much harder to get here now that you moved your dojo to the country."

"Yeah, but it was good business move and having more space has been good. More people are coming in and we have a lot more children starting."

Kaylee reached into her backpack and took out the package and a card. "Happy birthday!" she said with a smile.

Kevin, surprised that Kaylee remembered his birthday, replied, "Thank you. That was kind of you to remember." He opened the package. It was a photo of Kevin with Kaylee as a little girl in her karate uniform. Kevin smiled and opens the card. A large bill floated out and he looked at Kaylee perplexed.

"Put this toward a scholarship fund for kids who cannot pay for lessons. You have been like a father to me…I mean, sometimes you gave me some free karate lessons. It meant so much to me."

"You are such a special young woman, and you are clearly still the best. Are you still planning to save the world?"

"Of course!" she laughed. "Always!"

"You should consider working for the CIA or FBI. You can save the world that way."

Kaylee sighed. "I am not sure I am agency material."

"Oh sorry, I forgot…how's your sister?"

They chatted a while longer before Kaylee had to leave for work. Kevin thought that she was one of the toughest and most gorgeous women he had ever known, and he was so proud of her, but he also felt that Kaylee was wasting her talents. She would be an asset to an agency like the FBI or CIA and really could really save the world. He looked at the picture, then put it on the wall.

As Kaylee left she saw a few of the young men from the class watching her through the window. Kaylee gave them a bit of a show, slowly moving her leg over the motorcycle and stretching suggestively as she put on her helmet. Kaylee turned and blew them a kiss as she drove away.

# CHAPTER 8

Two silvery figures snuck up to a fence with a double gate. The padlock opened easily with a few twists of a lock pick. They turned, relocked the gate, and set fire to the lock. They moved around the fence until they came to another gate. Making sure that this gate was unlocked, they moved to the building. A tank truck rolled up to the building and one figure opened the door. The other grabbed the end of the hose and poured gallons of gasoline all over the floor.

Some vampires woke up and smelled gas, but it was too late. The silvery couple lit a match and the gasoline went up in flames. The fire spread quickly, killing many of the vampires. Some had to choose between staying inside and being burned by the gas fire or running outside and being burned by the sun. Vampires could be heard screaming. Some of the oldest vampires knew about the secret escape hatch in the floor. They scurried through the hatch to a space under the building where they were safe. As they huddled in the darkness they listened to the other vampires screaming for help.

Kaylee drove up to Ann's store, parked her motorcycle, and walked in. She glanced up at the sign saying "No Vampires" and paused. Ann was at the cash register, and there were no customers in the store. Ann was surprised to see Kaylee, who rarely came around anymore.

"Kaylee, how are you doing? I haven't seen you in ages. You don't seem to need much in the way of potions these days."

"I am good…umm, most of time. I mostly make homemade potions to save money. If I don't have something or I don't have time, I come here."

Ann walked to door and switched the sign to "Closed" before continuing the conversation. "Wait, it's almost impossible to make homemade potion by yourself without training or instruction. Hmm, impressive. So, what do you need?"

"I want a speed-up potion so I can see things that are moving quickly in slow motion. Does that make sense?"

"I don't think I have exactly what you want, but I have a couple of instruction books that might tell you how to make a speedy movement potion, if that would work." Ann walked over to a shelf at the back of the store. "They are not too popular because the potion work is difficult."

"I would like the book if you don't have the potion itself."

"Hhmm, it's not here. Let me check in the storeroom. I will be right back." Ann walked through a back door. Kaylee looked around at the books on the shelf and waited for her.

Eventually Ann returned triumphant, declaring, "Here you go!" and holding up a book. "I think I should introduce several of my witch friends to you so we can share our witchcraft secrets. Would that be something you'd like?"

"Why would they want to share their personal spells and witchcraft?"

"There are lots of reasons we come together," Ann smiled. "Sometimes we share experience, sometimes we share knowledge, and sometimes we share expensive ingredients. We could trade new ideas for potions. But we must maintain our secrets too. A witch shares within family bonds—that's normal. I did same thing with your mother all the time. If you are interested, you could join our coven or at least learn from us as we learn from you."

"Sure, why not?" Kaylee said nervously. She wasn't used to talking openly with other witches, having been exhorted by her dad to keep her powers a secret.

"All right, when we find best time to meet here with several of my friends, who are witches as well, we'll let you know. I'll need your phone number."

"Sure," Kaylee said. She wrote her phone number on a card. Ann was smiling, happy that Kaylee was part of her witchcraft family.

"Thank you. Here's the book. That will be $30." Kaylee handed her the money and waved as she left.

She rode her motorcycle home. Kaylee grabbed the mail and then drove into the garage. She closed the door and walked in the front of the house. She grabbed some supper from the crock-pot then, with her plate in one hand and a drink in the other, she went to her master bedroom and sat down at her computer.

Kaylee was eating when a voice spoke in her head, *You must finish those goggles by today*. The voice was powerful and made her gasp. Kaylee opened the book from Ann and began to read. Soon she picked up a pair of goggles from a box and began to work on the potion. After a while she managed to she set a spell on the goggles using the potion—a puff of smoke appeared around the goggles and they turned silver.

Kaylee put on the silver goggles and looked at a mouse cage she kept nearby. Inside were mice that had been turned into vampires. Vampire mice were much faster than regular mice. After a moment, her eyes adjusted to the silvery purple haze of the goggle lenses and she saw the mice. They were not running at their usual fast speed, but almost in slow motion. Slow enough that she could actually catch one in her hand if she dared. She dipped another set of goggles in the potion and while she waited for the potion to do its work she picked blood off her shelf to fill a bottle for the mice.

Eventually she left her desk and changed her clothes. Dressed head to toe in silver, she disappeared into the garage with a shower of sparkles. She gathered her silver weapons: an arrow gun, some silver webs, a silver whip, and a small silver box that tested vampires' ages. She popped back to the kitchen to grab some water when Grace came out of the basement.

"I have bad news to tell you," Grace said.

"Tell me when I get back."

"No, wait. I heard it was crazy and dangerous out there."

"I'll be careful."

"All right, but I still worry about you."

"I know," Kaylee said as she walked to the kitchen door. She disappeared leaving a few sparkles in the air.

Grace chewed her thumbnail. She was worried about her sister because she heard that something dangerous had happened. Grace was afraid that she didn't have the strength to protect her little sister. She reached into the fridge and drew out a bottle labeled "Cow Blood."

She poured a tall glass and stepped over Kaylee’s black bag to get to the microwave. She noticed some letters on the counter, the mail from earlier, but she didn’t pay attention.

## CHAPTER 9

The full moon shone down on the woods, creating shadows and turning the leaves silver. A small group of men were gathered in the shadows. There was a sense of urgency in all of them. Harvey Hall, deputy from the town of Acton, put his hand into his pocket. He was handsome and muscular with curly red hair, a neatly trimmed mustache and goatee, and penetrating green eyes. Next to him stood Frank Lopez, who looked nothing like his name suggested; he had long blond hair tied neatly behind his head and blue eyes. Even though he had a few extra pounds on his tall frame, it was clear he worked out. Scattered in the woods behind them were six deputies, all handsome and muscular. They were facing Eric Longshore, the sheriff from Millbury who was also a vampire. Frank handed Eric a picture of a pretty girl.

"This is Grace. She's been spotted in a number of towns in this area, but none of us have an ID for her. We need to find her."

Eric looked at the photo. She looked vaguely familiar, like he'd seen her years ago.

"Where is she from?"

Frank looked at Eric. "I've heard rumors that she's from Millbury." Eric looked a bit surprised at this news. "I've also heard that she doesn't allow anyone to come to her home."

Harvey echoed this concern. "She might be hiding something."

"Okay, I will look into this. I don't know her, but my deputies and I will do what we can to find her." He took the picture and slipped it into his pocket.

"We've had some more serious reports about the silver people attaching more vampires. Over the last few weeks it has been getting worse every day," said Frank.

"Something isn't right. We need to be extremely careful," added Harvey.

"We've been hearing the same in Millbury."

Suddenly the quiet of the night was broken when the deputy next to Eric gasped. They all turned to him and saw a silver arrow protruding from his chest. In an instant the vampires fanned out to catch the shooter who managed to escape into the darkness.

Kevin looked up at video screen and spoke in to a small microphone. "How many hits?" he asked.

The voice said into his ear, "Looks like four are dead, but we wish it were more."

The silver of his clothing shimmered in the dim light cast off the monitors. Some of the monitors showed normal video, while others showed infrared shapes throwing off heat along with darker shapes—vampires whose bodies contained little heat.

Kevin spoke into the microphone again. "I think we should close up for tonight. There's not much going on. Come in, everyone."

Silver-clad people were shooting in the daylight. A ray of sunshine hit his shoulder. He hissed in pain and moved further into the shadows. It was a small burn and healed quickly.

Kaylee hid her motorcycle in the bushes and walked into the woods a short distance. She sat down to listen quietly. About 15 minutes later, Kaylee heard a noise in woods. Proceeding with caution, she put on her goggles and got her weapons ready.

Eric walked alone in the woods, barely making any noise. Kaylee found him with her goggles. She waited and prepared a silver web. She flung it out and the web tangled in Eric's legs, dropping him to the ground. His growling mingled with a hiss of pain from the silver.

Kaylee ran to him and said, "Don't contact any vampire for rescue." Eric growled again as she continued, "I won't harm you, but I am doing research and I need your blood. I will test it, then set you free. I promise."

The handsome vampire stared at Kaylee with gorgeous hazel-green eyes. She seemed familiar, but he knew he was not acquainted with any of those silver people he'd heard rumors of.

Eric sniffed the air and sneered, "You're human! Ssss!"

"Yeah I am. Be quiet." She searched him for hidden weapons. It was a pleasure to search all six feet his muscular frame. He had dark blond hair that reached his shoulders. He was sharp featured and clean-shaven. She noticed that he worn no jewelry save for a dark stone wrapped in wire around his neck. It seemed rather at odds with his polished clothing and well-groomed good looks. She hurried and drew his blood.

Despite being angry, he was curious and asked, "What are you doing? What do you need those for?"

"Shhh! Hold still for a second. Almost done."

Kaylee opened the silver box from her belt and exposed half a dozen small bottles strapped neatly inside. She put a single drop of Eric's blood into each bottle. The bottles were neatly labeled 1900-1999, 1800-1899,1700-1799, 1600-1699, 1500-1599, and 1400-1499. After a few seconds, the bottle labeled 1500-1599 began to exude a purple glow.

Eric was weakened by the silver, but he was still pissed. "You brutally murder vampires!"

"Sorry, buddy, I want nothing from you but blood."

Eric closed his eyes and concentrated. He mentally sent a message to Scott. A long time ago Eric had marked Scott, his friend from the sheriff's office, allowing a telepathic connection. Scott's green eyes widened when he realized that Eric was in danger and he took off to find him. His muscular frame moved quickly and he had a grim look on his handsome mustached face.

Kaylee heard a noise from the woods. She grabbed her silver crossbow and notched an arrow. Scott, hiding behind a tree, was a bit too slow and Kaylee spotted him. Her arrow was off before she could even blink, shooting into his chest. Eric was stunned—humans couldn't move that fast, almost at the speed of a vampire. Eric gasped, "You murder vampires! What are you, human?"

Kaylee removed the silver web from his face and then slapped his cheek. "I warned you not to ask for rescue! If you had listened, he'd still be alive. This is *your* fault."

"Human bitch!"

Kaylee slapped his face again. "Shut up! Keep quiet and let me ask you a question before I set you free. This shows that you last time you were human was the 15th century, am I right?"

Eric was shocked, but didn't show it. "How did you know?"

"What did you do for a living when you were human?" she asked.

Eric tried to use his powers of mind control on her, but he suspected it wasn't working and that her goggles probably blocked his powers. Eric had no option but to wait for her set him free.

"All right, I'm done." Kaylee put her silver gloves back on and repacked her silver box back onto her waist belt. She notched another arrow on the crossbow in case anyone attacked her. "I will set you free, but don't be foolish. I will attack you if you provoke me."

Eric nodded.

Kaylee set him free very slowly, removing the ropes one at a time. Eric felt the heat of her movements and not just from the silver ropes. As each one was removed, he felt his strength again. Kaylee walked backward, turned, and ran. She hopped onto her motorcycle and started the engine.

Eric began to chase her on foot. She turned and shot an arrow at him, missing by inches. She turned a corner and sped home.

Eric stopped. The sound of the engine was gone, and so was Kaylee.

# CHAPTER 10

Kaylee looked around to check if anyone saw her appear and was relieved to find it was quiet at home. She drove into the garage and turned off the engine. Relief spread over her face as she got off her motorcycle. She hurried in the front door.

"Whew...he was hot!" she said to herself. "Too bad he's a vampire."

Grace heard Kaylee as she arrived home and walked upstairs from the basement. "You're home early."

"Yeah, this was my lucky day. Let me change my clothes and I'll tell you about it." Kaylee hurried from the living room to her bedroom, where she removed her silver outfit and got into regular clothes. Grace brought her blood drink into Kaylee's room. "Let me show you something," Kaylee showed Grace Eric's blood. "This is from the 15th century."

"Whoa, that's oldest vampire I've heard of. Who was he?"

"He didn't tell me his name, but he was very handsome with a hot body. Unfortunately I killed his friend. It was my second vampire murder today."

"Jeez, slow down, girl. Did he contact one of his marked people to rescue him?"

Kaylee nodded.

"Shit, this guy is a very old vampire. He's got power and a lot of it. You need to be very careful."

"Don't worry, big sis."

"I know you thought this guy was hot, but I don't want you with a vampire. You stick with humans. And be careful of a guy named Eric Longshore. He's like the vampire sheriff in town. He can be very dangerous."

"No worries, sis, I am not planning an attack. Come on, let me show you something." Kaylee led Grace to her workroom. She put Eric's blood on a secret shelf. She pulled out the second pair of goggles and handed them to Grace. Kaylee showed her how to change from night view to day view and infrared vision. There was a new vision that made everything look silver. "Here, look at the vampire mouse. I know you can see their movement with your vampire eyes, but now I can follow their movement too."

To Grace the mouse moved in slow motion. "Ha ha, this trick actually works."

"I was working on it today. It was easy."

Grace gagged. "Oh, that smells rotten!"

Kaylee grabbed the plate of her leftover dinner from earlier. "Sorry, I will be back in a second." She went to the kitchen, put her plate in the dishwasher, and started it. She scurried back to Grace. "So what was the bad news you mentioned?"

Grace sat down and looked quite serious. "Look, I am very concerned about us because vampires tried to find me to correct my ID info. I always tried to avoid them the best as I could. It is kind of difficult because we live in between two different worlds. Vampires are getting very cautious with those silver people attacking and murdering innocent vampires. There are rumors that some vampires are trying to trick humans. What happens if you go to a bar with no silver on and I can't get in because I don't have proper ID? How will I protect you?"

"Is this fear in the vampire world just because of these silver people?"

"Yeah, it is just a scare, but what are we supposed to do? I am not staying home forever and what about you? What if silver people attack me? Or vampires attack you?"

"Where did the silver people attack vampires?"

"It just started, maybe in Bolton or Acton or some town nearby. What if Millbury is next? Who knows?"

"I don't know what to think. I know that vampires and humans living together is forbidden, but this just isn't fair."

Both girls looked sad. "Kaylee, let's shake ourselves out if this mood. I think you mentioned that we are scheduled for shopping tonight, right?"

"That's right! I forgot. Let's go!"

They each scooped up what they needed to shop and met at the garage. Grace said, "I'll drive." Kaylee opened the passenger door.

"Wait," Grace said, "Do you have any silver on you?"

Kaylee chuckled. "Yeah. Look, I always have this on 24/7." She showed her silver jewelry.

"Good, you never know. You can't be too careful around vampires."

"You sound like you're my mama."

Grace chuckled, then started the engine and drove away.

They arrived at the mall and started to do some serious shopping. Soon they had new clothes in bags and they were having a pleasant time with each other. At one store Kaylee went to try on a new bathing suit. "What do you think? Is this too much color?"

Two stunning vampires watched Kaylee as she stepped out of the dressing room. The first one ran her hand through her thick blonde hair and whispered to her brunette companion, "Look there, she is damn hot."

The brunette vampire said, "Whoa. Yeah, that one's perfect."

They started to come closer, both eyeing Kaylee hungrily. Another human woman came out of her dressing room with a one-piece bathing suit and asked her human friends, who were waiting to try on clothes, "Does this looks all right?"

Her friends shook their heads, and one said, "Try another one."

The blonde vampire looked at the woman and said, "That's an ugly suit."

The woman was surprised and responded, "okay, I'll change it."

The brunette vampire sneered, "Don't bother changing it. You have an ugly body and there is nothing you can do about it."

The woman was upset. One of her friends spoke up, saying, "Excuse me, that was rude. Be nice to my friend." The woman disappeared into the dressing room.

The blonde vampire spoke up. "Hey, I don't hang around with friends who have ugly faces or bodies, got it?" Then she turned to Grace. "You look familiar."

Kaylee looked around at the heap of clothes near the group of women. She decided to change the subject. She picked up a bright blue suit. "Wait…let me show you," she said to the woman in the dressing room. "This will definitely look good on you, I guarantee you."

The woman looked out and said, "All right, I'll try it."

The brunette vampire chuckled, "Grace? I see you so very rarely! Where do you live these days? I she your's?" She chuckled, indicating Kaylee. "She seems so nice to be so hot."

"Too bad she's mine. Mind your own business," Grace replied. The human women nodded their agreement.

"No one was speaking to you, humans." The blonde vampire sneered. "Grace, where do you live?"

Grace chuckled, "I'm homeless, no address. Sorry!"

Kaylee chuckled too. The blonde vampire turned around and looked at Kaylee.

"My, aren't you attractive?" She gave Kaylee a long slow look from head to toe.

"Attractive, me?" Kaylee said. "So what's the problem?"

The blonde came over and got almost close enough to kiss Kaylee, stopping only when she saw her silver jewelry. She didn't move away, but she kissed the air in front of Kaylee's lips. "You look so perfect…care to join me?"

Kaylee still had on the bikini. She stepped back and waved her off, saying, "Uh-uh. Sorry."

Grace came over and got between them. "I don't need to tell you again, she's mine. Get lost. Got it?"

Kaylee chuckled and then went back into the dressing room to put her clothes back on. The blonde vampire woman looked at Grace. "You are lucky, but I will see you again. You are such a child vampire and I will have her." The two vampires walked away from them and out of the store.

The human women all let out a breath at the same time and laughed. One said to Grace, "They are so cruel."

"Yeah I know. They give vampires a bad name."

The human who was trying on clothes came out in the swimsuit that Kaylee had chosen. "I think I like this. You must have good taste in clothes," she said to Kaylee.

Grace turned and smiled. "Yeah, definitely. That looks better than other one."

The woman's friends agreed, "Yeah, that one is definitely a keeper."

A few moments later, Kaylee and Grace sat down in a café, Grace with blood to drink and Kaylee eating ice cream.

"Those vampires seemed to know you, Grace," Kaylee said. "Who are they?"

"They are definitely older vampires and I know the blonde one is named Evelyn Day. She's from somewhere near Waltham, I think. She is a bitch." Grace looked at her sister. "Kaylee, you always said that when you were 25, a whole quarter of a century old, you would be ready. So now that you are 25, what are you ready for?"

Kaylee sighed, "My angel wasn't really that specific, just that at 25 I'd be ready."

"I hope it is something wonderful. You deserve good news from your angel."

All of the sudden Grace caught sight of the female vampires sitting in a café across the food court from them. Grace sighed, "Don't look back. Those female vampires from the store are following us."

"That sucks. Let's use the stairs." They moved quickly to the entrance of the stairs, but the vampires followed them. Kaylee paused and whispered to Grace, "Once we get in the door, bend like you are sitting in a chair." Grace did as she was told and closed her eyes. Kaylee used her powers to transport them to inside the car.

"Whew. I am surprised she was that interested in following you. She must suspect you have powers." Grace started the engine and drove off.

Meanwhile, the blonde whispered, "Go quickly downstairs. I will go upstairs. We will meet right in the middle."

The brunette vampire sighed, "Remember, they don't allow us to move at full speed or show fangs in front of humans. What if someone sees us?"

"They won't. Remember, humans don't take stairs. They are lazy."

They entered the stairwell and started on either end, checking each floor for Kaylee. They met in the middle, both empty handed.

"Damn…Forget her," sighed the blonde vampire. They gave up and went back to the mall.

Grace was driving home when Kaylee said, "Grace, I am worried about you now. I'm not sure how to solve this situation with those silver people and vampirism, but I will try to figure it out. Can you stay home tomorrow night? Stay safe, for me, please?"

"All right," Grace agreed softly.

## CHAPTER 11

Eric Longshore and his deputies were sitting around a small conference table drinking blood. Eric was at the head of the table. All the deputies knew what had been happening lately with the silver people who had been hunting down vampires.

"We've had some unfortunate developments," Eric explained. "Not only have we lost our friend and deputy, Scott, but we've lost the Chinese deputy too. A deputy and my marked human, Scott, were killed today. A silver clad female attacked me. She was doing some research project on vampires."

"Was she alone? They usually work in teams," said Deputy Michael Johnston. Michael had light brown skin and startlingly blue eyes. His hair was braided with beads dangling to his shoulders. He had a neatly trimmed goatee and a thin mustache.

"What, is there a doctor for vampires now? You are lucky to still be here," said Joseph Chubnova, who had dark brown eyes and short coffee colored hair. He also had a trim mustache and beard.

"She set me free," Eric said softly.

"She set you free? Impossible! Silver people murder vampires!" said Kuruk Blackfeather. Kuruk looked every inch the full-blooded Cherokee he was—tall, muscular, with smooth reddish brown skin and long black hair pulled back in a thick braid. His eyes were so dark they almost looked black.

Changing the subject, Eric said, "Please go find Grace, but watch out for silver people. When dawn comes, get back here to sleep safely. It will only be temporary."

The deputies went out and Eric sighed as he started on some paperwork.

As they arrived at home from the mall, Grace asked, "Any news about the concert in California yet?"

"Not yet. Soon, I hope." Grace and Kaylee opened the doors of the car.

"Fly me in. These bags are heavy," said Grace.

Kaylee chuckled and held out her hand. Kaylee and Grace flew together to the second floor balcony and entered through the glass slider. Grace closed the slider as Kaylee dropped her shopping bags in her bedroom.

"I almost forgot again. Hold on for a second, I have something for you." Kaylee jumped to the kitchen to get her backpack. She then jumped back to her room, missing the mail on the counter.

Kaylee reached into her backpack and pulled out a five by seven framed photograph. It was a present for Grace—a photo of the two girls.

"Has it really been 10 years? This was a vampire anniversary photo, huh? Wow you changed a lot but I haven't." Grace reflected it as she looked at it. Kaylee put it on the wall. Grace and Kaylee stared at the new photo and an old photo of them together as kids. "You know, you will never see me grow old—no white hair, no wrinkles, and no dentures. I will always be young and beautiful. I am sad that I can't keep you forever because you will grow old and die."

"I can live with it. You can watch my children and grandchildren. I want you to pass on potions to my children and grandchild who are witches too."

Grace sighed, "You don't have a boyfriend, you're not married, and you don't have kids yet."

"I will find a good man eventually."

"How? It's impossible if you've never had sex or experience with a boyfriend. Come on, sex is good. Think of it like vitamins—you need it. You need to find a man. Look, some vampires out there can smell that you are virgin if you are not wearing silver. It's more likely they will target you. Come on, tell me: when will you lose your virginity?"

Kaylee chuckled, "Silver is my protection, but I promise you I will find someone soon."

Grace sighed, "All right, whatever. When you turn 80 years old, I can't picture myself in a photo with you and your wrinkles. I am not going to help you change adult diapers and I don't like that nursing home smell." Grace wrinkled up her nose.

Kaylee chuckled, "Nurses will change me, not you,"

"I wish you would live forever so we could fly together and do stuff together. I will feel empty without you."

"I wish I could live forever like you, but then I would have to drink blood. Yuck!" Kaylee yawned. "I am very tired. I am going to hit the sack early tonight."

"Go ahead, go to sleep."

"Good night."

"Good night, sister," said Grace as she left.

Grace was downstairs watching TV in the living room. The light from the TV reflected on all the surfaces, giving the room an eerie glow. She kept flipping channels, not finding anything interesting on. She flipped the TV off and opened a book. She was quickly bored. She thought about trying to go to Longshore Bar. She hated feeling so restless. She just wanted to go out and do something or find someone to do. She smiled wickedly. She hadn't been to Longshore Bar for a very long time. *It won't hurt me to go for a short time as long as I am very careful*, she thought.

Grace stood up and walked into the kitchen. She left her book on the counter and tried to find a pen to write a note. Her book covered the mail on the counter. Grace wrote a note for Kaylee, "I have gone to the Longshore Bar. Please don't be mad. It is just once, and I haven't been there for a long time. Love, Grace." She stuck the note under a refrigerator magnet.

Grace decided just run to the bar since it wasn't far, about three or four miles. Just as she was about halfway she realized she had forgotten her cell phone in the basement.

At the Longshore Bar, Grace was asked for ID, which she didn't have. An ID was required for all vampires. Deputies Joseph and Michael recognized Grace from her photo and they arrested her. They wore protective gloves and held her with silver chain. Grace groaned and small wisps of smoke rose up from where the silver chain touched her waist. The two deputies were talking, but too softly for her to hear.

Grace shouted to them, "I didn't do anything wrong. Why are you arresting me?"

Deputy Joseph said, "You have no ID. It's required for all vampires at all times."

Deputy Michael continued, "You need to get a new ID."

Grace gasped. She was stuck now. She knew that she was not supposed to tell them where she lived or any information about herself because it was a secret that she lived with Kaylee, a human. She had really screwed up now.

Kaylee woke up late in the morning, around 10 am. She went to the bathroom, then walked into her workroom. She donned a pair of rubber gloves and began to take out potions. She took plenty of bottles and a medium-sized pail with her. She walked to the back door and flew to a small barn. She floated above the floor because she didn't want to get dirt on her bare feet. She used the broom leaning against the wall to clean up the straw and cow poo, which got tossed into a large box. Next, she fed the cow and milked her. Finally, she drew blood and filled a couple of bottles up. She brought the blood and milk to a small table in the barn. She used a potion to test to make sure that the milk and blood were safe. She put back most of the equipment, then took the blood, milk, and pail back to the house. She put the blood in the fridge and poured the milk into a plastic gallon jug. As she put the milk in the refrigerator she noticed the note and read the message from Grace.

"Oh crap!" she said to herself. Grace hadn't kept her promise. Kaylee flew upstairs to bring the potion there, and then flew back to the kitchen. She took out some cereal, poured the cow's milk over it, and ate. She started to clean the bathroom and changed the sheets in her bedroom. She collected dirty clothes in a basket to wash. Kaylee carrier her dirty laundry into the basement and turned the light on.

"Good morning, sleepyhead, are you in there? I am doing laundry." Kaylee didn't hear any response. She put clothes into the washing machine and turned it on. She opened her secret storage area, but it was dark inside. "Grace...Grace?" Kaylee reached for the light switch and turned it on. She noticed the bed was empty, no sign of Grace. "Shit." Kaylee jumped to her master bedroom from the basement to find her cell phone and call Grace. She dialed Grace, but it just rang and rang. "Damn it." Kaylee held her cell phone and jumped to the kitchen from the master bedroom.

Kaylee tossed her cell on the counter and began to put food in the slow cooker to prepare for supper. Then she started madly cleaning the kitchen. She moved her book and noticed the mail from yesterday on the counter. She checked each piece of mail. Her eyes opened wide when she found a letter from California. She opened the letter and read it. The letter invited her to join a concert tour. It said she needed to be in California in September. Kaylee shouted, "Yes! Hooray!"

She was very excited and happy, her dream was coming true and she couldn't wait to tell Grace the good news. At same time she was worried about Grace. Even when she met someone, she was usually home by now. Kaylee called her again. Her phone started ringing and she heard the washing machine stop. Then she heard Grace's cell phone in the basement. Kaylee followed the sound down to the basement and all the way to the secret room, where she saw Grace's cell phone on her desk. *Maybe she just forgot it*, she thought.

Kaylee was scheduled to go to the gym to work out and lift some weights. She headed out and focused on her workout for two hours. Kaylee arrived home on her motorcycle and grabbed an energy drink from the refrigerator. She then started the water to fill up the tub. She took off her clothes and stepped into a bubble bath. She shaved and then relaxed by listening to music. She stepped out of the tub, put a robe on, and walked into her bedroom. She sat down to do her make-up. She had plenty of time to get ready for work at the strip club that night.

Kaylee jumped to the kitchen. The time was up for the slow cooker and she ate plenty of dinner with fresh milk. Kaylee was wondering where Grace was. Had she slept over at another vampire's house? She had done that before, but Kaylee still worried that something happened to her.

Kaylee prepared her stripper clothes: white high-heeled boots, silver jewelry, silver underwear, and little else. She threw her cell phone and goggles inside of her bag. She put her bag in her sister's car and drove to strip club. As she walked around the back, she frowned at the sign saying "No Vampires."

After work, she walked out of the strip club. Kaylee tossed her bag in the car, got in, and called her sister again. Still no answer. She drove home and checked for Grace, but there was no sign of her yet. Kaylee was getting worried and desperate. She tried to speak to her angel, *Where's Grace? Help me find her, please*. There was just silence.

Kaylee decided to go to Longshore Bar to check if Grace was there. Outside the bar Kaylee saw the hours posted and the rule: No Silver. The schedule for humans and vampires was Sundays, Mondays, Tuesdays, Wednesdays, Thursdays, and Fridays only. Vampires only on Saturdays. Perfect, Kaylee could go in since it was Friday. Kaylee wore regular clothes—a white camisole that showed her belly piercing and blue jean shorts with flat shoes. She took a quick look at herself and decided to change into her white high heel stripper boots. Kaylee used her silver sprinkles to switch from shoes to boots. Kaylee started to follow the vampire's rule and began to remove her silver jewelry, but something stopped her. She opened her bag and took out a small plastic zippered bag where she kept jewelry. She opened it and took out a thin silver bracelet. She put it on her ankle and zipped her boot up where it wouldn't be seen, but would still protect her.

Kaylee walked in and showed her driver's license as the host, Carolyn Shea, looked up and down to see the gorgeous woman who entered the bar. Kaylee glanced around. There was a small stage with dance poles on the left and right. On the right was a woman dancer wearing a sexy bikini and on the left was a man wearing sexy bikini bottoms. In the center was a small band with a dance floor in front of them. There were high tables all around. There was also a small bar to order food or drinks and a second floor balcony that looked like a small stage. Kaylee looked around at the people at the bar—still no sign of Grace. She sat and waited for a little bit. Then an idea popped into her head. Perhaps she could sing and Grace would hear her.

Kaylee asked the host vampire, Carolyn. Carolyn was very sexy with long blonde hair and spectacular hazel eyes.

Carolyn walked to Eric's office. She opened the door and said, "A *hot* human woman wants to sing in here today if that's okay with you?"

"Sure, go ahead," Eric said, at the same time curious who the woman was.

Carolyn walked back out to Kaylee and told her, "You can sing on stage. You just have to talk to the band."

Carolyn led Kaylee to the band and introduced her. Kaylee stepped up on stage and spoke to the three vampires in the band while they discretely sniffed her. "I know you won't know my song, but follow my rhythms, okay?" she explained. "Let's start with a basic 4/4 with a rock beat." They agreed.

Eric stepped out of his office and watched Kaylee sing. Both the vampires and humans looked very pleased with her song. Kaylee looked like she really enjoyed herself on stage. She was a natural performer. When song the song ended, the crowed clapped enthusiastically while Eric walked to Carolyn. They had a whispered conversation.

Kaylee bowed, thanking the crowed. The band was friendly. The guitarist said, "Awesome. I love your song. Did you write it?"

The drummer said, "Your voice was perfect. Great voice tone."

"Are you looking to be hired here as a singer?" the last band member asked. They couldn't keep their eyes off at Kaylee. She waved to the crowd before stepping off the stage. Kaylee went to leave the bar, but Carolyn stopped her.

"The owner wants to see you." Kaylee felt a strong urge to leave, but she went anyway. Perhaps she could find out something about Grace.

"Ah, sure, for short time," she agreed.

"Let me bring you to him."

Eric was sitting on the small stage on the second floor balcony. Kaylee was surprised to recognize him as the vampire she had attacked in the woods the night before. She hoped he didn't know it was her, unless it was too late now, and he had already watched her sing. Grace had warned her about him.

Eric stood up and held out his hand, saying, "Hi, I am Eric Longshore and I own this bar. Your name?" Kaylee couldn't believe it was him. She kept her cool.

"Tara," she lied as she took his hand.

"Have a seat, Tara. I don't believe I have seen you around here before. You have great talent as a singer."

"First time here today, and thank you."

"Would you be interested in working here part-time as a singer?"

Kaylee had a feeling that she was busted, but she also liked him. She tried to not show her feelings. "Let me think about it."

"Did you write that song you sang today?"

"Yes, I did. Most of time I write my own songs. I try to get ideas for new songs as much as possible."

"I am impressed with your talent. Are you are from around here?"

Kaylee didn't want him to know where she was from. "Waltham. I drove about 30 minutes to get here."

The band began to play a new song, something slow. Eric stood up and asked, "May I have this dance?"

"Sure," she said standing to head to the dance floor.

"Don't go over there, let's dance here."

"Oh...fine."

They started to dance together; his hand holding her's between them. As his hand brushed her skin, he felt her heart beat. Eric took a deep breath and smelled her fragrance. She smelled amazing, and his instincts tried to take over. He could barely stay in control.

"You smell beautiful, Tara, if you don't mind my saying so?"

As he held her, he felt his fangs emerge. His eyes opened wide with surprise, and he retracted them. He hadn't lost control like this in centuries. Eric stared at Kaylee for a moment then she looked up at him. She felt like she couldn't stop looking at him.

During the sexy slow dance together, Kaylee felt like she couldn't let go of him for a moment. She felt a bond with him, and at same time Eric felt the same thing. Eric's fangs popped out again. He felt out of control, something he wasn't sure he liked. Kaylee turned quickly so that no one else could see his fangs.

Deputy Michael Johnson saw them together. For as long as he had known Eric, he'd never seen him dance with a human before. Deputy Michael saw Eric's fangs pop out and that he'd almost lost control. This was not good.

"Sorry again," Eric mumbled to Kaylee. "I don't mean to scare you…umm. Maybe that's enough dancing."

Kaylee and Eric sat. For Kaylee this was love at first sight, but she tried to keep it cool and hide it. Kaylee knew that she couldn't date or fall in love with a vampire. Kaylee felt weird. She knew he couldn't be the right guy for her.

Eric moved closer to her. He tried to mark her, but she caught him. "Don't try any of that vampire marking crap on me!" she said and moved away.

Eric was surprised. He didn't think she knew about the talents that vampires had. Few knew, and even fewer could resist. "Sorry about that. Vampire instincts." The slow music stopped. "Can I get you something to eat or drink?"

"No, thanks. I have to go find my sister."

"Your sister? Do you think she has been here before?"

"I don't know, but I think so."

"Maybe I can help you find your sister? What's her name?" Eric really liked her too, and he hoped she would spend more time with him.

"No, I will take care of it, but thanks," she said as she stood.

"I hope you come here again."

"Maybe I will. Pleased to meet you, Eric."

"Maybe?"

"I am planning to move to California soon. I have a recording contract." Eric was crushed by the idea of her so far away.

"Really? How wonderful. Congratulations. It was a pleasure to meet you too. Good luck, Tara." Eric held her hand and kissed it.

Kaylee noticed he wouldn't let her hand go, and they stared at each other a moment. Eric chuckled, "Oops, sorry." He let go of her hand, and she turned and walked away from him. Eric stared at her as she walked out of the bar. Michael saw everything and came over to him.

Kaylee got into her car with caution. She started the engine and began to drive away. "Oh God, I am so stupid," she said to herself. Kaylee checked around to see that nobody could see, then she jumped with the car. Kaylee and car popped out at the driveway. Kaylee wondered if this was what love at first sight felt like. She tried to ignore her feelings about Eric and make sure that she would never see him ever again. Kaylee grabbed her bag and jumped to the kitchen from the car.

Back at the bar, Eric said to Michael, "Did you see that human woman walk out?"

"Yeah, dark hair?"

"Kidnap her. Do it now!" Michael suspected he knew why Eric wanted her so badly, but he listened to his order.

"Yes, sir," said Michael as he left. Michael stepped out of the bar and looked around. Where was she? He circled the bar and checked the woods. He looked down the road and saw no cars. It was impossible for a human to just disappear.

Eric waited impatiently at the bar. Could she finally be his soul mate? Michael came back to the bar. He told Eric, "She's gone. I cannot find her."

"Well, look harder."

"I found no car, or tracks, and no scent trail either. Why do you want her?"

"Go back and look harder! She was headed home to Waltham from here."

"I will try again, but she's gone."

"Obey me. Now go."

Michael noticed how serious he was. "Yes, sir," he said as he left.

Kaylee checked for Grace in the basement, but she wasn't there. Kaylee was quite anxious. She put on her vampire goggles and went in search of her sister. After a few hours of searching she came back. She tossed the goggles on her dresser and flung herself across her bed, crying.

At the same time, Michael came back to Eric at the bar. "I can't find her. I don't believe she's in Waltham."

"Don't tell our deputies. Keep this a secret between us. I hope she comes back again."

"Don't get me wrong, she's hot, but she's human. Why is she so special?"

"Mind your own business," Eric growled. Michael suspected that Eric had finally found love. *Will wonders never cease*? he thought.

Two sexy female vampires flirted with Eric after Michael left. He flirted right back at them. "Come with me…" he said suggestively, leading them to his office and closing the door behind them.

*She and Eric were dancing together very sexily and kissing each other. Slowly they started to strip their clothes off, then Eric popped out his fangs.*

*"Join me?"*

*Kaylee bent her neck to accept his bite.*

*"Yes," she said breathlessly as Eric bit her.*

Kaylee woke with a start from the nightmare and felt her neck. It was so real.

# CHAPTER 12

Kaylee decided to focus on where Grace was. She looked carefully through the house one more time just to be sure. *Grace, please just tell me where you are*, she pleaded in her head.

She was eating a few bites of a late breakfast when her angel spoke in her head: *I can see you are upset about Grace being gone, so I will take you to find her tonight. Wear silver clothes, and don't bring potions. I will lead you into woods and I will remove your powers before you enter the vampire area. You will understand. You are ready.*

"What? Why? Am I going to become a vampire? Is Grace all right?"

*Yes, you will become one and Grace is fine.*

"Why you are you leading me to become a vampire? What about my record contract? It has been my dream."

*Yes, you are ready. You are on your path at the right time. This recording contract might not happen now, but it will someday. Trust me, I am protecting you. Please follow these orders.*

Kaylee was scared, but she trusted her angel and it was important that she find Grace alive and well.

Kaylee was given a list of what to pack. She gathered some important documents—files copied from the computer, her spell book, bills, bank information, and insurance forms. She recalled memories and gathered several pictures of her family. When Grace had made the basement workroom into a bedroom she found that their dad had copied old videos of their family from when they were growing up. There were a bunch of them, and now Kaylee noticed one that she'd never seen before. She stuck it in the VCR and began watching it. It started with a shot of Dave telling his girls that he loved them. She decided to stop watching and tucked it in her bag so she could share it with Grace.

Her motorcycle was in the garage. She put her backpack next to it and put some of Grace's clothes in the saddlebag. When she'd gathered everything on the list, Kaylee flew off the balcony and dove into the pool to cool off and unwind. She swam a few laps and then lay out to dry off in the sun.

Kaylee put on a terrycloth robe and sat by the pool looking at pictures from her family album. Was this the end of her family tree? She went to check and see if she'd forgotten anything and found two tapes left on the shelf.

*Kaylee and Eric were dancing together very sexily and kissing each other. Slowly they started to strip their clothes off, and then Eric popped out his fangs.*

*"Join me?"*

*Kaylee bent her neck to accept his bite...*

Eric's eyes popped open, and he jerked his head off his desk. He'd fallen asleep. He had to stop thinking about Kaylee because he'd failed to get her. He's lost her and she'd move thousands of miles away. It was too late.

Kevin, wearing a business suit, walked up to a large steel door. He had to show his ID and then have his fingerprints and retinas scanned. Finally he arrived at an office door inside the CIA. Ben Sullivan, director of the CIA, waited for Kevin Douglas' arrival. Everyone else was seated around a large square table ready for a meeting. They all had on suits and wore their CIA badges. Ben gave a speech about building offices in each state and hiring more people. They were still waiting for the President's signature.

After the CIA meeting, Kevin asked the director, "Why should we use equipment against vampires? Out there people complain taxes being high and wanting them lowered. Many people want to use our funds for humans, not for vampires."

"I'm sorry you feel that way. People get voted into office and they make policy that we follow. Wait and see what happens. There's nothing I can do about it."

"All right. Whatever they vote for, I am in either way."

Ben started to suspect that Kevin knew about something illegal that was going on. Ben has never quite trusted Kevin's loyalty. Kevin had been passed over for a promotion and Ben had gotten the job. Kevin was his right-hand man, but it had to be difficult for him sometimes.

Kevin wondered why it all started against vampires. In the past they had given vampires equal rights, but now people were challenging this and things were started to get ugly. He didn't like this at all, but he has no choice but to work for a living.

Kaylee got dressed in black leather pants and a white camisole top. She carefully made up her face and did her hair. Her feet were still bare. She cooked a big dinner with steak, mashed potatoes, corn, and cheesecake for dessert. These were her favorite foods, and for her very last human meal she was going all out.

Kaylee put on silver outer clothes and placed her goggles on her head. She added some weapons—her belt with the silver web and her cross bow. She looked at herself in the mirror and then opened the sliding glass door. She flew down to the barn. She took care of the cow and left plenty of food for her.

Kaylee jumped back to her room and put on black boots. Then she flew down to the front door. She took a last look at the family picture. She stepped backward from the front door and then jumped off to the garage. She put on her goggles and started the motorcycle.

The voice in her head led her. She arrived in an open area and parked her motorcycle in some brush for coverage. The angel spoke in her head: *No crossbow*. She removed it and returned to her motorcycle, leaving it in the bag. Kaylee walked into the woods a little distance where she saw a big rock with cliffs. She heard a noise in woods and hid. A couple of deputy vampires walked in a different direction from where she had been going. She let them pass and kept silent.

Kaylee noticed that they looked like they had walked off the cliff. She crept forward to see where the path led. Kaylee looked down the cliff and saw a wooden log and a big rock wall. Her angel said in her head, *This is the vampires' secret lair. You have to pull the wooden log back and it will open, but get in fast because it closes quickly. Remember, once you are inside your powers will be gone.*

Kaylee was scared to go forward, toward her death. She took a deep breath and paused for a moment. Then she pulled the wooden log and moved inside quickly. She started to feel nervous, but she knew Grace was there. She tested her powers and confirmed that they were not working. Fear rose up in her, but the voice in her head assured her she was on the right track.

In the distance she could see torches and skeletons lying in crypts along the wall. The skeletons were old, covered in spiders and dust. She started moving forward with caution. As she moved forward, she saw three circles on the wall that looked like doors. Two were similar and the third was smaller.

Kaylee decided to go in the small door on the right side. She found twisted stairs with a landing about five or six steps up. In the middle of a large circle, there were six chairs around three tables. It looked almost like a courtroom. Skeletons occupied the chairs and their clothing suggested that they were very old, possibly from the 1600s. The women looked like pilgrims, and there was clearly at least one skeleton of a Native American wearing traditional clothing. Some had died violently with what looked like bullet holes in their skulls.

For a moment, Kaylee heard footsteps and voices chatting. Someone was coming to the courtroom. She hid inside the wall of the second landing. The first person that came in had on a white wig with curls like George Washington. Kaylee couldn't see who it was.

The vampire deputies came in next wearing a whole lot of black leather and fangs. Grace was with them, held between vampires. Kaylee's eyes flew open wide. Grace was wrapped in a silver chain, obviously a prisoner.

Eric, adjusting the wig, opened a large book and read, "Grace Dailage, is that correct?" "Yes."

"I don't have a record of your history or even simple things like your address. Who marked you? How many beings have you marked so far? How long since you were human? I need proof of where you live. If we get all this information correct and confirmed, I will set you free."

"I have been a vampire for 10 years, but no one marked me, sorry. Get me a new ID. Now are you happy?"

"How many have you marked?"

"I have never been marked, nor have I marked anyone."

"If you aren't marked then who was your maker? Do you have another vampire helping you?"

"No one adopted me. I am completely alone."

"Alone? What is your address?"

"You don't have to know where I live. My private life is private, if you don't mind."

"You can't have an ID without an address. Have you been living underground for the last 10 years?" Everyone chuckled. "One more time, where do you live? If you refuse to cooperate with me I will sentence you now and keep you until you tell me what I ask."

Grace was frustrated. She couldn't tell them the truth and put Kaylee in danger. She snapped angrily, "Vampire laws suck! You are an asshole!"

"Fine. Enjoy your sentence." Eric stood and turned away from Grace.

As the deputies took Grace out of the courtroom, Kaylee suddenly jumped off the balcony. The deputies were surprised to find a human in their midst.

Grace was surprised that Kaylee had come to rescue her—it was stupid, foolish, and dangerous.

Kuruk hissed, "Silver!"

Michael shouted, "How did you get in here?"

Joseph yelled, "Kill the silver bitch!"

Eric growled, "Human blood! Seize her!"

Grace gasped, "Oh no!"

The deputies attacked Kaylee, and she fought them with her black belt in Karate and silver weaponry. Eric recognized her as the human woman who had captured him in the woods. Grace was terrified that Kaylee would get hurt or killed. Kaylee continued to hit, kick, throw sliver weapons, and fight three vampires simultaneously. As the fight wore on, Kaylee's breath became labored.

Grace called frantically, "Jump! Now!"

"I can't," Kaylee panted.

"Forget me, go save yourself. Jump!"

Kaylee held up her hands in surrender. "Stop! I don't have strength like you guys. I give up. I will be cooperative, just stay back, please? I am human and fragile."

The deputies started to move away from her. Grace gasped, shocked that Kaylee was giving up.

Eric removed his jacket and sped toward Grace. She was surprised when she recognized him. Kaylee looked at Eric, and he finally recognized her as well.

"Surrender," he said softly, holding a knife to Grace.

Kaylee was still breathing heavily as she said, "Set her free and you can have me instead. Deal?"

"Deal."

"No!" Grace shouted. "Don't trust him! Jump!"

Kaylee's breath was starting to return to normal as she admitted, "I don't have a choice."

"Don't sacrifice your life for me!"

"Silence!" Eric said to Grace. "Go on," he urged Kaylee.

"This is my older sister, Grace Dailage. She doesn't know who marked her because I killed her maker, a male in his late 20s. I keep her as my marked vampire more or less. She is my only sister, the only family I have. She can't give you her address because I am human and we live together."

Everyone was surprised at this. Grace was crying blood tears as she begged, "Jump! Please!"

Eric, confused, yelled, "What's *jump* mean?"

Grace was silent for a moment. She clearly didn't want to tell him. Kaylee looked at him and said, "To escape."

Grace was shocked. "What? Are you out of your mind?"

"Silence or our deal is off." Eric looked at Kaylee. "You attacked me back in the woods and murdered my marked man! You also killed her maker! You brutally murdered vampires!"

"I have only killed two vampires so far," Kaylee said. "I am telling you the truth."

Joseph shouted, "She was one of them! On of the silver people!"

Kuruk hissed, "You betrayed us!"

Michael said, "I don't need your sympathy."

Kaylee felts helpless as they blamed her and accused her of brutality. Eric yelled "Enough! Let me take care of this!" The deputies were silent. Eric said, "Go on."

"You're mistaking me for someone else. I am not with those silver people. I am just doing research on vampires. I don't normally harm any vampires. I am worried sick about Grace and her being attacked by the silver people. I think they need to be stopped. I don't want to lose her. I came to rescue her here because I love her. I am on your side and I can help you."

All the deputies were confused. She seemed to be telling the truth, but it sounded like a story.

"May I talk to Grace alone for a few moments?" Kaylee asked. Eric considered this. Finally he nodded his assent and stepped aside.

Kaylee walk toward to Grace, removed her silver gloves, and held out both arms. "Keep your distance," warned one of the deputies. Kaylee stopped. All the deputies moved backward and watched them. Kaylee made sure they couldn't hear her talking.

"My angel sent me here. She took my powers because I am ready now, I am going to be like you," she whispered into Grace's ear.

Grace's eyes flew open wide. "What? Wait, you're sure?"

"Yes."

Grace looked upset with Kaylee. However, she now understood why Kaylee had no powers to jump from here to save herself. She looked at Kaylee with sadness and defeat in her eyes.

Eric asked, "Done?"

"Yeah," Kaylee said.

"Remove all your silver now."

"Set Grace free first, then I will do it," Kaylee replied.

Eric sighed. "Set her free," he ordered Kuruk.

Kuruk did as Eric ordered, and Kaylee requested, "Give her blood now, please."

Eric, exasperated, said, "Bring her a drink." Michael did so, and Grace drank greedily. The blood helped her recover from the silver exposure, and she quickly got her strength back.

Kaylee said, "Thank you" as she began to remove her boots. She proceeded to strip off all her silver until only her mask and goggles remained. They were all curious to see who she really was. Suddenly Kaylee said, "Eric, please can we discuses this privately?" Grace and all the deputies were confused.

"How do you know my name?" Eric asked, looking at her closely. "Did you come to my bar last night?"

Grace was confused. "You know him?"

Kaylee removed her goggles first then removed her mask. Eric was very surprised. It was the woman who had danced with him last night. "Tara?" he gasped.

Michael suspected what was going on. He recognized Kaylee and knew that Eric had danced with her. However, he kept silent.

Grace was confused. "Who's Tara?"

Kuruk and Joseph hadn't seen her at the bar, and they were puzzled by everyone's confusion.

Kaylee said to Grace, "I attack him in the woods, and I was at the bar last night looking for you. How did they capture you?"

Grace guiltily admitted, "They arrested me at Longshore Bar. I am so stupid. If I'd listened to you in the first place we wouldn't be here today."

"I suppose your name isn't Tara," Eric said. "What's your real name?"

"I am Kaylee Dailage. I came to the bar because I was looking for Grace."

Eric's anger was mounting. He moved closer to Kaylee and growled. His fangs showed.

Kaylee gasped, "No, don't!" Her head was almost on his chest, and she was shaking with fear and desire. Eric and Kaylee stared at each other for a moment then Eric walked away from her. He was shaking with rage and fear—fear that his feelings were true and that he loved her.

"I don't care about your bullshit story!" he yelled. "You will never get out of here alive! You murder vampires and you broke vampire law! No human knows this court exists! And Grace, you broke the laws! You are supposed to leave humans and your old life behind!"

"She's different than you think. She's my sister."

"She is the same as all humans. You didn't have a maker to teach you these things, so I will do it now. Stay away from humans!" These are our rules, our laws. Vampires and humans cannot live together."

Kaylee said, "Wait, calm down. How can you stand up against silver people on your own?"

"Our laws will take care of it, but not you, human!" Eric spoke to Grace again. "Never ask humans for help, ever!" Then he turned toward the other sister and said, "Don't do any research on vampires anymore! Vampires don't have doctors!"

Kaylee felt frustrated that Eric was yelling so much. Kaylee walked toward Eric and slapped his face. Eric growled at her. Kaylee gasped.

Grace said, "Stop, don't scare her."

Eric said, "Quiet!"

Kaylee begged, "I want to make you an offer."

All the deputies looked at each other in disbelief. They had never see any human who would say such words.

Kaylee continued, "I want you to make me one of you."

Michael's voice was low as he said, "What?"

Eric's growling showed the turmoil of his emotions—real anger, confusion, and love. This allowed her to walk around the table to avoid him attacking her, but she tripped by the stairs. Eric smashed a candle held in a human skull. She looked afraid but didn't take her eyes off of him. Eric was very emotional because he loved her and knew that she was breaking laws. He didn't want to lose her because of vampire laws and traditions. Eric ordered Michael to hold her, and he did.

The other deputies were excited at the prospect of killing a human tonight. Kuruk asked, "Can I scalp her?"

Joseph said, “Let her skull replace the one you broke.”

Kuruk added, “Yeah, get it over with! She is too much drama.”

Grace begged, “No, please!”

Eric and Michael stared at each other for moment then Michael’s eyes turned away from him.

Eric said to Kaylee, “Tell me the truth. Are you with the silver people?”

“No, I’ve never met any silver people or even seen them. Think about it. I’ve come to you alone twice and I have not hurt you. The two times I killed vampires it was in self defense or defense of Grace. I want to learn to be a vampire healer. That’s why I’m doing research on vampires.”

Joseph added, “Hey, you don’t know if she was one of them. She could lead them here. Look at her. She still has the silver clothes. Let’s just get it over with and kill her. ”

Grace yelled, “How dare you think she was one of them when she has a vampire sister! Come on, human or vampire, either way she would support our side against silver people! She wants to maintain vampire equal rights because of me!”

Eric asked Kaylee, “Why do you want to be one of us?”

Kaylee knelt on the floor and begged, “Please let me become a vampire. I want to stop the silver people. If I prove to you that I am not with the silver people, will you let us out of this trouble? I mean, like you said, I broke the law by trespassing here, right? I am offering a deal.”

Joseph started, “Wait…”

Eric was pissed off. "Don’t talk,” he said to Joseph. All the deputies fell silent.

Eric took Kaylee by the arm. He looked at her, trying to use his powers of mind control. *Test…what do you think of me?* Mind control wasn’t working.

Kaylee felt like she walked on air around him. *You are handsome and hot. You scare me and excite me at the same time.*

Eric wanted to kiss her but couldn't because the deputies were still there. Eric changed the subject and his tactics. He looked deeply into her eyes. "Tell me your address."

Grace sighed, "It doesn't work."

Eric turned around to look at Grace. "What?"

"She is trained to resist vampire imprinting," Grace said to Eric. Eric turned around and felt anger. He growled at Kaylee and grabbed her arm. He threw her down on the floor. All the deputies looked at each other for moment.

Michael said, "Trained?"

Grace ran to Kayle to be sure she was all right. Kaylee was doing okay, without any broken bones. "Yeah I am fine," she reassured Grace, "but guess what? I got the recording contract for three years as a singer in California. I should be heading out next week, but it was the wrong path for now. That was the biggest dream of my life."

Grace was surprised that she has some good news. "What? Oh," she sighed, "It's all my fault."

"Forget it. I don't want to leave without you," Kaylee said to Grace. Hearing this story, Eric realized for sure she was the woman from last night.

Grace cried and sighed, "Damn it. Thank you for taking care of me, you are the best sister and adoptive maker. Oh, I will miss your scent. I love you."

"I love you, too." Grace and Kaylee kissed each other on one cheek then the other. Suddenly Grace sniffed her. She knew Kaylee was still wearing silver because it covered her virgin smell. Grace said in a low whisper, "Remove your silver."

Kaylee whispered back, "Shh, don't let them find out I am a virgin."

Grace was confused. "But the silver kills you after you wake up as a vampire."

Joseph sneered, "Vampires are forbidden to love humans."

Kuruk added, "Right."

Grace turned and said, "Don't tell me what to do! I will cry for her! Believe me, vampires rarely have love relationships. They don't work out. All I have is my sister."

Eric and Michael looked at each other for moment, then looked back at Kaylee and Grace. Michael suspected Eric might be one vampire who *did* fall in love.

Kuruk added, "Vampires doesn't have relationships. It is forbidden."

"Eric," Grace said, "I am done, but one thing, please taken her with you. Protect her for me."

Eric sighed, "I am willing to protect her." Eric ordered Michael to take Grace away from Kaylee, then he sat down beside her.

Kaylee whispered, "Set me free like I did you back in to woods. Please?"

Eric stared at her for moment, thinking about setting her free. He touched her face gently and leaned down to her neck. She felt his breath on her skin, and it have her goose bumps.

Grace was upset and crying blood tears. "I can't watch her die." She turned around.

Kuruk joked, "Oh poor young thing."

Eric bit Kaylee, and she cried out. Grace heard her screaming and dropped to her knees on the floor. The vampires moved closer to Eric and Kaylee, getting excited by the smell of blood. Eric fed until Kaylee was completely dead. He got up, walked to his table, and used a napkin to clean up his mouth. *That was the most amazing blood I've ever had*, he thought. Joseph came over and began to suck some blood from her wrist, but Eric stopped him. "We can't drain her completely dry. I want her to come back." His deputies were surprised that he was planning to keep her marked after all.

Grace was still crying on the other side of the room. Joseph wiped his mouth and said, "Oh, this was real healthy blood. Obviously she was fresh and clean." Joseph walked to Grace and said, "Your sister still has plenty of blood in her. Do you want some?"

Grace gasped, "No, you sick bastard."

Joseph chuckled. "Accept what you are."

Kuruk and Michael both sampled Kaylee's blood, wiping the red liquid from their mouths with a smile.

Kaylee was completely dead on the floor. Eric said to her sister, "Grace, I am done, so you can look at her." Grace walked over to Kaylee, sobbing.

Kuruk sniffed the air. "Hmm, deliciously warm blood. I had almost forgotten how good that smells. I do want equal rights, and know that this is the price, but it smells *so* good."

Michael nodded, " Fresh always tastes so much better."

Joseph, curious and a bit shocked, said, "Is this for real? Are you going to let her become one of us?"

Eric gave them all a hard look that let them know he was serious. Then he said to his deputies, "Take Grace to a cell."

"What?" Grace shouted. "I thought you were supposed to protect me! Why are you still keeping me?"

"Of course I will set you free after we discuss some things in private, if you don't mind?"

Joseph took Grace, and Kuruk picked up Kaylee's dead body and brought them both to a cell.

# CHAPTER 13

Michael and Eric were alone. Michael was puzzled and said, "I have never see anything like that in my many centuries. You broke the law and our traditions. You were supposed to kill her for trespassing, but you are planning to let her become one of us, aren't you?"

Eric had the idea that they could use her against the silver people, and that way he could still be with her. "Let's see what she's offering; at the very least we gain a vampire. We need to increase our numbers."

Kuruk and Joseph rejoined them after they had brought the women to the cell. Eric asked, "What do you think of her?"

Joseph said, "She should become a new skull on the table. Don't let her to be one of us."

Kuruk added, "I don't know, but you broke the law. You are the boss and can decide what to do with her, but I don't want to be at risk of going to prison. She could lead the silver people right to us. We don't know if we can trust her yet."

"This is too risky for all of us. You can't take her offer. We need to keep our own laws and traditions." Joseph hit the table with his fist.

Michael was thoughtful for a moment before saying, "We lose many vampires' lives out there now because of the stupid silver people, so what can we do about it? How is this going to change that fact?"

Eric paused. "Let's wait and see what she's offering. I think it might speak to Michael's point."

Joseph crossed his arms over his chest. "Oh come on. If any other deputy vampires find out what you did, you will be a skull on the table for breaking the law. Forget her to save yourself."

Eric felt guilty. "Well, I admit that I broke the law, but look at her. She took on three experienced vampires and held her own for a long time. What if we used her skills against the silver people? Tell me what you think."

Kuruk didn't think for long. "Good idea. Let's use her abilities to fight like a vampire."

Michael was skeptical. "Yeah, try her. If she can't do it, we've lost nothing."

Joseph was adamant. "No, we must keep traditions and honor our laws! A human broke in here and must be killed. Her skills don't change anything! We can handle the silver people ourselves. Besides, one of them must die because they are of the same blood. Our law forbids marking one of your own family!"

The deputies were puzzled. Kuruk asked, "What? I am not familiar with this law of not marking your own family."

Michael responded, "I don't care about this anymore. Many vampires have already lost their lives so far to these silver people and to humans."

Joseph suggested, "Why not set up new laws?"

Michael shouted, "Forget about the laws! Now we need to get focused on the silver people and how can we deal with them!"

Kuruk snarled, "I would chop off the heads of those silver people."

Eric chuckled, "Kuruk, that's your response to everything. Look, only a few humans are the silver people. We should rebel and ask for our equal rights again." Eric looked at Joseph. "I don't need to add new laws. I am in charge of this, not you, Joseph. Let's see what she's offering. If it doesn't work, we can always fall back on the law. She broke the law, plain and simple. Agreed?" They all agreed, and Eric continued, "Look, please keep this secret. Tell nobody."

To Eric's relief, they all agreed. He still wanted her, but at the same time he didn't want to tell them the truth about how he felt.

Joseph chuckled, "You broke the law and traditions of our race."

Eric chuckled but with little humor. "I don't have much choice but to use her."

Kuruk asked, "What about Grace? What's their address?"

Eric and the deputies headed over to the prison cell. Grace was crying and holding her sister's dead body.

"Bring the backhoe and met me there in the woods, but please watch out for silver people," Eric said to Joseph.

"Yes, sir," Joseph said as he left. Eric open the prison door, picked up Kaylee's dead body, and put it on his shoulder. One of the deputies took Grace out of the cell.

Grace asked, "Where are we going?"

"You talk too much. Follow me."

It was nearly dawn. Michael had a gun and knife and led the group. Eric followed and was carrying Kaylee on his shoulder. Kuruk's old-fashioned backpack held a small shovel inside.

Grace felt frustrated not knowing where they were going. They arrived at a spot in the woods where Joseph waited with a backhoe. Grace noticed that it was drilling two deep, dirty holes. Joseph hopped off the machine when they arrived. Eric dropped Kaylee on the ground.

Grace said, "Hey don't drop her. Take it easy."

Eric sighed, "Shut up. She can't feel a thing."

"Why are there two holes in the ground?"

Michael hissed, "Shh! Keep your voice low. Silver people might be out here."

Joseph sighed, "Ah, this was a waste of my time. Look, both of you sleep in the holes. It will soon be dawn. So in you go." He pointed at the hole.

Grace gasped, "What? No! This isn't a protected place. You broke your word to Kaylee."

Kuruk said, "Oh, stop complaining, crybaby. This is definitely a protected place."

Eric turned to the Grace and said, "You need to go in there."

"Why don't we stay the cell, where Kaylee will be safe from silver people? Look, this is disgusting with all the dirt and bugs."

Eric felt frustrated. Kuruk grabbed a shovel and covered Kaylee up with mulch and flowers.

Michael smiled, "Since you have no address, you can sleep next to her."

Grace knew she had no option. "Okay, fine. I'll go in." Grace got in the hole.

Kuruk smiled and said, "Good girl. I lived through this many times in my centuries. Have fun and enjoy the experience."

Michael sighed and warned, "The sun will kill you soon if you don't hurry up."

"See ya tomorrow," Eric said as he shoveled dirt over her. They covered the dirt with mulch and flowers.

Joseph sighed, "Whew. Do young vampires always complain this much?"

They left them there and headed back. They were safe and clear from silver people and went to rest for the daytime.

Instead of sleeping, Eric thought about Kaylee. At sunset, he found himself alone standing on the ground next to where Grace was buried. A few minutes later Joseph came up behind his back, his silver knife drawn in his leather-clad hand. Eric said, "Check to see if there are any silver people around."

"I haven't seen anything," Joseph said.

All of a sudden Michael came toward them from in front of Eric. Joseph reached behind his back, hiding the knife and glove. Kuruk came up and stood beside Eric. The deputies waited for Grace and Kaylee to wake up. Finally Grace dug herself out and saw the deputies standing and waiting.

"Where's Kaylee?" she asked.

Joseph stated, "Kaylee is still in the ground."

Grace wiped her dirty clothes, dust flying everywhere, and said, "Jeez, this is disgusting."

Kuruk sighed, "She *never* shuts up."

Eric sighed, "Keep quiet, and don't let silver people find us."

Kaylee's angel was inside her dead body protecting her. The angel said in Kaylee's head, *I am leading you into a vampire's life. This is the fate that I chose for you when you were born. You still have the power that I gave you. You can keep it as you wish. There are some new powers that will manifest once you come out. You will need to learn your new powers of witchcraft, and those that will translate into vampire powers.*

*Your vampire powers will automatically be transferred to you when you wake up. You won't need any training to use them. You will need to be trained to use your witch powers. Some of your new power is from witchcraft, and you should keep doing that always. You can touch silver, walk in sunlight, continue to make some potions, and fly and jump like you do now. You will never eat or get bloodthirsty. It is important for you to embrace vampire life and leave your human life behind.*

*Also someone who truly loves you can break the vampire curse. Someone will bond with you and from a triangle with Grace. The triangle will protect you when you need something or need to protect your identity for short time. Silver will always be there for you forever. I made both you and Grace a new hybrid vampire and rulers because you are blood sisters, but you are extra strong and have some powers Grace doesn't. You will be the ruler of the vampires in all the world's universites. If Grace dies the all of the vampires will die except for you. You will live alone forever because you don't feed and can't produce vampires. You need to live with silver because it feeds your energy. Try to figure out what you are, learn about your new self.*

*"You can't die because you are strong and powerful. You need to be a survivor. Please stay strong and survive. You need to protect Grace. It's most important to make vampires safe. Your mother died because of you. I took her because I didn't want her to see visions of your or Grace's future. Your mother's power to see visions of the future needs to be passed on to one of you. You can choose who will carry this power.*

Kaylee knew Grace had been jealous when they were younger because she had no powers, so she said to her angel, "Let Grace have it."

*She can't view the past. It only works to see forward, and she will keep it forever. Now on to other matters, first of all you need to protect the vampires by stopping the silver people. I will give you a list of four kinds of creatures you must destroy. They will be strange creatures. They will appear about every three to six months. You will need to kill them within the borders of each country on Earth.*

"Do I have to go alone against them?"

*No, you will find a team. Find the four different strange creatures, and then you must kill old hybrid vampires. They are the only ones who can stop everything from happening.*

"Why do we need war between new and old hybrid vampires?"

*The world needs to change, and the old vampires and rulers are unable to do that. We need them to pass on so that the new leadership will accept equal rights. You and Grace will become that new leadership and unite both groups. I am going to leave you until you complete the things on the list. I will see you again, Kaylee.*

The angel left her.

*Wait a minute, wait!* Kaylee shouted in her mind, but the angel had left her completely.

Grace started to worry that the silver may have weakened Kaylee and that she couldn't dig herself out. "Help her out," she said to the other vampires.

Joseph crossed his arms over his chest. "No, let her dig by herself."

Eric sighed, "Ah, the young have no patience."

Grace knew that Kaylee still had some silver on her. She decided to dig by herself to help Kaylee. "Oh, I smell silver."

Michael thought Grace was crazy. "Smell silver? She hasn't any silver with her." Grace grab a shovel and started digging. Kuruk laughed and made a crazy sign behind her back.

Joseph laughed, "Whew, good thing she isn't my marked. She's mentally ill." The deputies laughed.

Kaylee was still in the ground when all of the sudden the earth quaked. Grace and the deputies heard strange sounds from below the ground. Grace gasped and started to move back from where Kaylee was buried. The noise became louder, and then sand and dirt were thrown at the deputies and Grace. They shielded themselves as Kaylee emerged from the ground. She flew straight up in the air and floated. All the deputies and Grace gasped. Kaylee shouted. She was scared when her angel left. The deputies shared a look of panic and quickly ran into the woods. But Grace stayed. She looked up in the air, watching her sister. Kaylee shook her body to get rid of the dirt and rubbed her hands to clean them off. She smiled. She still had powers.

"Kaylee, are you all right?" Grace asked.

Kaylee looked down to see Grace on the ground. She flew down fast and landed on one knee next to her. Kaylee was so relieved to see that Grace was safe. Grace gasped and stared at her sister. "Silver eyes?"

Kaylee was puzzled, but she believed her sister—her eyes must have turned silver. "Come on, let go home," Kaylee said. Grace looked happy and Kaylee was too. Kaylee took her sister's hand and flew them both away.

The deputies stopped running and turned to see the girls disappearing.

Joseph gasped, "What the hell was that flying thing?"

Michael added, "What is she?"

Kuruk gasped, "And we *still* have no address?"

"Let's get back to the office before we meet any silver people out here," said Eric.

Kuruk asked, "Is she dangerous to us? Should I have scalped her head?"

Michael added, "I have never seen anything like this. What should we do with her?"

Joseph sneered, "See I told you. I don't trust her, she should be dead."

Eric was worried because he thought Kaylee was out of control and he could be in real trouble if other vampires found out he let her become a vampire after killing two of their kind.

"Just shut up," he said. "Let me think of what we can do about her." Eric hoped that she would be cooperative and not tell anybody that he broke his laws.

When they got back home, Grace said to Kaylee, "I am thirsty. I will be right back." She stepped out of Kaylee's bedroom. Kaylee looked at herself in the mirror. It was like seeing a whole new person. She had silver eyes, white skin, and fangs. Grace came back with two glasses of blood to drink. She handed one to Kaylee.

"Look, I will never get bloodthirsty or hungry for food."

Grace was confused. "What? That's impossible."

Kaylee laughed softly, "I still had silver underwear on me when I was died, remember?"

"That didn't kill you?"

Kaylee pulled her pants aside to show her silver underwear. "No."

Grace looked confused and surprised. "It looks like it isn't bothering you at all."

Kaylee chuckled, "Look, I will explain everything." Grace sat with her on the bed and Kaylee began talking.

# CHAPTER 14

Eric and Michael were in the office. Michael turned to Eric. "We must find Grace and Kaylee tonight. What if silver people attack Kaylee or something?"

"If they found out we broke the law, they would punished us all together. We have to find them ourselves before the silver people attack."

"Why did you let her become one of us? This will get us in trouble. Come on, I am marked by you and I don't want to lose you. I am also your best friend."

"That you are," smiled Eric.

"What's the deal about Joseph? Can we trust him? He is still pretty new our office. He's been here for what—five, six months? Do you think he would tell anybody?"

Michael and Eric knew Joseph might be dangerous since he was so new. He might not have the same loyalty. They felt they could trust Kuruk more because he had been with them so long, but then again he was his own brand of trouble.

Eric was nervous about how his actions might play out. "I know, but let's wait and see how things go. Come on, I expect the others to be here soon."

"I hope Joseph keeps quiet," Eric said to himself. They came out of his office and into the main room. In a few moments they were joined by Kuruk and Joseph. They came in with one case of 12H-blood. Joseph opened the case and gave everybody one.

"Sorry, I've made a mess," Eric said, "but we must act now and search for Grace and Kaylee. We need to keep looking, even if it takes all night until dawn. Is that clear?"

Michael looked serious. "Yes, sir."

Joseph and Kuruk didn't like the idea because they could get in trouble because of Eric. Joseph said, "You should do this by yourself—it was your mistake. You should take responsibility for making Kaylee a vampire."

"Enough Joseph," Eric said pointing at him. Kuruk and Joseph looked at each other for a moment. Kuruk spoke up, "It is only us? Do you think we have enough people to find them?"

Joseph nodded. "Right, why don't we ask somebody for help finding them?"

Eric was angry with Joseph. "Don't ask anybody for help. We can do this ourselves."

Joseph was silent for a moment, then said to Eric, "Yes, sir."

Kuruk looked at Eric. "If other vampires find out about this, you will be trouble. This would be easier if you kept to the laws."

Eric came close to Kuruk's face. "Shut up. Don't say a damn thing about me! Find them! Got it?"

Kuruk was silent for a moment, then said, "Yes, sir."

"What if it doesn't work? How are we supposed to find them with the silver people still out there? It seems like bad timing," said Michael.

"If we find her, we should kill her for breaking the law. We should have kept our traditions and laws safe," said Joseph.

"No, don't kill her. She can help us. I prefer you kill the silver people instead."

Kuruk was thoughtful. "What if she lied or if she was one of them before? What do we do with her then?"

"Killing her would be so much easier, and it would save you all from my trouble," said Eric. "But I still think she can help with the silver people."

"What's about Grace?" asked Michael.

"If we find Grace then we find Kaylee. We know that Kaylee risked everything to save her sister. See if you can use that relationship."

Soon the meeting broke up and they were on their way. Eric was in turmoil. Kaylee had broken their vampire law. By tradition and law he should have killed her on the spot. He was very confused and guilty. He had made a huge mistake and broken the law, and on top of that he'd gotten his deputies mixed up in it too. How could he have fallen in love with Kaylee at this time? Vampires had formidable laws on love between humans and vampires and even between vampires themselves.

The sisters each took hot steamy baths. They went to bed as the first rays of dawn were coming up. Grace was resting in the basement and Kaylee lay on her own bed. Once she fell asleep, she began to float in the air. They rested all day. Kaylee was sound asleep in her bedroom, the sun shining on her, but it didn't hurt at all. Kaylee's body floated toward the sunlight. The sun drew her like a magnet.

Kaylee felt the light on her eyes and woke up with a start. She stared through the curtain on the window, which had slid apart. She panicked and plopped down. Why did she float while she rested? Once she got comfortable again and was almost asleep, she opened one eye to see if she was floating again. She was.

Grace woke up and walked upstairs. She saw Kaylee floating as slept. Grace stared at her while she floated. "Kaylee?"

Kaylee woke up, noticed that she was floating, and then stood on the floor. Kaylee was puzzled. "Why do I float when I sleep? Is that a vampire thing?"

Grace shrugged her shoulders and chuckled, "It isn't a vampire power that I know of. Maybe it is a witch thing? It is awesome."

"Whew. I have to figure out what powers I have and how to use them."

Grace giggled, "It's good to have you back."

They went into the kitchen. Grace sat while Kaylee took blood from the refrigerator. She gave the blood to Grace and looked at the cow's milk. She was a bit sad that she could no longer drink it.

"Are you going to try milk? Or try blood?"

"Not blood, but I will try milk." Kaylee poured a very small amount in two glasses. She took a tiny sip. Grace was curious and stared at Kaylee. Kaylee's tongue touched the milk. "Yuck!" She retched in the sink. "That was the grossest thing ever I tasted."

Grace laughed, "Maybe blood works for you."

Kaylee didn't want to try blood because she thought she would hate it. "I don't think this will work for me." The idea of drinking blood gave her the shivers.

"Try it like you did the milk," her sister coaxed.

Kaylee sighed. "Okay, let me have sip from yours." Grace gave it to her. Unable to believe what she was doing, Kaylee's tongue touched the blood. "Oh, gross! Yuck! This is definitely not for me, but milk is even worse."

Grace laughed. "That was some face you just made! I wish I had a camera!"

Kaylee gave the glass back to Grace. "Grace, while I was dead, an angel came and talked to me. She gave me powers and told me things. One of the things she said is that you are going to have Mom's power to see the future."

Grace just sat there, dumbfounded. "What do I do?"

"Now that I'm a vampire too, it is doubly important that we stop the silver people."

"Right…umm, how come I can't see the future by now? Do I have to do something?"

"I don't know. Maybe wait a little while? Oh, damn, I forget my motorcycle back into woods. I have to go get it. You want to come?"

"Sure, why not."

Kaylee still has her extra goggles from her workroom, so she took one pair for herself as much out of habit as needing them. She was still getting used to her new powers. Grace and Kaylee flew to the woods. Kaylee put her goggles on and they walked into the woods on an old path.

"If the deputies find us, you need to be careful about what you tell them, especially about our new hybrid. Hold on, I can read those people's thoughts right now! Oh, this is really weird," Grace said.

"Silver people?"

"No, definitely deputies…. They are looking for us now." Grace had a faraway look on her face as she learned her new powers.

"Hurry, you stay hidden in the trees and stay still until I get back." Grace nodded as she tucked herself against the tree.

Kaylee walked carefully along. She was still about 30 feet from where she had parked her motorcycle in the bushes. Suddenly, she saw a vampire shape. With her night vision goggles it was purple against a gray background. The vampire was behind a tree. She moved so they could see her.

All the deputies had their fangs out and were full-on vampire. Eric stared at Kaylee alone from a distance. Eric yelled, "Seize her!"

Suddenly the four deputies came at Kaylee while Grace was hiding so that nobody could see her yet. Deputies fought against Kaylee alone. The movements were so fast a normal humans would not be able to see them. Steel weapons glinted and clanged as the five fought. Kaylee was surprised at how much easier it was to fight as a vampire without getting out of breath or fearing injury so much. Deputies noticed that her karate skills were strong and that she was very graceful. Joseph shouted, "She's too strong for us!"

Eric came to Kaylee with his ancient sword. "Stop," he commanded. "Stay and work with me."

"Do you honestly think I would listen you? You put us in dirty holes and thought it was safe for Grace! You filthy liar! You didn't protect her when I asked you to!" Eric and Kaylee put their swords in front of their faces in salute.

Eric looked around. "Where's Grace?"

"Oh I don't know, somewhere. Maybe shopping?"

Eric was frustrated and angry. He growled and attacked Kaylee. She defended herself well, meeting his years of experience with her natural grace and martial arts training. Finally, Kaylee beat him, holding a sword at his throat.

"Why do you care about Grace?" she asked Eric.

The deputies moved closer. Kuruk, ever focused on the present, asked, "So what's your address?"

Kaylee, not turning from Eric, said, "I live in cave. No address, sorry." Kuruk didn't take that well and drew a sword to attack her. Kaylee moved her sword from Eric's throat and fought Kuruk. Eric, not wanting to miss an opportunity, thrust his sword at Kaylee. Kaylee met his sword and fought him and Kuruk. When Joseph tried to jump her from a tree, she pulled out a small silver whip and wrapped it around his ankles. She dropped him to the ground. After besting the deputies, Kaylee dropped to one knee next to Eric.

Deputies now understood that she had been transformed into a vampire without any training by her maker. Eric shouted, "Stop!" He looked around to include his deputies and Kaylee." Let's make this quick. I want your cooperation against a common enemy, the silver people. They are out here and can find us at any moment. Let's move someplace safe to discuss this."

"How am I supposed to trust you? You hurt Grace."

"Come on, this isn't a safe place to talk. What if they attack us right here?"

Joseph had slipped off and then yelled that he had Grace. He held her in a silver rope around her hands.

"Good, *now* I want you to come with us," Eric said to Kaylee.

Kuruk went to seize Kaylee, but she threw a silver web that hit Joseph's face. She ran to catch Grace, then lifted Grace because she knew she couldn't run while silver was on her. Kaylee sped to the motorcycle, hidden in the bushes. Kaylee put Grace on the back seat of the motorcycle. She hopped on but didn't start the engine. Eric ran and caught up just as they jumped to the garage.

Inside the dark garage, Kaylee turned the light on. Eric grabbed Grace and held his sword to Grace's neck. Kaylee was surprised. She hadn't realized Eric was so close behind them.

"Don't hurt her!" she shouted. "I will cooperate with you."

Eric lowered the point of the sword. He looked at everything inside of the garage. "Where are we are?"

"This is where we live."

"You live in a garage?"

"No, up there." Kaylee pointed up at the stairs.

"What's your address?"

Kaylee was silent for a moment. Eric waited impatiently for her answer. He lifted his hand to hit Grace.

"Hey! Take it easy," Kaylee said to Eric. "We live at 2 Maple Terrace in Millbury." Eric let Grace go. "Don't come closer to us."

"Tell him everything so that he will understand," Grace said to Kaylee. Kaylee nodded.

Eric held up his hand. With his other hand he dialed his cell phone to call Joseph. "Bring a van to 2 Maple Terrance, Millbury, this instant." Joseph told the others, who were quickly on their way.

Kaylee headed out of the garage. "Where are you going?" Eric asked to her back. Kaylee led them out of garage. She turned to go in the door, but the door was locked.

"Shit. It's locked. Do you have a key, Grace?"

Grace shook her head no and said, "Just jump."

Eric looked panicked. "No, wait, no jumping! If you do, I swear I'll kill her!"

Grace turned to Eric. "Don't be stupid. She needs to get in the house."

"If you let me jump inside, I will open the door for you to come in. Please don't damage anything in my house, all right?"

Eric held Grace tightly when Kaylee disappeared. She reappeared a moment later. "Come in." She started to turn on some lights.

Eric sniffed the air. "Does anyone else live here? It smells like humans."

"It must take a while for the human scent to leave. It is just the two of us. This has been our house since we were little." Kaylee removed her goggles and puts them down on the counter.

Eric stared, shocked, and said, "What the hell are you?"

The van honked outside, and the deputies were on the doorstep quickly. As they came in, they stared at Kaylee's eyes. Kuruk added his usually loquacious hiss to the conversation. Joseph peered closer. "Are they for real?"

"What the hell is this?" Michael asked.

Kaylee was silent for moment. Grace said, "Don't panic, guys, she won't harm you."

Eric said to Kuruk, "Check her weapon. All her silver must be removed if you can." Kuruk checked her black leather jacket. There was silver inside and outside. "Take it off," he growled.

Kaylee was cooperative and removed her jacket. Then she removed her silver belt and started removing all her silver weapons. Kuruk continued to growl as he held open a bag for her to drop silver stuff into. The deputies were rather shocked that she could touch silver so easily.

Eric ordered the deputies to check the house for other occupants. The men quickly dispersed and in a few moments "clear" could be heard from all points. Grace and Kaylee stared at each other. They knew what was in Kaylee's workroom. Luckily it was locked, and none of the men could get in without her.

Eric called everyone together again. "You guys take Grace to the van. I will be there in a few moments, Kaylee and I have something to discuss." The group filed out and Kaylee and Eric were alone. Eric said, "Keep your distance. Now go upstairs." Kaylee led him upstairs to her bedroom.

"This is my bedroom."

"I know. Do you have any more silver on you?"

"No, there is nothing here." She held up her arms to show him they were empty.

"Now strip. I want to make sure you don't have any silver hidden away."

Her eyes widened in surprise and fear. "I have no other jewelry or piercings. Really."

"You are a vampire now. Get used to being nude in public. It is part of our culture."

Kaylee chuckled, "I am not afraid to show you my body. There is just nothing there to see."

"Either strip or I'll call down and have my deputies hurt Grace." Eric crossed his arms over his chest.

With no choice but to do as he asked, she began to strip off her clothing. "All right," she said to Eric. She stripped down to just her silver underwear.

"See? You lied; you do have silver on. Remove them now."

"I don't feel right without silver on me."

Eric moved toward her. "Removed them now!"

Kaylee and Eric stared at each other for moment. Kaylee felt vulnerable without silver on. It had been so long since she hadn't worn silver. She removed her underwear and threw them through the window, out to the balcony outside.

Kaylee began to dress, and Eric moved backward a little. "Good riddance. So now there's a locked door that I need you to open," he said to Kaylee. Kaylee knew he meant her workroom. Slowly she led him to the door of her workroom. The door looked rather ordinary, but she knew it had special locks. Kaylee didn't want him to go in, she feared he would destroy it.

"Wait, wait," she said. "I lost the key, but there is nothing there, just storage. We haven't used it in years."

"Open it now!"

Kaylee and Eric stared at each other for a moment. Kaylee begged, "I don't want to break anything in the house. When I find the key to open it I promise I will show you."

Eric suspected that he knew what was going on in there. It must have something to do with her witchcraft, and it must be something very important to her.

Eric looked at her hard. "Is there anyone in there?"

"No! It is just an old storeroom."

"All right, let's go to the van."

Eric walked behind her as they walked out of the house. She turned off the lights as they went. As they stepped out, she locked the door. Eric noticed this and secretly unlocked the door before closing it. They entered the rear door of the van to see Grace there with Michael and Joseph. Kaylee got in with them, and Eric closed the rear door and got into the front passenger side. Kuruk drove. He smoothly pulled away from their house. Eric looked back at the house, planning to return again.

Kuruk drove them to the vampire law offices. They got out and brought Kaylee and Grace back to a cell.

Eric said to Grace, "You go in." Grace walked into the cell. Kuruk and Michael fixed a sliver chain on her cell.

Grace was feeling pain from all the silver. "I am tired of silver." They ignored her plea and left, closing the door behind them.

Kaylee was pulled toward another cell, separate from Grace's. "Why can't I stay in the same cell with Grace?"

Eric held her arm. "No, I want you to stay separated." Eric opened the door to the cell next to Grace's and pushed Kaylee in. Joseph and Kuruk set a silver chain around the cell door while Eric held a gun pointed at her. Kaylee looked at them and mocked, "Ahh, that feels good." Joseph and Kuruk stared at each other for a moment. They couldn't believe it. How could a vampire like silver?

Eric said, "Forget it, remove the silver." He looked at Kuruk and Joseph. They looked astonished.

"What?" said Joseph.

Kuruk asked Eric, "How can we watch her without silver?"

"Follow my orders. She won't go anywhere without her sister."

Kuruk took off the silver as he shook his head in disbelief.

Eric gave Joseph a gun. "You stay in case she tries to escape. I will be back within less than an hour." Eric turned to Kuruk and said, "Come with me." The two men turned and walked out the door, leaving a surprised Joseph watching Kaylee in her cell.

Eric and Kuruk picked up Michael and drove the van back to Kaylee and Grace's house. They double-checked that no one had come in while they were away. Eric stood in the kitchen while the other two men searched room by room. Eric found the letter from the record company under a magnet on the refrigerator. He read the letter and put it in his jacket pocket. The others came to the kitchen. The house was clear; now they just had to figure out what was going on inside that locked room.

They headed down and stood before the locked door. Michael and Kuruk stood back. Eric kicked the door, but nothing happened. He hit it with his shoulder, but once again nothing happened. He waved to Kuruk to do the same. Kuruk tried, but nothing budged the door.

"Go get some tools from the workshop outside," ordered Eric. Both Kuruk and Michael ran to the workroom. The men returned with a variety of tools, and the three set to work on the wall around the door. Finally, they gained access to the room.

Eric turned the lights on. Kuruk, Michael, and Eric came in, and they stared at the workroom. There were potions all over the table and ingredients on the shelves. Every space was covered. There were pictures on the wall. One showed Grace and Kaylee—Grace had fangs and it looked like Kaylee was about15 years old. Another looked quite recent—Grace looked the same though Kaylee had changed a lot.

Michael looked around and said, "What the hell is this? Is this a witch's room or something?"

Kuruk and Eric both stared at the pictures.

Eric said, "She told the truth. They have been living together, human and vampire."

Kuruk added, "Yeah, but she didn't say she was a witch, did she?"

Michael found the mouse cage. "Hey, look at this cage. I think she has mice that are vampires inside this cage."

They looked at the cage and saw that there was blood in the water bottle. They were surprised, believing that only humans could become vampires.

Kuruk asked Eric, "How is this possible?"

"I don't know. I've never in all my centuries seen anything like this."

"No wonder she has powers. Obviously she was witch before she was turned. Now can she be both a vampire and a witch?" Michael wondered.

Kuruk picked up a bottle. "Should we destroy her potions?"

Eric said, "No, don't break anything. I have idea. These things are clearly important to her. Let's pack them up and bring them to the office. This may be another weakness of hers and we could use it as leverage."

They packed quickly, putting the boxes of bottles and ingredients in the rear of the van. They went back to the office. Eric opened the door for Grace while Michael and Kuruk unlocked the silver chain.

Eric said, "Come out, I need to talk to you." Grace stood with Michael and Kuruk. Eric then opened the door for Kaylee. "Come out, please, and let's have good behavior. I need to ask you some questions." Eric spoke formally to Kaylee, "Welcome to vampire territory. You are new to this life. There are a few things you need to understand. You are marked by me and you need to follow my rules and vampire laws. I manage the deputies in this town and the surrounding area. You need to obey the deputies as well.

"I have never seen anyone who had vampires powers and sliver eyes in our history or who could pick up their vampire skills so fast. Since you seem to have additional powers, I am going to have to use additional force to guarantee your good behavior while you are learning the rules. I will hold both Grace and your witchcraft supplies. Will this guarantee your cooperation?"

Grace and Kaylee knew the importance of the potions and ingredients. Grace looked stricken.

Kaylee gasped, "Did you go back to my house and break the door? Where are my potions?"

Eric held up the framed picture and showed it to Kaylee and Grace. "How old were you when Grace became a vampire?" he asked Kaylee.

Kaylee yelled, "First you need to tell me where my potions are! I won't answer your questions until you tell me that they are safe."

Eric looked satisfied. "Those potions are important to you?"

"Yes, I've worked hard to create them. Some of them are irreplaceable. Tell me where they are!" She flew over to Eric and looked him right in eye. Joseph moved quickly and pointed a gun at her, then moved toward Grace. They knew her weakness now. Joseph pointed his gun at Grace. Eric and Kaylee stared at each other. If looks could kill, they'd both be dead.

Grace spoke up, "Take it easy, both of you. Kaylee, please. Come on."

Kaylee dropped to the ground and moved back. "Pay attention. I asked you a question," Eric continued, "How old were you when Grace became a vampire?"

All Eric got from Kaylee was a glare. She set her fists on her hips, and her lips were in a tight line.

Grace answered for her: "She was 15."

“I am speaking to Kaylee,” Eric said, not taking his eyes off Kaylee.

“Grace is right. I was 15,” Kaylee said. “Pease don’t destroy my potions. Tell me where they are.”

“Your potions are here and safe.”

“Can I see them?”

Eric turned to his men. ”Kuruk, bring them over here.”

Kuruk pulled a small wooden cart over. It looked like there should have been a donkey or small horse pulling it. There were some boxes covered by a blanket sitting atop the cart. Kaylee sped to the wagon and checked to see if there was any damage to the potions. Kaylee examined the boxes, and once she was assured they were intact, she glared at Eric again. “Don’t touch them again, or I’ll ki—”

Eric was amused by this threat. ”Kill me?”

Grace pleaded, “Don’t Kaylee., look, he found your materials. I think it would be best to follow his orders for now. Tell him everything and I think he will understand.”

“Interesting,” Eric said, “You listen to her better than to me. Tell me about yourself and why those potions are so important.”

“Let Grace tell you everything that you want to know about us,” Kaylee said, seeming exhausted. “I don’t feel like talking.”

Grace was full of concern for her sister. “I will answer your questions, but I think we need to let Kaylee rest.”

Eric looked at the sisters. “Okay, go on. You talk and she can rest.” Grace began to explain everything.

# CHAPTER 15

The men were dressed in silver from head to toe. They all wore silver headgear that hid their identities. The men were concealed in the woods waiting for vampires. They had been tipped off that there had been some vampire activity in the area. Kevin spoke into a small microphone. He too was dressed in silver, with only his head exposed. He asked, "Any activity over there?"

A quite but firm voice answered in his ear, "Still nothing, sir."

"Okay, come on in. We can go by Longshore Bar. It is a known vampire bar."

The lead man gave a quick command, "Let's go! Back in the truck." They moved into the back of a plain white 18-wheeler. Kevin moved to close the rear truck door. Then he jogged to the passenger door, hopped in, and they drove away. The truck parked in a large parking lot near the Longshore Bar. In the back, the men waited, silent and ready to attack.

Grace began to speak to the deputies and Eric. "Please keep our secrets. Please don't tell anyone other than the deputies."

"Deal. I get it, but first of all I need deputies feed on your blood, just a few drops. It will help to clear up your waste. Many new vampires need this." Kaylee held out her arm to follow his order.

Grace was shocked. "Wait, what was that for?"

Kaylee turned to her sister. "Grace, it's okay, it won't hurt. Will it?" she asked Eric. He shook his head.

"No, it's not okay. Kaylee, don't let them do it."

Eric ignored Grace. "Michael, go ahead." Michael bit Kaylee's wrist and started to suck her blood. All of a sudden, Michael started screaming in pain. His fangs burned up in a puff of smoke. They quickly re-grew, but Michael was choking. He couldn't breathe due to the blood in his throat. Kaylee looked at the blood on her wrist. It was silver.

Grace gasped, "Silver blood!"

Kaylee was worried. "Honestly, I didn't know I had silver blood. Wait, I can save his life." First she healed her wrist.

Eric ran to Michael. "Silver!" He turned and growled at Kaylee. Michael was his best friend and his trusted ally. Kaylee understood his panic. She moved over to the boxes that held her potions. "Relax, I am making a potion to save his life right now. Please give me a space!"

Grace gasped and came over to Kaylee. Grace knew that she had never done something like this before. Kaylee ignored her and focused on the work at hand. Grace was quiet, not sure what she should do and not wanting to get in her way.

Michael started to weaken and collapsed to the floor. Kaylee continued to make her potion, pulling things out of boxes. Michael started coughing, and his body shook uncontrollably.

"I feel like someone stuck a stake in me," Michael groaned through gritted teeth. Eric glared at Kaylee for hurting Michael.

"Is he dying?" Joseph asked in alarm.

Kaylee set up a few potions on the table. She picked up a book, which she flipped through quickly. She stopped on one page and read a line. Then she added something to a final bottle.

Grace looked worried. "Hurry up, heal him!"

"I know. Let me concentrate. " Kaylee walked up to Michael with a syringe in her hand. She took blood from his arm and walked back to the table.

Eric was angry. "If you don't heal him, I swear I will kill you."

Kaylee gave him a level look and kept working. She took a few drops of his blood from the syringe and put two drops in to the first bottle. The blood changed from red to black—bottle one had failed. Then she did the same to the next bottle. It failed as well. Kaylee looked nervous. In the third bottle, she performed the same test with two drops of Michael's blood. Grace was afraid for Kaylee. What if she failed to save his life? Grace came over to her and said in a low whisper, "How do you know it will work?"

Kaylee whispered back, "I already tested some of this potion on the vampire mouse." Grace thought, *This might not the same as a mouse*. Grace was afraid she would fail and that the vampire deputies would kill them.

Kaylee looked at the third bottle. The blood stayed red—that was good. It didn't stay in a drop form, but she'd have to risk it.

"I think I have found a cure," she announced. "Put Michael on the table now, and give me space." Eric and the other deputies moved in quickly to get Michael on the large wooden table. Kaylee looked at Grace and said, "Trust me." She grabbed her spell book and moved to stand next to Michael. She looked for the right words to speak and took a powder, a potion, and a bulb syringe to the table. Kaylee moved Michael to sit a sitting position. "Drop this in your mouth and swallow it. Trust me." She held out a small potion for him to sip. Michael opened his mouth and swallowed it. Kaylee put her hand on his arm. "Stay in this positions for a few seconds, then you can lay down." Michael listened to her and did as she asked.

Kaylee ripped his T-shirt off and looked at his skin. It changed color in a wave and looked like acid was eating at him. Kaylee threw the powder over his stomach and started speaking powerful words. The powder began to spread across his skin. After a few moments the powder began to coalesce and form a ball. It was as if the powder were pulling the silver from his body through his skin.

"Is the pain less now?" Kaylee asked.

"Yeah, I think so. But it still hurts."

Kaylee kept her hand above his abdomen. "I am processing the silver now. Hold still, it may still hurt on and off when it comes out of your mouth" All the deputies and Grace watched carefully. Kaylee spoke more works, her hand above his chest. Everyone began to crowd closer, curious.

Grace spoke up: "Everyone please stay back. Give her space."

Everyone moved back a little. After a moment, a small silver ball came out of Michael's mouth, and Kaylee sucked it up with the bulb syringe. Michael's color suddenly started looking more normal, and his breathing returned to normal.

Kaylee asked Michael, "How are you doing now?"

"I am feeling much better."

Grace clapped her hands and let out the breath she was holding. All the deputies let out their breath too, disbelief on their faces.

Kaylee squirted the silver into her hand and showed the deputies the silver ball. The deputies stared it like they couldn't believe what they were seeing. Kaylee looked at Michael and placed a hand on his shoulder. "You are healed completely, but you should rest for a few minutes."

Kaylee turned to Eric. "Bring him a drink." Eric made a face. He didn't appreciate being ordered around. Nevertheless, he went and got his friend a drink. He clapped Michael on the shoulder and handed him the glass. Kaylee walked toward her potions and cleaned up. She closed the book and looked up at the deputies.

Joseph looked at her and held out his hands in surrender. "Silver blood? Stay away from me!"

Eric looked at his friend. "Are you feeling well? Healed?"

Michael opened his eyes wide. "I can't believe it, she healed me completely. How did you do that?" Michael got off the table and dropped to one knee in front of Kaylee. "Kaylee, thank you for saving my life."

"You're welcome. I am actually a professional doctor for vampires. I know that silver can kill you slowly because vampires don't eliminate waste in the same manner as humans. It needs to come out either from their mouth or the other end."

Michael looked surprised, "Oh."

Kuruk made a face. "Jeez. TMI."

Joseph looked at Michael. "Don't come near me."

Grace said to Eric, "See, I told you she was different and not like other humans." Grace was proud of her sister and beamed, both at being proven right and for the great work Kaylee had done.

Joseph considered Kaylee. "I've never heard of a vampire with silver blood or eyes. This is the oddest thing. I don't know what it makes her."

Eric looked at Kaylee. What she did was amazing. She helped someone who had imprisoned her. Her compassion was wonderful. He was stuck because she had silver blood and he was falling in love with her, but couldn't be with her.

"You surprise me, Kaylee," he said. "Silver doesn't kill you, yet you are a vampire or at least I think you are. What *are* you?"

Carolyn, the host from the Longshore, was in the woods. It was chaos. The men in silver had come in and attacked the vampires. There had been silver arrows and bullets flying everywhere. She had slipped out the back door and, after tripping over a wounded vampire, escaped into the woods. She called out for help.

Kaylee sighed. "I know this sounds too much for you, but I need to have my silver back."

Eric looked at her. "Are you telling me you need it like food?" She nodded. "Okay, you can have your silver back, but only the silver that isn't a weapon. Remember, I can still hurt Grace or destroy your potions."

Kaylee gladly dug through the silver they had taken from her. She found some silver clothing and jewelry and began to put it on. She was tired from healing Michael, but the silver energized her. Kaylee felt good. For a moment, she went full vampire, her fangs emerging. They quickly retreated. Kaylee was confused, but she found this new and interesting.

"Ohhh, this must be an after-effect of the magic I performed," she said to Grace.

The deputies looked confused. Kuruk asked, "Witches can transform?"

Grace chuckled, "Sweetie, you have no idea. Look, please keep this a secret.... Wait!" she said suddenly. "Oh Goddess, silver people are attacking the vampires at Longshore Bar. Right now!"

Joseph asked, "How do you know?"

"I am psychic. I see visions. Witch family, you know.... A witness is coming. She is going to need help."

All the deputies were silent and held their breath. Just as predicted, Carolyn came rushing in. Her clothes and hair were a mess of blood and leaves. Grace looked at Kaylee and quickly reminded her to cover her eyes.

Kaylee looked around. “With what? I don’t have sunglasses.”

Grace got an idea. “Put you goggles on.” Kaylee turned her back to Carolyn as she put her goggles on to keep her seeing her silver eyes. They sat Carolyn down and Joseph brought her a glass of blood. “This is urgent,” she said breathlessly. “The Longshore Bar is on fire. Some vampires were killed by the silver people.”

“Damn it,” Eric growled, turning to the deputies. “You all stay here. Don’t go out. I will be right back.” Carolyn and Eric left the office and Kaylee moved her goggles onto her head.

Back at the truck, two men in silver were brought back injured. Others were searching the woods for vampires who had escaped. Eric and Carolyn sped into the woods where they could see a great distance. Eric saw that his bar was on fire. Eric used his cell phone to report the blaze to the fire department. His second call was to the human police to let them know that the silver people had attacked vampires and destroyed his bar.

Kevin was wearing street clothes inside the truck as he cared for the two injured men. One had a broken rib, which he taped, and the other had a broken leg. There was little he could do other than immobilize them until they could get to a doctor. He glanced at a video screen from time to time to watch for vampires near the truck.

Suddenly, the sound of sirens cut through the night. Police cruisers and fire trucks arrived at just about the same time. The firemen set to work putting out the blaze. The police began to sort out the situation.

One officer asked, “Did anyone witness this?”

Carolyn, who was sitting with Eric, said, “I did.”

The officer walked up to her and asked her what happened. “The silver people attacked the vampires. Some of the vampires disappeared or escaped. The silver people were firing weapons around the bar and then set fire to the bar with gasoline.”

“I can’t help the vampires who are dead, but I can help with the property damage. Who owns the bar? I am going to need that information.”

"Here is my contact information," Eric said, trying to restrain his frustration over the situation. "What should we do next?"

The officer took his card and put it in his notebook. "After this, I will report this to my commander. Then we will contact the Vampire Human Rights Agency. They will decide what to do next and any punishment, since this appears to be a human/vampire issue. In the meantime, I am going to do some questioning of other witnesses to confirm her story."

Back at the office, Kaylee looked at Grace. "Close your eyes. Tell me where you see silver people." The deputies were on alert the moment they heard the question. They knew what Grace could do.

Grace closed her eyes. "Silver people are in a different part of the woods from Longshore Bar. Some of them are getting ready for another attack and two are injured."

"Where?"

"I don't know, but it looks like woods everywhere to me."

"I have an idea. Let me put on my silver clothes. I can go into the area and the silver people might just be fooled long enough for me to get close to them."

Grace opened her eyes. "Bingo."

Kaylee started to get all her silver clothes on. She stripped and got dressed again, remembering Eric's statement that vampires are not modest. "Perfect, here I go."

Michael moved in front of her and said, "No, this is a very bad idea. You can wait until Eric is back."

Joseph agreed, "He's right, and you were told to obey us in Eric's absence."

Kuruk crossed his arms and looked big. "Don't go. Eric said he would destroy your potion or kill Grace if you didn't obey."

Grace threw up her hands in exasperation. "Oh come on, he will understand."

Michael turned to Grace and said, "Eric is many things, but understanding isn't usually one of them."

Grace closed her eyes and said, "I can see that certain actions will lead to success if she goes now. It will take a few days to finish this. If she doesn't go or if things go differently or change, there will be more delays in time and this will take longer to resolve."

The deputies stared at Kaylee and Grace. They had seen some amazing things from these sisters, but Eric had told them to stay, and the order of a maker was powerful.

Grace gave Kaylee a quick hug and whispered, "Please be careful."

Kaylee put her goggles on and said, "Yeah, I will see you all soon." She jumped from the office to the woods, leaving the deputies to stare in amazement at the space she had just occupied.

In the woods, Kaylee changed her goggles to an infrared view. She floated above the air and noticed several heat signatures below. She flew down to the ground silently. She walked into the woods and heard the silver people talking in the background. They were a fair distance from her. Two of them were chatting to each other and to someone else on the radio. They weren't trying to be silent and were relaxed. They never noticed Kaylee floating above them.

Kaylee heard one man say, "Nothing much tonight. I heard lot of vampires will be celebrating at a lake in the woods tomorrow night. We need to bring a lot of men there."

Kaylee walked up to them. The first man was confused by her appearance. She looked different—her clothes were fancy and she was definitely a woman. The second agent looked at the first. "I didn't know our agency had women in this division yet," he said. He figured that he hadn't heard that they hired a few women in their agency. It would certainly be a welcome change on dull patrols.

Kaylee said, "I am new, I just stared. Tell him about tomorrow. I will see you back at base."

The first guy said, "All right."

Kaylee walked away from them. The agent called on his microphone, "We are leaving now. There was nothing to find, but we have some information."

Kevin was confused. "What are you talking about? Never mind, come back in now. We have to get to the hospital."

"Everybody go home, hop in the truck," the agent said to the silver people and Kaylee. All agents began to leave the woods. One of the agents jogged up to the lead field agent.

Kaylee walked in with them. She stopped and started to go back into the woods. "Hey, wrong way," one agent called.

Kaylee responded, "I dropped something over there. I will meet you at the truck." Kaylee backed out a bit and then when it was safe jumped back to the sheriff's office, where she was surprised to find Eric waiting for her. "The process was completely successful! Hey, why are you holding Grace?"

Eric said to Kaylee, "Change your clothes this instant!" Kaylee noticed Eric was angry, but she listened to his order. Kaylee move her goggles atop head. They she picked up the leather clothes on table, waved her hand over them with a glittery spray in the air, and she was changed. She put her silver clothes on the table. "I told you to stay until I get back!" Eric growled. "Just obey me."

Kaylee didn't back down. "Wait, I can stop the silver people. Isn't that what you want? I kept my word, remember?"

"Remember you are marked by me, you have to follow my orders."

Grace was exasperated. "Eric, you make no sense! She can help us! Don't be angry over little things! You don't have powers like her!"

Eric turned around and yelled "Grace, don't talk me that way. Even if I am not your maker, I am still the leader of this community. Show me respect."

Grace started, "Look, tell me—"

"Silence!" Eric yelled at Grace.

"May I speak?" Kaylee interrupted softly. Eric turned to look at her, then studied the assembled vampires.

"Who set her free without my authorization?" he demanded.

Michael looked at Eric and took a step forward. "I did. Try to listen to them explain for once." Eric was surprised at Michael. They had known each other for centuries, and it was unexpected that Michael would challenge him so. All the deputies were silent—they were surprised that Michael was brave or foolish enough to speak out.

"Michael? Are you out of your mind?"

"We need her, and you need to listen."

Kuruk supported Michael. "Boss, you should listen to Michael. She is only two days old, and she kept her words against the silver people, so let it to be."

"She is my marked. It is my responsibility to train her. What if she got out of control and took humans? We just don't know how she'll be yet."

Joseph raised an eyebrow. "I don't think she was out of control."

Grace laughed. "Train her? Ha ha."

Michael cleared his throat. "I understand your point of view, Eric. You need to train a new vampire. You trained me. Remember, it wasn't an easy transition. But this is new territory. Kaylee isn't like the rest of us. She isn't having a problem with control, and she doesn't need help adjusting. Consider her unique situation—her training will need to be unique as well."

Kaylee kneeled on the floor and begged, "As my maker, let me speak. I am sorry, I made a mistake once. However, our plan works against the silver people. I want permission to try tomorrow to help rid us of some of the silver people. May I?"

Eric growled at her.

Michael said softly, "You are stubborn. Let her help."

Eric growled again.

Kaylee looked up at Eric and said, "My maker Eric, I am not trying to take over, but I want to help. If you want to get to know me better, let me take you to my house."

"Why your house?"

"I need a spell book and several potions back there."

"All of your potions and ingredients are here."

Kaylee looked at him and smiled. "Yes, *most* of them are right here, but you didn't get everything."

# CHAPTER 16

A large white truck sat in the garage at a federal agency. A handful of silver-clad people were in the locker room changing into their normal clothes. They put their silver weapons in a safe room.

Kevin sat alone in small office wearing his regular clothes. He was on the phone and looked up to see one of his lead agents about to head out. He hung up the phone and motioned him into his office.

"I heard that you got some intelligence on a vampire gathering tomorrow. Where did the information come from?"

"Another agent gave it to me. At least, I thought she was an agent. She was dressed in silver, although it was not exactly standard issue."

"That's impossible. We don't have any female agents in this division. We need to find out who she is."

The agent rubbed his hand over his face. "Sorry, boss, but I don't know who she was. I just thought she was one of us."

"Forget it. Go see who might be up for some overtime to go after a few more vampires."

"Sounds good, sir."

Kevin finished up his report and closed up the office. As he went in to the elevator he met up with his own boss, Ben Sullivan.

"Ben, I am glad I saw you," he said. "I have a report here from tonight's raid. I ended up sending everyone home early since we had two injuries. We got some intel on a big vampire meeting tomorrow. We are still working to check out the validity of it. Also, I need to leave the office early tomorrow to check on something. Can you run the afternoon meeting?"

"That should work just fine. Let me know what you find out about the information, okay? And be careful, I don't want any more injuries." Ben took the report from Kevin's hand.

Kevin was planning to head over to visit an old friend tomorrow. He just had a gut feeling about Kaylee and that she might have an idea about this mysterious silver-clad woman.

Eric agreed to take Kaylee back home. The group held hands, and Kaylee jumped Eric and the deputies to the sisters' house and landed in the foyer behind the front door. The girls led them to Kaylee's workroom in the basement. Grace noticed that Joseph was quite curious about a few of the potion boxes that were in the room.

"Joseph, don't touch them! Please just look," Grace said to Joseph.

Eric looked suspiciously at Kaylee as she bustled around the workroom. She noticed his look and said, "Look, you hardly know me. I've been a vampire for what, two whole days? This is my area of expertise. You have to trust me on this, okay?"

Eric nodded. "It has been a busy few days for me too, with my bar being burned and the silver people attacking and…you."

Kaylee smiled. "I understand. Well, Grace and I can help. I depend on her psychic abilities and she depends on my powers."

"Let's get what you need. Where is it?"

"Right there," she said, pointing at the wall.

"An empty wall?" Eric's eyebrows rose.

Kaylee winked and said, "Open sesame." She moved her hand over the blank wall and an opening appeared. She reached in and removed a few things. "That's all I need, and now I need my motorcycle."

They both turned to the door when they heard a car come up the driveway and park.

"Expecting anyone?" Eric asked.

"No. I don't let anyone know where I live. Duh!" Kaylee couldn't let friends know where she lived in case anyone found out that she and her vampire sister lived together. They ran to the living room and Kaylee peered out the curtain. Kevin was removing his seatbelt. "It's Kevin. He was my sensei, I took karate lessons from him for 15 years. Please don't hurt him. Wait in the basement."

"I've had enough of humans for awhile. Just get rid of him quickly, or I will kill him," Eric growled. She reached over and kissed him lightly. Her kiss had quite an effect on Eric, and as he went downstairs he had to retract his fangs.

Kevin tucked his CIA badge in the glove box and walked up the steps. After just one knock Kaylee opened the door. "Hi, Kevin! This is a surprise. Don't you look nice in a suit? Come in."

Kevin came in and gave Kaylee a hug. "Hi, sorry it is so late, but I keep meaning to give this to and forgetting. I drove by and saw a light, so I thought I'd take a chance you were home. Hey, what's with the silver eyes?"

"I am a bit of a night owl. They are contacts; what do you think?"

"Not sure about them, but they are great on you. Oh, here's the video. It is of you in karate lessons when you were a little girl. I thought you might want to have it."

"Oh, that is so kind of you. Thank you much." She pretended to stifle a yawn.

"Next time I will call you before I come over. You take care, okay?" he said as he hugged her goodbye. She knew that she wasn't supposed to see any humans once she became a vampire. She knew she would miss him terribly. He'd been such an important part of her life when she was growing up.

Suddenly Kevin's direction changed. He decided to get back to the agency instead of going home. He wanted to spy on Ben to see what he was up to. Could it be something illegal?

Eric headed back upstairs. Kuruk, Michael, and Grace were talking while Joseph was curious about those potions. He noticed the vampire mice in the cage and just had to open it to check them out. He opened his hand, and one jumped up on it. It bit him, and he pulled his hand out quickly.

Grace turned quickly. "Don't touch it!" It was too late; Joseph had left the lid open. The mouse escaped. "Where did it go?" Everyone started looking around.

Joseph pointed to a hole in the wall. "I think it went in there." Back upstairs, Eric asked Kaylee, "So how far did you get in karate?"

"I am a black belt with a few degrees. Not sure what is going to happen now," she said sadly.

They heard shouting coming from the basement. They looked at each other and headed down. They passed an open door that was clearly Grace's rooms. Eric noticed that it was a pretty bedroom and he could see her bathroom with a sink and big tub, but no toilet.

"Was this Grace's room?" he asked. "No toilet?"

"Of course. We put this in together for her needs."

Eric was impressed that they had found a solution of sorts. Grace's rooms were well hidden and showed a surprisingly good knowledge of vampire needs.

When they got to the workroom, Grace looked frustrated. "It was them!" she said, pointing to the deputies. "The mouse escaped."

"Holy shit. Where did it go?"

Grace and Joseph both pointed to a small hole in the wall. Kaylee glared at them both and picked up a small bowl and a screen made of silver. She put the bowl on the ground and poured blood from a small vial. She spoke some words of power and heated up the blood.

"Everyone get your feet off the floor. I don't want the mouse distracted or for you to scare it," directed Kaylee.

Everyone climbed up on chairs and tables. Kaylee hovered the deputies to get their feet off the ground. Then she flew above the bowl and waited. After a few moments they finally saw the mouse sneaking up to the bowl. She scattered some magic on the mouse and immobilized it.

"Bring me the cage," Kaylee ordered. Grace put on a leather glove and meekly brought it to her. "Good, there's no damage to the cage."

Joseph couldn't believe it. "I've never seen a vampire animal before. How did you do that?"

"I made it using Grace's blood, some magic, and science."

"What do you think would happen if it escaped?" Eric asked. "Could it make more vampire mice?"

"I think so. And I am not alone in that thought. That is one of the reasons that it is not legal to create vampire animals."

Kaylee tidied the cage and gathered a bottle that attached to its side. She put some warmed blood in it. "Let's take it with us. I need to run some tests. And don't touch my things again," she warned the crowd.

Joseph humbly said, "I didn't expect it could get out."

"Okay everyone, let's go," commanded Eric. "Kaylee and I are going to get her motorcycle. You all take the van and this creature back to the office." He indicated the mouse.

Eric and Kaylee jump together to the garage where it was dark. Kaylee turned the light on, grabbed a key, and tossed it to Eric. "Drive Grace's motorcycle," she ordered. She threw her leg over her own motorcycle and put on her helmet. "Where do you want me to park?"

"Let's go to the Longshore. I want to check up on it."

They enjoyed the ride together. They arrived at the ruins of the Longshore Bar. Eric motioned for Kaylee to follow him and they parked their cycles behind a rock outcropping. They covered the motorcycles with brush to hide them. Eric and Kaylee walked over to the blackened ground.

"The silver people set this fire just to hurt vampires," Eric said angrily.

"I have to stop them."

Meanwhile, three men in silver drove up the long driveway to Kaylee and Grace's house. They rang the bell, but no one answered. One called out. Still no one answered, so they slipped in. The three separated and searched the house. After a few moments, they called, "All clear."

"Come to me in the basement," called one man, and the others joined him. He had found some fabric sticking out of a wall. The three of them struggled, but they got the door open to Grace's room. They found a big studio with a bedroom, a huge tub and sink, a living room, and a desk with a computer.

"Someone must have been keeping a vampire in here," observed one man. "Let's check the garage."

"Help me pour gas over their garage," said the third man when they arrived.

They poured gas all over the house, disabled the fire alarms in each room of the house, and set fire to the garage.

Back at the office, Kaylee set her potion on the desk and started unpacking her backpack. She pulled out all sorts of silver weapons and potion-making gear.

Kuruk asked, "Would these potions work for me if I learned to make them?"

Grace walked up and said, "Sorry, neither you or I can make the potions work. For this to work, you need to be a witch and know how to make the potions. Both pieces need to be there for all the magic to do its thing."

"Was it true what your angel said about those four strange creations? I have been around a long time, and I've never see any quite so strange as you," Kukuk said to Kaylee. Kaylee didn't respond. She was too focused on getting ready to meet the silver people tomorrow.

Grace, on the other hand, jumped right in to answer. "An angel just told her. Probably means that the angel needs her for some reason because she has the powers to stop them."

The deputies and Grace debated about angels for a few moments. None of them recalled seeing or hearing angels or anything else when they died. Eric was silent but listened to their conversation.

Kevin drove to the agency and parked his car. He sat there for a moment, thoughtful. He picked up his badge and headed into the building. He had to pass a number of checkpoints to get to his office. He didn't want to be discovered by Ben. He headed to his office, avoiding anyone who knew him.

He stood so he could see Ben's office but no one could see him. Finally he saw Ben leave his office and head to the bathroom. Kevin entered Ben's office as quickly as he could. He stuck a bug under Ben's desk and hurried out again.

Ben returned to his office unaware that anyone had been there in his absence. Kevin returned to his own office and listened to Ben's office bug. He kept having to remind himself to relax. No one would know who he was listening to by just looking at him. Suddenly, he heard Vice President David Lawrence and Doug McDonald, who sat on the governmental finance committee, come into Ben's office.

Kevin sat up, listening intently.

Ben: Hi, come in and have a seat.

McDonald: I am going to push through legislation to increase taxes to pay for the Silver Agency.

Lawrence: Even if we get the Senate to agree, people might be unhappy. They will just have to get used to it. It is the President who I am not sure about. He may not agree to sign the bill. We need to get rid of him so I can take over.

Ben: Who is going to kill the President?

Kevin's eyes opened wide as he listened. He realized that the Silver Agency had been operating without Presidential authority.

Lawrence: I already took care of it. Don't worry. The process will work if the President is suddenly lost.

McDonald: Sounds good.

Ben: If our plan goes smoothly, gentlemen, I will see you at the White House tomorrow at 8:00 pm.

The men left the office, and Kevin quickly recorded the conversation. He hid a copy of it in his office and took the other with him as he left for home, where he could think more about what he'd learned.

Grace whined to her sister, "I am thirsty. Can you stop now and get something to eat?"

Kaylee sighed, "All right, I will take a break." Kaylee walked away so she could jump home to get Grace blood from their cow. "Grace, watch my potions."

"Do I have to babysitter them forever?"

"Yeah," Kaylee smiled as she disappeared.

Kaylee returned almost immediately. There were scorch marks on her clothing and her shoes were smoking. She collapsed on the ground.

"Are you all right?" Grace shouted, rushing over to her sister, her babysitting job momentarily forgotten.

"Our house was on fire. It had to be those bastard silver people who did this. No one else would have burned it. I could see what remained of my extra gas can outside the garage."

"Good thing we took your potions out of that house."

"How could they get in?"

Eric cleared his throat. "It might be my fault. We might not have locked up after we stole your potions. I unlocked the door when you and I were there, and then used the unlocked door to get back in to take the potions. I don't remember if we locked up again afterwards."

"It doesn't matter," Kaylee said. "We are all safe, and even if they hadn't found the house unlocked, they may have burned it anyway. Fire doesn't need an open door. Besides, that is what insurance is for."

"Look your leathers. I think they are ruined," observed Kuruk.

Eric was impressed once again with Kaylee. She was taking the loss of her home well.

Kaylee looked at her sister, who was starting to look like she was getting sick. "I will be right back, Grace."

She jumped to a store. She grabbed two cases of A- and H-Blood from the cooler of the closed store. She wished she had some cash to leave on the counter, but it was not to be tonight. The two cases of blood made a thump on the table as she plunked them down. She handed one to her sister, who started drinking right away. The deputies looked at the blood and then at Kaylee.

"Where did this come from?" asked Joseph.

"Don't ask," said Kaylee looking defiantly at him.

Eric said to her, "Stealing?"

"What choice do I have? It isn't like I can just order it or go to the grocery store for it. I was human until two days ago."

"Do you do this often?"

"No, and if I had any money on me now I would have paid for it." Kaylee went back to work on her potions. All the deputies helped themselves to the blood. Only Kaylee and Eric didn't take any.

Kuruk observed, "Good think you have a powerful sister to look out for you, Grace."

"She's the best," Grace beamed.

Eric excused himself and went to his office. He grabbed an H-Blood before he went. He wanted Kaylee to know that he understood doing something for family sometimes made up for breaking the law. Besides, he hated A-Blood.

# CHAPTER 17

Grace and the deputies talked to pass the time while Kaylee finished her potion.

"I wish I could fly like Kaylee does. Wouldn't that be great in traffic to just to fly over it?"

"I wish I could fly like my sister too," Grace agreed. "I've always envied her ability to fly, and it is amazing to watch her do it outside. In some ways I am glad she's a vampire now. My heart would break thinking about her no longer being around to fly on a moonlit night."

Breaking the tension of that emotional revelation, Kuruk asked, "How long will it take for those potions to be done?"

"It depends. Probably she will be done in less than an hour, but it could be another day or so. Some of her more complex spells and potions can take weeks to complete. Even after all that mixing and waiting, she still has to say certain incantations or spells over them to make everything work correctly. I don't know how she has the patience for it all."

"We need to move faster if we intend to meet the silver people tonight, Kaylee," Joseph called. "How much longer do you anticipate this taking?"

"Should be less than five minutes. Then I have to test it." Kaylee didn't even look up from her book.

Eric came out of his office and asked Grace to join him in there. She walked in slowly and looked around. At first glance it looked like an ordinary office with a large desk and two tall filing cabinets. It also contained a painting of a vampire taking down prey and there was an ancient scroll in a holder on top of one of the filing cabinets. The other had a vampire skull on it. Behind his large wood desk was a shield that looked straight out of Arthurian legends. His penholder was in the shape of a skull.

"This is the paperwork for you to sign," Eric explained. "It shows your maker's name—that can stay blank—the date of you becoming a vampire, that it wasn't consensual, and your address. Sign here." He indicated a line near the bottom. "I will get you new ID number. Look,

I put down that Kaylee is your marked and that you adopted her as such. It keeps it legal."

"Thank you," Grace said softly while signing the paper.

"I think I've got something," Kaylee said suddenly. "Anyone volunteer to use my silver crossbow?" She stood up, smiling.

Kuruk was first in line with a grin. He loved weapons, especially sharp ones. He reached for it, but Kaylee stopped him. She handed him a set of leather gloves, then the weapon.

"I will float over there," she said as she indicated the other side of the room, "and you try to shoot at my chest, okay?" She put on her goggles and headed over to the other side of the room.

Kuruk aimed the crossbow at her and let an arrow fly. Kaylee caught the arrow in her hands as if he had just tossed it to her. He tried again, and once again, she was able to catch it in her hand.

"How does that work? Is it a power of yours or the goggles?" asked Joseph.

Kaylee grinned. "The goggles help to slow the motion of silver objects. The arrow just moved slowly enough in my perception that I could just catch it."

Joseph asked, "Can I try the goggles?"

"No, these are silver, so you can't touch them. I can make another set of goggles for each of you, for when the silver people come. And I can line them so you won't touch the silver, okay?"

Kaylee set to work coating the goggles with her potion and covering the parts of the goggles that touched skin with fabric so they wouldn't burn the other vampires. Joseph was first in line to try the new goggles. He carefully put them on and noticed they had a colored background.

Kuruk set up to shoot at Joseph, who was still wearing the leather gloves. Kuruk let an arrow fly and Joseph ducked in plenty of time. He wasn't quite sure he wanted to catch silver arrows just yet.

"Live fast," commented Joseph.

Kuruk shouted, "Whooo! My turn!"

Joseph lifted up his head. He took the silver arrow from the wall and walked up to Kuruk. Kuruk put on gloves and donned his goggles. He prepared to be shot by Joseph. "okay, shoot."

Joseph let loose an arrow and Kuruk caught it. "Whooo!"

Michael grinned, "Live fast."

Kaylee passed out the goggles to all the deputies and Eric. They tried them out like kids with a new toy.

*Ben, Doug, and David were in Kevin's bedroom. Kevin and his wife were asleep on the bed. Ben kicked the bed to wake them up.*

*"You almost gave me a heart attack. What are you doing here, Ben?"*

*"I found the bug under my desk."*

*The three men took out their guns and pointed them at Kevin and his wife. David asked, "Where is the copy of our conversation?"*

Kevin was talking in his sleep. His wife woke up and looked over at him. He only did that when he was under great stress. She patted his shoulder gently and then went back to sleep.

*"No! No, no. I didn't do it...wait, I won't tell anybody!"*

*His wife was confused. "What? What are you talking about?"*

*Doug said, "He works for the CIA, and he is full of lies"*

*"You work for the CIA?" Kevin's wife asked, shocked.*

*"No, of course not," he lied.*

*Ben scowled at him, "If you don't tell me where the copy is I will kill her!" He held the gun up to her head and pulled back the hammer, the clicking sound of the gun was terrifying*

*"What about the karate business? I thought you taught karate!" his wife sobbed.*

*"Tell me what I want to know, now!" shouted Ben.*

*"No. I won't tell you."*

*Ben shot his wife twice in the head. Then turned the gun on Kevin.*

*"Where is it?"*

*"No."*

*Ben shot Kevin once in the heart.*

Kevin woke up in a sweat, he was shaking all over. He looked over at his wife and put his hand on hers, relieved to see her sleeping so soundly.

Eric asked Kaylee to join him in his office. "I am sorry about your house. You are taking it well."

"It is only a building. What is most important to me is here."

"Good. Look, here's your paperwork it just needs your signature. I already signed that I am your maker, the date you became a vampire, and your address. It is all set, so I will get your new ID number soon. We can worry about the fire burning down the address later." Kaylee signed the documents. "Welcome to our immortal world." Kaylee stared at the penholder made from a skull. "You okay? Does this scare you?"

"No, I am interested in your ancient vampire style. Can you teach me how to make them?"

"Not many vampires are made these days, and we don't usually teach such things to young vampires. I have a question for you. The other night, when you killed Scott, did you use your goggles to help you slow down his vampire movement like you did with the silver goggles?"

Kaylee felt guilty and was silent for moment, "Yeah, goggles were necessary when I was human."

"Ah, I figured. Umm, you were different than I thought."

"Are you really from the 15th century?"

"Yes. Look, sorry if I didn't believe you other night. Were you really planning a singing career like you said?"

"Yeah, I have always dreamed of being a singer. No matter. I can try it another time, right?"

He looked at her thoughtfully then said, "That's it for now. You can go."

"Thank you for the ID. And thank you not giving me a hard time about breaking the law when I stole the blood." She kissed his cheek and walked out of his office.

Eric wasn't sure what do. He wanted a woman for the first time in decades, perhaps centuries. Many women had caught his eye for a few hours, but few were as intriguing and as frustrating as Kaylee. He opened his top drawer to look at the letter he had taken from her refrigerator. Eric decided to keep it for now. He left his office to rejoin the group. As he did he heard Kaylee instruct his deputies to take a few drops of blood from Grace.

"Why do they need my blood?" Grace asked her sister as they were cleaning up the table Kaylee had worked on.

"I want them to protect you, you are important. Please just do this for me. I can't do it because of my silver blood."

"Can you tell me why?"

"You don't need to know why, just trust me."

"Eww, no. I won't let them taste my blood until you tell me why." Grace stamped her foot to emphasize her point.

Kaylee knelt down before Eric. "Eric, allow me to speak the truth to her." All the deputies were curious about what she would tell her.

"If you know something, then tell her," Eric agreed.

Kaylee stood up. "If you drink the blood of another vampire and it is given freely, then you share a bond. This bond allows you to know when the other is in danger. I think it might allow them to know when you are experiencing any strong emotion, perhaps including physical pain."

Eric was shocked. "You knew this all along?"

Michael asked Eric, "Did you tell her this?"

Joseph said, "This is an ancient secret. Usually this bond is reserved for master and marked or deputy. It is very serious that you know this."

"It shouldn't matter how I learned it or when in my life I learned it. I know it," Kaylee said. Eric was impressed that she didn't back down from Joseph who was an old and formidable vampire.

"Let me have a word privately with Grace, okay?" Kaylee asked the deputies. No one responded yes or no. Kaylee pulled Grace to one side of the room and spoke a few words of power to make their conversation totally private.

Michael stood next to Eric and asked, "How does she know that?"

Eric whispered back, "I have no idea. I didn't tell her."

Kuruk's voice was low as he asked, "Is she psychic too?"

"I have no idea. She seems to come out with something shocking every few hours," said Eric tartly.

Joseph solemnly said, "Kill them. They should not know about our ancient secret. They must be psychic, and we cannot afford that kind of liability, especially in these turbulent times with the silver people."

Eric knew that to some extent Joseph was correct, but he was an aggressive soul. There were moments when he wished he could fire Joseph and be done, but Joseph knew too many secrets. "I will handle this, is that clear?"

Joseph realized he had overstepped his boundaries. "I apologize. It won't happen again, sir."

Eric was uneasy with Joseph. He was new to their office, having only started about five months ago.

Kaylee tried to explain to Grace, "If they feel you are in danger, they can come help. I might not always be right there, and there are many of them. Let them help protect you. Your powers are important and I love you."

"I love you too. I wish I could see the future for everyone. I've never really seen into your future. Eric seems to block me. Joseph I get, but he's fuzzy. Everyone else I can see clear as day."

"We can figure it out after we stop the silver people," Kaylee said taking down the magic barrier.

"Now that you are free," Eric interrupted, "I would like a word with my marked alone. Come," He indicated his office and Kaylee followed. When they got to his office, Eric demanded, "Tell me everything this time."

Kaylee squirmed. It was like being in the principal's office. Eric leaned over his desk to look directly in her silver eyes. "It is just the two of us here. Tell me."

"I know I haven't been a vampire long, but I have more abilities than even ancient vampires. My knowledge of vampire physiology and my skills as a witch…well, they make me this way, okay?"

"Look, you don't have to keep secrets from me. Normally a marked can't keep big secrets, but there is no way I am drinking your blood." They both smiled. "Now, if you have any other secrets or learn anything else you think is important, you tell me first, okay?"

"Yes…sir." She let out a breath she didn't realize she was holding.

"Part of why I want to know is to make sure you can't overpower me. I am the leader of the vampires of this town. Talk to me and obey me, clear?"

Kaylee nodded. "I am listening to you. And don't worry, management isn't my thing. I just want to be a singer. My potions and healing are just part of who I am." He was surprised at this admission. Most vampires he knew were more power hungry.

"Good. Let's go back and get ready."

In the other room Joseph asked Grace, "You are psychic. You don't have information on our deepest secrets, right?"

"I can't see in the past. It only works forward," Grace responded.

"But how do you know things from the past?"

"Enough everyone, we can figure this out later," Eric interrupted. He walked up to Grace and held her wrist out. "Bite," he commanded. Grace bit her wrist and showed everyone that her blood was red. He then told his deputies to take her blood. She healed her wrist when they were done.

"Grace, can you read our thoughts?" Eric asked.

"Not all of them. I can read Michael's and Kuruk's easily, but I can't read yours or Kaylee's at all. Joseph's in and out."

"Good to know."

Joseph was worried. He was not sure if Grace knew about his plan because she could read his thoughts on and off. Joseph hoped that she wouldn't read his thoughts. "What do you mean by on and off?" he asked Grace.

"I don't know why, but sometimes I can read you and other times I can't."

Kaylee wished she could be part of that circle and that her sister could read Eric. There were many questions she would like answered about that man. Kaylee knew she was falling in love with him, but did he have feelings for her?

"Umm, are we supposed to rest here?" Grace changed the subject, indicating the office with a wave of her hand. Eric realized that the sisters were homeless and it was up to him to help them find shelter for the day.

"For the moment we are going to use this as a base while we deal with the silver people. After that you can stay at Scott's house."

"Sure, thanks." Kaylee felt very odd about moving into the house of the man she had killed.

"You're welcome. Now everyone try to get some rest."

They prepared to rest. The vampires laid down on tables and couches in the office. Kaylee floated above the ground about eight to twelve inches near Grace. Eric noticed Kaylee floated while she rested.

"Why do you float? That is not typical of vampires."

Kaylee closed her eyes. "It is a witch thing."

Eric closed his eyes. Grace smiled and said, "Makes making your bed in the morning a snap."

Kaylee smiled and laughed.

# CHAPTER 18

As the sun rose, so did Kevin. Not that he'd slept much, but he didn't want to wake up his wife. She had to go to work too. He decided he was just going to remove the bug from Ben's office so he would stop worrying about it being found and getting in trouble.

Kevin showered and dressed quickly. He was at the office very early, thankfully before Ben and his secretary arrived. He slipped into Ben's office, a folder in hand just in case he needed a cover story. He grabbed the bug and disposed of it without being observed.

The copy of conversation weighed heavily in his hand. He thought about leaving it in his office safe, but with Ben around he thought that might not be a good idea. He put the recording in his pocket for now.

Coffee called to him, so he went down to the lobby to get some. As he rode the elevator down he had an idea. He grabbed a coffee to go and headed over to his karate studio. It was too early for classes, and no one was around when he went to his office and stashed the recording in a filing cabinet there.

Kaylee was worried about her cow. She found Grace in the afternoon and shared her concern. Together they found Eric.

"I need to go check on my cow," said Kaylee. She looked quite serious.

"I must still be asleep, I thought you just said you were worried about a cow," Eric smiled at her.

"We have a cow at our house. Grace drank the cow blood and I drank the milk. It worked out well for everyone, the cow included, as she was very well taken care of. I want to see if she's okay after the fire."

"Wait. You forgot about the sun, baby."

"Did you just call me *baby*?" asked Kaylee, surprised.

"Why yes I did. You are a baby vampire and you forgot that the sun is still shining."

"Oh, that's not a problem. The sun doesn't bother me."

"Really?" Eric was surprised.

"Yep, that's my sister," Grace bragged to the disbelieving vampire. "If she said she can, she can." Then Kaylee jumped to show them.

Kaylee jumped outside the house. She blinked a few times from the sun. She'd have to get some sunglasses. She looked over at the barn. It was still intact. The fence was still fine too, but one piece was broken. Where was the cow?

"Damn it," she said aloud. She stared at the ruins that had once been her house. The sight cut her heart. She went to check on a few other things that had been stored in outlying buildings and in the woods. But she found no cow.

She jumped back to the office and Grace. "The cow is missing, but the barn is fine."

"Our cow was kidnapped?" asked Grace, surprised.

"I have no idea. It is just gone. The fence is broken. It must have escaped."

"Obviously you didn't burn up in the sunlight," Eric reflected. "Did you have any problems?"

Kaylee smiled. "I think I am going to need sunglasses now. The sunlight hurt my eyes more than it used to."

"Good to know that there are some vampire changes in you," said Eric sarcastically.

Kevin's son Mark worked with him at the karate studio. They worked opposite hours so they rarely saw each other. Mark was the same age as Kaylee. He was surprised when he saw his dad in the office. "Hi, Dad, how's your day going? You look tired."

"Yeah, I am. Look buddy, I have to go do some errands. Can you take care of things here for a while?" He planned to give the business to Mark when he retired. He was a good kid, just a bit inexperienced at the businesses side of things.

Kevin headed to his agency office and ran into Ben coming out of the building as he was going in.

"Hey Kevin, I left some things on your desk. Can you review the files and fill in some missing details before we submit them next week?"

"You got it, Ben," Kevin said, trying to sound cheerful.

"Great. I will see you next week."

As all the vampires were up and starting their day by drinking their morning breakfast. Eric brought some blood over to Kaylee.

"No thanks, I don't drink."

"That's true. She told us last night, and she hasn't touched anything since," Michael added. The others agreed.

Eric sighed. "I must have been in my office last night when you guys drank. You walk in the sun and you are not bloodthirsty. What else?"

Kaylee thought for a moment. "Guess that's it." She smiled.

"How can you survive without being bloodthirsty?" Eric asked her.

"She feeds on the energy of silver," Grace replied.

"What else could it be? Next you are going to say you need sun to stay healthy," Eric said, exasperated.

Kaylee dressed in silver clothes and gathered her silver weapons. She put on her goggles and looked around. She was ready to go.

"Go kick some silver ass for me, sis!" Grace said.

"I will," Kaylee grinned. "Watch out for my stuff. It's all I have aside from you."

Kuruk was staying behind along with Grace. "Get a silver scalp for me," he said.

Kevin and his men put on their silver suits. Their faces were protected by silver masks and special glasses. Kevin had not put his on yet and was finalizing plans with the driver. They were checking their weapons when Kevin paused, looking at them getting ready for battle. If anything happened to him no one would know about Ben's plans....

Kaylee found her motorcycle where she parked it. She started the engine and pulled out onto the road.

Kevin hopped off the truck and closed the door. He looked out into the woods. The driver grabbed his coffee and accidently spilled some on the floor. He leaned down to shake his pant leg where the coffee landed, his head ducking down from the window of the van.

Kaylee rode a few miles down the road when she noticed a large white truck pulled off the road. *Car trouble*? she wondered. She didn't see anyone at the wheel and figured they were walking to the next phone.

Kevin was peering into the woods when Kaylee drove by. He opened the rear door and called, "Time to hunt vampires, gentlemen." The men filed out, weapons at the ready. Kevin got back into the truck to run the operation. He flipped on the monitors and checked the cameras. Some showed normal views while others showed infrared views.

Kaylee parked her motorcycle in the woods and covered it with some brush. She walked through the woods, looking at everything through her goggles, and then started looking for heat signatures in the woods. She saw a few small animals, but that was it. She decided to fly up over the trees to get a better view. She saw the heat signatures of about 50 people encircling the woods. She flew down to get a better look. She adjusted her goggles when one of the men noticed her.

"Who are you? We don't have any women on our team." He could see she was wearing silver and then realized she had no heat signature.

"I am here to protect vampires."

A second silver agent walked over. "What? You protect the vampires?"

"Arrest her!" said the first agent.

Kaylee popped her fangs and hissed to scare them.

The second agent screamed, "She's a vampire!" Kaylee pushed him away, but she didn't know her own strength now that she was a vampire, she sent him flying into the woods. Other agents joined in the fight as they realized she wasn't on their team.

The agents shot her with a light as bright as the sun. It had no effect on her and she threw a small net at it. The weights on the net shattered the light. The agents rushed at her and fought hand-to-hand. She defeated them all. She didn't tire,

Back at the office, Grace grabbed Kuruk's arm. "Kaylee is being attacked!"

"I thought you couldn't read her."

"I can't, but I can read the silver people. They are fighting her. And I think she's kicking ass!" she said with pride.

Kaylee shouted, "Come on, don't be chicken! How do you feel now that *you* are being hunted?"

Kevin was watching some of this from his truck. He heard her shout, paused to think, and then found a file on the computer. In a few seconds, he heard singing. Soon agents were returning to the truck. The first few came in and one sat next to Kevin to report back.

"There is a silver woman out there. She's a vampire and she's handing us our asses."

"What?" He spoke into a microphone, "Return to base. Retreat. I repeat, return to base."

The agents returned to the truck. One agent moved quickly to get the doors open and haul people into the truck. Kevin yelled, "Hurry! Let's move!" Agents rushed in and reported seeing a Silver Vampire. "Is that everyone?" asked Kevin anxiously. One of the agents was working the monitors and was talking on the microphone.

"Sir, I think that is everyone," the agent said to Kevin. They had lost a lot of agents. He closed the door and looked at the monitor showing the back of the truck. He saw a silver-clad woman fly up to the doors. Since when did vampires fly? This was new and unexpected.

He turned to the agent manning the monitors. "Tell the driver to *go*!"

The driver started the engine and pulled away quickly. Kaylee flew next to the driver and reached into the truck. "Vampire!" the driver shouted. He worked to get the window up and keep driving. Kevin watched on the monitor, helpless to get a weapon to the man.

Kaylee opened the door and ripped it off the truck. She yelled, "Pull over!" The driver didn't stop. She reached in and pulled him out of the still-moving truck. The truck went down a small hill, and sparks flew as it ran into a metal fence.

Kevin sat helplessly, watching this on the video monitor. Normally he would have led the charge to face an opponent, but he was deeply conflicted. He pulled on a mask and donned a set of safety glasses.

Kaylee ripped open the back of the truck. "Who is in charge here?" she demanded.

Kevin stood up and faced Kaylee. She grabbed his shirt and flew with him away from the truck. She dropped him on the ground. She flew into the woods, leaving him alone for a few seconds. Kaylee came out of the woods again and Kevin gasped at her speed. He started to run back to the truck, but she overtook him in the blink of an eye. He was scared. He had never seen this side of her before.

Kaylee reached out and grabbed the silver-clad man again. She growled in his face. He begged her to stop, and she reached out and tore off his mask.

"Kevin?" she shouted, stunned. *Kevin is the leader of the silver people! How can this be?* she thought. She felt betrayed. What happened to all that he taught her about respect and honor?

"I am here to save the vampires," she said. "You tore their lives apart. I will fight you with every breath in my body. I can't believe this is how you were going to save the world."

Grace's eyes opened wide. "Kevin Douglas?"

"Who is that? Human or vampire?" asked Kuruk.

"Kevin was Kaylee's karate teacher since she was, like, three. He was always really good to her. Treated her like a daughter. He has a son about the same age."

Kevin held up his hands in surrender. "Kaylee, I know you are angry with me. This is not exactly the way I wanted to introduce you to this part of my life."

"Really?" she said sarcastically.

"Kaylee, I know this won't be easy to hear. But I need your help."

# CHAPTER 19

Kevin said, "I know that you want to save the world, even as a vampire. I can't imagine that being a vampire will change who you are inside. I will do anything you want to get you to help me. I can work to make peace between vampires and the silver people."

Kaylee was angry and felt betrayed. "How can I trust you? Why are you doing this? Do you hate vampires? Do you hate me too now?"

"Just assume I am not happy to see you are a vampire, but I can live with it. I am between a rock and a hard place, and if certain people find out about what I know, they will kill me and not think twice about it. Let me explain. I work for the CIA. My boss, Ben, manages the agency and I am his assistant manager. Ben is power hungry and a racist. Not against humans, but against vampires."

"You lied to me all these years? You are sick. I trusted you."

"I didn't lie to you. I also own the dojo. And I am your teacher." He paused and took her hands in his. "Some of the people from my agency are planning to do some very serious things." He wasn't quite ready to trust her fully with all the details. "I wasn't sure what to do about it until I saw you as a vampire with new powers. Then I knew that I needed your help. Please, help me save the world, for humans *and* vampires."

"Why can't you do this yourself? You can speak out, or quit."

"It is far too complex a task for just one person. Can we go to Washington, DC today? Come with me."

Kaylee was confused. She had known Kevin her whole life. Could he have been working for the CIA the whole time?

"I don't hang around with humans. I am no longer interested in helping humans anymore."

"Trust me, this isn't just about humans. If we can accomplish this, vampires will have civil rights. This could change things for both of us. If you help me, afterward you never have to see me again if that is what you want. I will leave your life forever. But please help me now."

Kaylee stared at him. She had known him for so long, and he seemed serious. She felt conflicted and didn't know what to do. But he had been so good to her…she had to know more.

"Put your mask back on so no one sees who you really are," Kevin told Kaylee.

"Where are we headed?" she asked as she began to replace her mask and goggles.

"The truck."

"What? I can't go there. It is full of vampire killers. I am a vampire now, Kevin, in case you've forgotten in the last two minutes!"

"I just need to give them some orders so no one will follow us to Washington. With your mask on you will look like you blend in."

She desperately wanted to believe him and stop the silver people. She took his hand and they flew back to the truck.

"I have never seen a vampire fly before. Is this a power they keep hidden?"

"No," was all she would say.

Kevin walked quickly back to the truck door. He tried to open the door and could hear voices inside. "Don't panic. I'll get you out."

Kevin tried to open the back but it wouldn't budge. It had been damaged when the truck went down the hill. He turned to Kaylee. "I need your strength." Kaylee opened the door and threw it away from the truck. Kevin helped get the men out of the truck and called an ambulance with security clearance. Those who were unhurt were taken back to the agency office to change back into civilian clothes and debrief while the injured men were taken to a secure hospital.

Kevin and Kaylee flew the distance alone. They landed on the roof by a helicopter.

"Keep low. We just need to get into that door," he said, pointing to a door next to an air vent. It had a guard standing beside it. "We need to get a key to get into the helicopter."

"What? Can *you* flying this thing?" she asked in a whisper.

"I flew them when I was in the army." Kaylee was surprised. He'd never mentioned flying helicopters before. What else could he be hiding?

Kaylee flew back to a better spot to see and retracted her fangs. They were able to spot a second guard watching this entrance. Kaylee stood up and walked over to them as if she were taking a break from work. They didn't find it odd at first that there was a silver-clad person at the hospital, but a second later realized there was no other door on the roof other than the one they guarded.

"How did you get up here?"

"I am Tarzan's wife, Jane." Kaylee knocked both of them down and opened the door gently, not knowing if there was someone inside. She saw a guard sitting at a table. He noticed the change in the air when she opened the door.

"What are you doing? How did you get up here?" he said, standing up and drawing his weapon. She knocked him down before he could finish his thought.

"I flew," she said as she began to walk away.

Kaylee came over to Kevin and let him know it was clear. He looked at her. "Can you fly me to the door?"

"Humans! You can't do anything without help." She smiled and for a moment, missing their old friendship. She flew him over to the door. "Now you are on your own. Go get what you need."

He returned a few moments later with a key in hand. They went over to the helicopter and got in. Kevin had her put on headphones so they could talk as he flew the helicopter away.

"How long have you worked for the CIA?"

"About 20 years. They recruited me partially because I had the studio. It was a great cover."

"So why are we hijacking a helicopter and heading to Washington, DC? Can you tell me now?"

"We are headed to the White House."

"What, to see the President?"

"No, to save him. He is set to sign some important legislation to give vampires more civil rights. This will close our agency. If Ben has his way, the President won't sign the bill and our agency will be permanently funded."

"How are they going to stop him?"

"They are planning to kill him. And you need to stop them."

# CHAPTER 20

Grace was sitting with her hands on the table in front of her. Her eyes were closed. Something was wrong.

"Kevin?" she said to herself in disbelief. She could see him, but she didn't see Kaylee. The other vampires had returned to the office when it was clear that there would be no silver-people killing tonight. The arrival of the ambulances to clean up Kaylee's mess had made it far too dangerous.

"Grace, where is Kaylee? Is she with Kevin?" asked Eric softly.

"Yes, Kevin is with Kaylee and they are… in a helicopter flying!"

"What? Why would they need a helicopter? Where are they headed?" asked Eric.

Grace opened her eyes and looked at Eric. "They're going to the White House to save the President."

Kevin looked over at Kaylee. He spoke in to the microphone. "Do you have your cell phone?" She nodded. "OK, give it to me. I don't want this to be over a channel that is likely monitored." She handed him her cell phone. He plugged it into the communication line of the microphone. He dialed a long number and then spoke at length, identifying himself. Finally he was talking with the right person. "Tell the President not to sign the bill until I get there. There is a plot against his life. Now I am going to land at the helipad next to the White House. My companion and I are wearing silver clothes. There is just the two of us, don't shoot."

They landed and ran over to a man in a dark suit with round glasses framing his deep blue eyes. "Sir, I am Jason Smith. I am part of the President's security detail. Can you give me some information about your intel?"

"I have a recording of a credible threat made against the President's life. The threat was for tonight and revolved around the bill on vampire civil rights."

Kevin spoke with Jason. "Use my name and get Jack Hopkinton at the Pentagon to come over to help. And tell him to bring some weapons to the party."

Jason called Jack Hopkinton, who sprang into action.

Meanwhile, David, Ben, and Doug were in meeting with the President before the bill signing. They looked at each other for a moment when they heard the helicopter land so close to the White House.

The President looked up at the men. "Am I in danger?" he joked after seeing their expressions. A few members of his security detail listened to their earphones while scanning the room.

"Not to worry Mr. President. We are all well-trained agents here. We'll protect you," said Ben.

The President looked at the bill for a moment and paused. "Gentlemen, let's table this for a short time while I confer with my security detail." He got up and spoke with one of the men protecting him.

Kevin said, "You go up on the room and look carefully for any snipers. They did say "shoot" on the tape, so look for a gun. I am going inside the White House."

Kaylee flew up on the roof and began searching.

Ben reached into his pocket for his gun. He thought he could pull it out and pretend to protect the President, but another agent aimed his gun at him, deciding to shoot first and ask questions later. Unfortunately for him, Ben was a faster shot and the agent fell to the ground. The Secret Service Agents surrounded the President who didn't know who he could trust anymore.

Jason and Kevin met in front of the White House. They heard the gunshot in an upstairs room. They raced up to see what was going on. It was clear that agents from all sides were shooting at each other.

"I don't know who to trust!" Jason gasped.

“Never mind, just go save the President!” They pulled out their guns and were ready to help the President.

Kaylee heard lots of gunfire from inside the building. She flew in and ran down the corridors. She found the gunfight easily. The Secret Service were trying to get the President out of the room and away from the threat. Some agents lost their lives trying to protect him. In a last moment of valor, one agent who had been shot handed the President his gun so he could protect himself.

As Kaylee strode up to the fight, all people could see was that she was a Silver Vampire. Ben, David, and Doug were as confused as was everyone else to see a silver-clad vampire in the room. The CIA Agents were trying to slip out and kill the President in the process. They wanted it to look like it was part of the gunfight.

Kaylee pulled out a small sliver of silver. She spoke a few words of power, and the sliver turned into a six-foot long weapon. She used that stick to bang, hit, disarm, and even knock away bullets.

The President tried to sneak out of the room, but that wasn’t working. He crawled under a desk, relived that he couldn’t be seen.

Kaylee had seen him, however. She moved quickly to the desk and touched his shoulder. “Stay with me,” she said to him.

The President turned and looked at Kaylee. All he could see were her fangs. “Please don’t kill me,” he begged.

“Shh, be quiet. I am trying to rescue you.”

Jason and Kevin tried to reach the meeting room where the President was hiding under a desk.

Kevin called Kaylee’s cell phone. She picked up. “Where are you?” Kevin asked.

“With the President, upstairs from the fighting.”

“Good, stay there. I will be up there in a moment.”

David called the sniper, “As soon as you have a shot, take it.”

Doug had both the President’s daughters with him. When the girls heard this, they started to cry.

Kevin looked at Jason. “She has the President and they are safe for the moment, upstairs.”

“Who is she?”

“You will meet her. Come on, let’s go.”

Kaylee noticed a silver bullet coming toward them through the window. She had her motion-slowing goggles on. She grabbed the President and pushed him to the ground. The bullet hit a framed picture on the wall. Glass flew everywhere. The President looked at her and realized that she had just saved his life.

Kaylee was relieved when, suddenly, Kevin and another man came in. Kevin came right over to the President. “Are you okay, sir? I am Kevin Douglas from CIA. You need get out of here immediately.”

“Wait, my kids are their bedrooms not far from here. I want to know they are all right.”

“Sir, we need to take you to safety first, then we can check on your daughters.” Kaylee smiled at this, and her fangs showed just a bit.

“She’s a vampire! I will not move until I know my daughters are safe.”

“She is no harm to you. You stay with her, and I will check on your girls.”

Kevin ran out of room and found Jason. Kevin told Jason the story and they went to find the girls together. A sniper tried to shoot the President one more time.

“Hide under the desk now. Don’t move until I get back,” Kaylee said to the President.

*Kevin was right*, he thought. He always thought that he was a good judge of character and he thought he could trust this Silver Vampire. She had already saved his life once.

Kaylee stared through the broken window and noticed another bullet coming toward her. She moved out of the way. The sniper stared through the scope in disbelief. *How can anyone move that fast*? he wondered. He looked at his gun and then back through the scope. Was there something wrong with his gun or with him?

Kaylee jumped to stand next to the sniper. She stood there for a second before he realized he wasn't alone any longer. She bared her fangs at him and knocked him out cold.

The President snuck out from under the desk by crawling on all fours. He thought he could make it out of the room and find his girls. He was wrong. Ben walked up and held a gun to his head. At that moment, Doug and a fellow agent took the girls hostage and headed to a rooftop helipad.

Kaylee popped back into the room with the sniper. He was still holding out his hands as if he had a gun in them. Kevin and Jason ran in just in time to see her punch the sniper and watch him crumple.

"Where's the President?" asked Kevin.

Kaylee indicated the desk. Jason looked behind the desk and then at Kaylee. "Nope, there is no one here."

"Shit. That is where I left him to go get that guy."

Jason looked at Kaylee hard. "Who are you?" he asked.

"Kaylee Dailage," she said as she held out her hand to Jason who, with an incredulous expression, shook it and introduced himself.

"Okay, now that everyone knows each other, we should find the President," said Kevin. Go check the security camera video and see if you can find him."

Jason went to the security room and checked the video monitors. None showed the President. He talked to the agent in the room and together they went back to the videos to see if they could track his movements.

"Stay here," ordered Kevin, who went to check on the President's daughters. After a moment, Kevin came back. "I can't find them."

All of a sudden, Kevin and Kaylee heard a helicopter on the roof fly away fast and then the shouts of soldiers on the stairs. "Damn it. Go to the roof. I will call you." Kevin rushed out of the room.

Kaylee flew up to the roof through an open window. From this vantage, she could see a sea of reporters by the gate. She was careful not to be seen as she waited for Kevin and Jason.

Kevin came into the security room. Jason whipped out his gun and pointed it at him for a fraction of a second before realizing who it was. Jason relaxed.

"Did you find anything yet?" he asked Jason. The other agent in the room was rewinding the video feed to show the President. The scene ran in reverse at high speed until Jason said stop, now play. The screen showed Ben, his overcoat slung over his arm covering his hand, pointing to the President who was getting into a limo. Ben got in after him. They rewound the video some more to find the President's daughters and soon found Dave shuffling them into the helicopter that they had heard leaving the White House earlier.

Jason told the agent to make copies and send them to his office. They heard footsteps. Jason and Kevin drew their guns and stepped out in to the hallway. They were greeted with a harsh "Freeze!" spoken by a sergeant. The pair held up their guns in surrender. The sergeant bade them to come with him, but Kevin refused to move.

"Call Jack Hopkinton and tell him it is Kevin Douglas."

"Red Unit 2 to base. I have an agent who wants to talk to the commander. Said his name is Kevin Douglas."

Someone was speaking into the earpiece of the sergeant, and the mood relaxed.

"Sorry, sir. The commander said, we will help you in any way you need."

"Soldier, I need you to take a tape the agent in the next room is preparing to my office and secure it. Let no one, I mean no one other than myself, this man, Jason Smith, or Kaylee Dailage, have the tape. Is that understood?" Jason stayed with the sergeant. This tape is critical."

"Yes sir." The sergeant stepped back and entered the security room. His men stood alert in the hallway.

Kevin called Kaylee. "The President was taken hostage in a black limo. Ben is with him. Can you find him before they get too far?"

"I will try." She hung up. Her battery was getting low.

He ran out of the White House into the parking lot. He looked for a car and found one with an open door. He flipped the visor hoping for keys, but no luck. He hotwired the car and drove out, breaking the gate as he went. Kevin sighed, “Damn it, I am too old for this.”

Jack shouted orders with amazing speed and organization. Ambulances arrived to take care of the injured, and the coroner arrived as well.

Kaylee flew along the road looking for the limo. She tried to be inconspicuous, but it was really no use when she was wearing silver head-to-toe. People stopped and stared, some shouted, all were amazed.

She found the limo a few blocks away and floated down to the door. She ripped the door off and peered inside. A bride and groom were startled from their champagne toast. The bride screamed when she saw Kaylee’s fangs.

“I am so sorry, wrong limo. Oh, and congratulations!”

Kaylee flew back up and more carefully searched for the limo. Crowds stopped to see her, and traffic slowed a few times as she passed by. “I hate cities,” she said to herself.

After a moment she found a limo that looked like it could be the right one. Not wanting to repeat her earlier mistake, she watched it for a few seconds. The car swerved a bit, and the passenger side door opened. The limo driver was tossed out. Kaylee flew down to catch him and helped him to safety. She flew up to the limo and tried to look inside. The windows were mirrored so you could see out, but not in.

Ben stared at the window. “What the hell was that? Do you know her?” He pointed out the window.

“No, I don’t know any flying Silver Vampires,” the President replied.

Kaylee started to bang on the roof of the limo, startling the man driving. He began to lose control. The car swerved. A young boy riding his bike panicked as the limo came closer to him. He froze in place, the limo swerving right at him. He held his breath, expecting the car to hit him.

Kaylee flew right at the boy at top speed, grabbing him and lifting him up in the air as the limo hit the boy’s bike, flinging it up in the air. She deposited him gently on the ground nearby. His bike landed a second or two after he did. People standing nearby gasped.

The air was filled with the sound of sirens as Kaylee continued to pursue the limo. Police officers began to shoot at her, thinking she was a threat to the limo. She called her silver staff to her. It materialized quickly and she was able to knock the bullets away.

Kaylee resumed her chase of the limo, now with police cars in pursuit of her as well. A civilian in a large truck was shocked by the sight of her flying over a limo and crashed into the first police car, slowing down her escort.

Kevin called Kaylee while she was flying. "Did you find the President's limo?"

"Yeah, I am chasing them now."

"Is that a siren I hear?"

"Yes, the police are chasing me."

"Stay with the President no matter what," Kevin urged before hanging up. He raced to find her, following the sirens.

Ben tried to look out the window to follow Kaylee, but she kept moving above the limo where he couldn't see her. "Damn that flying witch. What is she doing?" He pointed to one of his henchmen. "Try to shoot her. I am not sure it will work, but it might slow her down so we can get by."

The agent rolled down the window and stuck out his gun before he began to shoot. After a few shots, Kaylee flew down and pulled him out of the car. Ben and the President turned to see the man rolling to a stop on the side of the road. The President saw Kaylee resume her chase of the limo. He wasn't sure what was going on with her, but he was glad that someone was able to keep up with the limo. It gave him hope.

"Lose her!" Ben shouted to the driver. The driver did his best to use every trick in his limited repertoire of driving moves to lose her. The car got more difficult to follow. The driver went up and down streets and changed speeds in an attempt to get rid of her.

"I've had enough of this," Kaylee said, pulling out a small silver knife from her boot. She threw it at the rear wheel of the limo. This set the limo on a crazy course, but didn't stop it.

The driver turned down a tunnel expecting that Kaylee could not follow them through. As they turned, a woman pushing a stroller started to cross the street a couple of blocks away. As the limo got closer the baby started crying. The young mother looked down at the baby just as the limo was nearly upon them. Kaylee, undaunted by the tunnel, flew faster to catch the stroller and the mother and pull them to safety. Other shoppers on the street stopped and stared. It happened so fast that few had time to understand what was going on, let alone react. The mother clutched her baby, crying as she realized what just happened. The woman in silver had just saved her baby's life.

While Kaylee was distracted, Ben stopped the limo next to a taxi. He pulled the President out and the limo driver pulled out his gun. The driver slid in beside the taxi driver and waved his gun, shooing the man out of his taxi. Ben dug his gun into the back of the President, forcing him into the back seat.

Kaylee saw the limo stopped just ahead and sped toward it. She broke through the back window and flew straight out the windshield. She flew around the side and alit on the ground next to the limo. She peered inside and saw that the vehicle was empty. She picked it up and turned it on its side.

She turned to find a man standing next to the limo. He shrugged, "They stole my taxi. Do you want their car?"

"What color taxi do you drive?"

"Yellow."

Kaylee went to fly again, looking for a yellow taxi. How could there be this many yellow taxis in the city?

Ben opened his phone and called David. "I need a helicopter to come get this silver woman following us."

"No problem, I will take care of it. Leave your phone on so I can track your location and give it to the pilot."

David was back on the phone as soon as Ben hung up. He watched the helicopter depart. It had just brought him and the President's daughters to this location. He waved a gun at the girls and moved them along the grass path.

Kevin was frustrated that he couldn't find Kaylee, so he turned back to the White House to see if he could help her from there. Surely Jack could help him protect her. He called Jack only to find that he and Jason were together.

"Jack, I need your help to find an agent. She was following the President in the limo after he was captured."

"I'll do whatever you need. Just tell me where to meet you," Jack said.

"Okay, come to the command center in the Security Office at the White House. Use my name to get in. I will be waiting for you."

Ben sat beside the President watching the road ahead and giving orders to the driver. The President looked back and saw the silver woman flying. He winced when a car hit a light post after watching her fly by instead of watching the road. He reached up and tried waving, but that did no good. He started to bang on the window to get her attention.

Ben turned. "Stop banging or I'll shoot. I don't have to shoot to kill to make you miserable. I can shoot off your kneecaps or, with one call, I can have your daughters' kneecaps shot off. Now stop!"

"Where are they? Don't hurt them, please!"

"Then shut up! Do what I say and they will be released unharmed."

The President nodded. Ben shouted at the driver to go faster. The driver was getting flustered.

The crowd watched as Kaylee flew up to the taxi and threw a silver knife at the vehicle. She shattered the rear window. They began to take pictures and videos. The driver continued on. She landed on the roof and stabbed the driver's leg through the roof of the taxi with a long spear.

Ben and President gasped. The President shouted for help through the broken rear window. Ben pointed his gun at the President. The driver slowed down from his injury and Kaylee flew down behind the taxi. She grabbed the rear bumper, hoping to stop the vehicle. The bumper came off and the car sped away.

The driver felt the loss of blood and passed out. The taxi continued to move forward, but now there was no one controlling it. It sped into a tunnel, passing a blue minivan. The four-year-old girl in the back seat looked up to see Kaylee fly by.

"Look at the silver lady flying."

"Honey, no one can really fly," said her mother.

"Look," said the girl, pointing.

"Yes, I see her. Whoa," gasped the mother.

Two deaf students from Gallaudet University were driving in the beat-up sedan behind the minivan. They too saw Kaylee fly by, and their hands flew excitedly as they signed to one another. In the blue minivan, the mother's cell phone rang and she moved to answer it, slamming the brakes enough to send her groceries flying. A can of soup got caught under the brake. She panicked and tried to slam on the brakes only to find the pedal stuck. She panicked and pressed the gas pedal. She leaned on the horn to warn other drivers. Kaylee turned to look at the minivan. She didn't understand why the minivan wouldn't stop, but the look of fear on the driver's face was clear. She flew back and the students watched her. The minivan hit the rear of the yellow taxi, and the car hit the back of the minivan. Air bags popped all over the place and all the cars crashed to a stop.

Kaylee flew back to find that the driver of the car was trapped because her air bag hadn't deflated. She pulled out a small silver knife and popped the bag. The driver had a bloody nose but seemed otherwise unhurt.

The students were shaken up as well. They had been unable to hear the horn or the sirens. Kaylee stood on the roof of the car as it skidded down the road, like she was surfing. There was fire on the road beneath her. That was the image the TV cameramen captured, as well as a few civilians using cell phone cameras.

Kaylee hopped down and ripped off the door of the car to help the driver out. She signed, clearly upset. The student explained that they were all deaf in the car and that they were all right.

The President and Ben were both shaken up by the accident. Kaylee flew over to them and helped the President out of the taxi. Ben reached for his gun and tried to shoot the President, but she quickly grabbed his hand with the gun and broke his wrist. Ben screamed.

"Sir, are you okay?" she asked the President.

"Yes I think so." He took a step back, remembering that she was a vampire.

"I am going to put my arms around you and fly you out of here, sir. Don't worry, I won't hurt you."

He looked at her for a second and took a breath. "Okay, young lady. Let's go."

She reached around his waist and they flew off. The crowd that had gathered gasped and cameras flashed.

The President was afraid of heights, and this was really high. Kaylee held him securely. Still, he was happy when she set him down in a deserted alley. They could hear a number of televisions through open windows blaring public emergency broadcasts asking for any information about the location of the President. The President ignored the pleas of the television to call 911 if they spotted him. "Who are you? CIA?"

Her phone started ringing. "Shh," she said as she opened her phone.

"Do you have the President?" asked Kevin.

"Sorry it took so long. He is here safe with me right now. Meet us at the tunnel…"

Her cell phone battery decided to give up at that moment. Kaylee looked at her phone and swore.

"Kaylee? Kaylee? What tunnel? Damn!" Kevin said to himself. What tunnel could she mean? He wasn't all that familiar with Washington, DC, but he would do his best. There couldn't be that many tunnels in DC. "Ah-ha!" he said to himself. He looked for where traffic was backed up and located the closest tunnel.

"You stay here and don't move this time." Kaylee had found a reasonably safe location away from the street. "I will be right back. I need to find Agent Douglas." She took a step up and then flew off.

A helicopter came swooping toward her. A man in fatigues leaned out of the open door and began to shoot at her. She pulled a silver web out of a pocket. *The silver itself will be useless against a helicopter, but a net on the other hand...* she thought. She threw the web and it caught in the tail rotor. The helicopter couldn't steer. Luckily it was right above a building and half landed, half fell on the roof.

She flew on, searching for Kevin. Jack and Jason had found his car and were following it. Jason called him. "We are right behind you. Pull over and you can ride with us."

Kevin pulled over and watched in the mirrors on the car as a large military vehicle drove up behind him. He was grateful they were on the same side.

The air space above Washington DC was well protected and the Air Force quickly found Kaylee. They flew behind her in an attack helicopter with lethal and non-lethal weapons. The pilot smiled, thinking they even had a few tricks up their sleeves that no one would expect. He popped a few bullets in front of her. She didn't slow. Next the pilot tried a non-lethal sound pulse to knock her out of the air. It didn't stop her—it only seemed to irritate her. She turned and flew up to the helicopter. She pulled on the skid and dragged it down to the roof of a nearby building.

The President looked around the alley. He knew he should stay put until the Secret Service found him or that silver woman, but when he started getting hassled by the two homeless men who lived there he had to leave. He walked out of the alley and tried to orient himself so he could find the police or get back to a federal building. As he started walking, a couple passed him. The woman kept staring at him. She turned around and touched his shoulder.

"Aren't you the President?" she asked.

"Sorry, no. But I get that a lot." He smiled and walked on.

Her companion was not so easily brushed off. He pulled out his cell phone and dialed 911 as the President hurried away.

Kaylee found Kevin as he got out of the car. He jumped when she landed next to him. Jason and Jack got out of the vehicle, and the four of them stood on the grass. Jason looked at Kaylee and asked, "Where is the President?"

"I can take you to him if you like. But let me just take one of you so I can bring the President back here."

She held out her hand, and Kevin took it. Kaylee jumped with Kevin to the alley. "Where the hell is the President? He's escaped twice!"

"He's probably nearby, let's just go look," suggested Kevin.

Kaylee sped out of the alley. Kevin ran after her, breathing heavily, "Wait for me."

Kaylee couldn't hear him because she was too far ahead already. She stopped when she heard sirens coming close to her. The police stopped not far from alley where she had left the President. They pulled over and stopped a man and a woman to question them. The couple pointed, and the police went in that direction. Kaylee was faster. She caught up to the President and walked beside him.

"Sir, I need to get you to safety."

"Good. That alley was not safe for anyone. I had to leave."

"That's fine, sir. Can you take my hand? I will take you to some friends who can keep you safe."

"Okay," he said as he took her hand. They jumped to the alley where Kaylee had left Kevin. There was no sign of him.

"This is crazy. First you disappear and now Kevin! What is this?" The President looked a bit sheepish.

The police were all around the area. Jack and Jason pulled up across from the alley. They heard the commotion on the radio and knew that this was where they needed to be. They parked in a bus zone.

In the alley, the same homeless men accosted the President. "Hey, I own this alley, get off my property." One yelled and flailed his arms. The President stepped back. Kaylee put her arm out in front of the President and growled loudly at the man. She bared her fangs and the man all but flew back into his cardboard box.

"Please stay here for a few minutes while I look for Kevin. I don't think these people will bother you again. I am just not sure who to trust aside from Kevin, so please stay while I look for him." She flew out of the alley hoping that he would listen.

Kevin had run down the street, looking for Kaylee. He really needed to exercise more, perhaps lead more classes at the studio. He was out of breath. The police were shouting and their radios were abuzz with news of a person wearing silver having been sighted with the President. All officers needed to be on the lookout for anyone dressed in silver and hold them for questioning.

Kevin ducked behind a building where Kaylee spotted him and floated down next to him. The police officers nearby caught her movement and raised their weapons. "DC police! Raise your hands above your head and remain where you are!" One shouted at Kaylee.

She moved at incredible speed to call her silver staff. When the officers saw the staff suddenly appear they started to shoot. Kaylee was able escape injury, and after a moment the officers paused. She whipped the staff around her body and used the power to smash the hood of a cruiser. A few of the officers lowered their weapons and just looked. The lead officer held his ground and didn't miss a beat.

Kevin took that moment to slip into the background and eased himself out of the situation. He needed to get to a location where Kaylee could meet him.

"I said, remain where you are and put your hands in air. Drop the weapon now!" An officer demanded.

She looked at him and showed her fangs. He fired one shot above her and returned to his stance. She decided that he wasn't going to back down, so she lowered her staff and flew off. She didn't need to hurt him just because she was angry.

Kaylee dropped down near Kevin. Without saying a word, she took his hand. They flew over the area, and she jumped them to the President.

"Thank you for waiting for us, sir. I was getting tired of babysitting the two of you," said Kaylee. "This is Kevin Douglas, and I think he can help protect you."

"Young lady, I think you are probably the best security I could ever ask for," he smiled at her. "Are you two with the CIA?"

"I am," Kevin said, "and as for Kaylee, well, let's save that discussion for later. Right now we need to keep you safe."

The police fanned out and began searching the area. Dark sedans drove up to the join the police cars. Men in dark suits poured out of them and started to search the area. The two groups made for a formidable search team. Kevin didn't like their odds—soon they would be discovered and he still wasn't sure who he could trust.

Jason and Jack heard the commotion and were well positioned to see the standoff between the police officer and Kaylee. Jason and Jack looked at each other for a moment. They ran back to the vehicle.

Jack asked Jason, "Where are we going?"

"I have an idea. Let's see if we can get them to come to us and get the President to safety." They drove off trying to blend in. After a few turns, Jason drove the vehicle down an alley almost too narrow for the wide military truck.

Kaylee exhaled, feeling safe, but it was a moment too soon. The police and Secret Service just start down the alley. Kevin put his hand under the President's elbow. "Shit, here they come."

They noticed lights flashing into alley. They pulled back against the alley wall and stood very still. Kaylee whispered, "Both of you go up to the roof, fast. Stay on the roof and keep out of sight."

They listened to her order and began to quietly climb up the ladder. "Faster!" She said and they climbed faster.

Kaylee turned around to look at the police and agents. She prepared herself and her weapons. She listened to the two men as they reached the roof. She flew up and flipped over a car, blocking the alley. She flew up a short distance and then came down hard on the roof of the card, denting it. With her staff in hand, she landed in front of the car, crouching, ready for a fight.

Kaylee stood up and lifted the car. She flipped it over so it landed upside down on top of one of the Secret Service cars.

The two men watched her from the roof. "There is so much destruction. What is she doing?" the President asked.

"Saving the world, sir, saving the world. That's my girl."

Jason and Jack maneuvered the vehicle to the back of an alley and turned to park behind a building. They heard the commotion surrounding Kaylee and knew that would distract everyone. Jason pulled out his phone and called Kevin.

"Kevin, are you all right? Where are you?"

"I am here with the President, and we are fine. We are on the roof of a building."

"Can you identify the building or describe where you are? I think we are very close by."

"Sure, Jason. The walls of the building are dark brown, four stories high, and we are facing the road, we can see a building with faded white paint, a building with an Italian restaurant on the first floor, and…I can't really tell anything about the building behind us."

Jason was turning around as Kevin spoke, trying to orient. Taking a deep sniff of air to find the smell of marinara sauce, he broke out into a smile. "I think I have you now. May I speak with the President?"

"Of course, here he is," said Kevin passing the phone to the President.

"Who am I speaking with?"

"Sir this is Jason Smith with the FBI. I am here with Colonel Jack Hopkinton. We are coming up to get you. The battery on this phone is dying so I cannot talk long. Are you all right?"

"Son, this is not my best day, but I am not hurt."

Kaylee shouted, "Enough! Why are you hunting me? What do you want from me?"

Suddenly a helicopter came and hovered in front of her. It swung a large light toward her. When it was switched on, it was as if a slice of day was coming from the helicopter and shining on Kaylee. She blinked and put her arm over her face.

"This is ridiculous," she said to herself. She flew over to the aircraft and grabbed the light operator by the shirt. She flung him out on to the ground, knocking over a few agents and officers in the way. To the surprise of the soldiers in the helicopter, she took control of the light and swung it to shine on the police officers below. The officers covered their eyes and turned away.

"How does it feel when you have a light shined in *your* eyes?" she taunted. Kaylee moved over to push the other occupants of the helicopter out. Then she turned her attention to the pilot. She climbed forward and knelt behind him. She tapped him on the shoulder to get his attention and when he turned, she gave him a big smile with fangs and all. She picked up the headset from the seat next to him. She spoke into the microphone without putting on the headset. "Don't come back for me. Leave *now*!"

The pilot paled as she smiled again, fangs showing to full effect. She moved quickly back to the open door and jumped out. She flew to the roof. The President and Kevin looked relieved. Kevin was an excellent agent who knew when he was in over his head.

Kaylee touched the President on the elbow and said, "We must leave."

Kevin looked around and said, "No, no, wait. We need to wait until Jason and Jack get here."

Kaylee was not looking forward to babysitting four men who couldn't seem to listen "No, no, forget them."

Kevin gave her a very stern look. "No, we are going to wait. We just spoke to them a few moments ago. They will be here quickly, Kaylee. Just wait."

"Call me Silver."

"Silver?"

"Yes. I am a new person; I need a new name."

Kevin looked at her. The new name might have as much to do with being different as with ID card issues, but he wasn't going to argue. She wasn't the little girl who had done a cartwheel when she passed her first belt test. No, she was quite different. "Silver it is," he smiled.

The police had brought in more of the large lights and were using searchlights to find them. The trio hugged an access door to stay in the shadows. No matter which way they moved, the light trapped them.

"Sorry, Silver, can you break those lights?" Kevin pointed to the lights that were blinding them. She looked at him, picked up a rock, and smiled. The pebbles began to sail through the air.

Jason and Jack looked around the roof to see if there was any sign of the President or Kevin.

In the sudden darkness, Kevin held the President's arm.

"We need to stay low and find better shelter. They don't know it is you with me, but I fear that might not stop everyone. Not everyone is happy about the bill you were going to sign tonight."

They hugged the outer edge of the building, moving toward a ladder that came over the edge of the building. Just as they got close, a head popped up. It was Jason. They stepped back to let the two men onto the roof.

The helicopters returned in numbers. Kaylee looked at Kevin and pointed to the lights on the helicopters. They were too far away for her to hit them with rocks, so she extended her silver staff and flew off. After a moment, one helicopter went dark. Soon all the choppers were dark, and in the confusion, the rear rotor of one helicopter tipped into the blades of another and they both went down.

In this confusion and smoke, Kaylee headed back to the roof. She touched down just behind Kevin and Jason. They both jumped and she smiled. "Just me, boys!"

"You scared the crap out of me," panted Kevin. "Okay, I need you to stay out of sight. Silver, I need you to keep an eye out for any more helicopters. We need to get the President off the roof."

"I don't know if I can stay with you guys. All you do is tell me what to do. I want to end this. I have to go back where I belong. Understand?"

Kevin started toward her, "Kayl—"

"Silver!" she corrected.

"Sorry, Silver. We need a moment here. This is Jason Smith and Colonel Jack Hopkinton. We have a lot to discuss and we cannot stay here. Where to next?"

Kaylee was silent for a moment. "All right, I will find a safe place to stay. You guys stay together—don't move. Really, just stay here." She looked at the President who smiled. She flew up and then disappeared.

The President looked at Kevin. "Tell me what's going on. Why do you two wear silver?"

"What is strange to me is that someone was trying to kill you and your security detail wasn't there. And they let you leave the White House. I think we need to trust Kaylee and Kevin," Jason said, looking at the President.

"I know what is going on," Kevin said. "And I have proof. It has to do with vampire rights and the bill you were to sign tonight."

Kaylee flew around the area, trying to stay close to buildings to avoid the police. It was starting to quiet down, but that was more so because humans were going to bed than the police leaving. They were still out in force. She spotted a hotel that seemed pretty quiet and checked out a few rooms that were dark. She landed on the third floor balcony of one and checked the sliding glass door. It was locked, but a bit of jiggling loosened it. Kaylee slid the balcony door of Room 305 open just enough to slip through. No one was in the room and it looked unoccupied. Even the toilet still had paper across it. The big king-sized bed looked perfect.

Kaylee jumped back to the roof in time for Kevin to explain, "I have the original and a copy of every word of their conversation." He showed them a small disk in his hand.

Kaylee moved closer and they gasped. They hadn't heard her come back. "Sorry, I found an available location. Each of you touch me, now." They followed her order. She jumped them into the hotel room.

"Now, just how do you do that?" asked the President curiously.

"I've known you most of your life, and you are just full of surprises these days. I feel like I am meeting a new Kaylee," confessed Kevin.

"I am a vampire now. I am here for one reason and one reason only. I need to stop the silver people hunting down vampires. If I can find out what happened to my cow, that's a bonus. But for now, we must end this war."

The President, Jack, and Jason were confused.

"You wear silver. I thought you were with the silver agency," said Jack.

"I am not familiar with the whole silver suit thing. What's going on?" said Jason.

Kaylee sighed. "Ask Kevin. Look, I am not here to babysit you guys. You are safe here for now, but no phone, no TV, no lights, don't flush, don't answer the door, and keep out of sight. I am going back to my own kind, if you don't mind. Don't worry, I will right be back."

With that, Kaylee jumped.

"Look," Kevin said, "I can explain everything. Okay, *almost* everything. I am the assistant director of a secret agency within the CIA. I have known Jack here for a long time. We served in the Army together and I knew I could trust him. Kayl… I mean The Silver Vampire—I have known her since she was three. I'd trust her with my life.

"I overheard a conversation between my director, Ben Sullivan, and two others. They were plotting not only your downfall, Mr. President, but also a way to fund the Silver Agency long into the future."

"What exactly does the Silver Agency do?" the President asked.

"We hunt vampires, sir."

"Exactly what does that mean? Are you trying to say that you use federal money and personnel to kill vampires without authority?"

"Yes sir, that is what I am saying. Sometimes we also cripple vampire-owned businesses, but mostly we hunt them."

"So it would not be in your agency's best interest for me to sign the bill giving vampires stronger legal protections and greater civil rights."

"That is what is at the root of Ben's attempt on your life. With you out of the picture, your Vice President could take over, not sign the bill, and fund the Silver Agency at higher levels."

This made sense to the President, Jason, and Jack, but the President was very concerned that they were doing illegal things without authority. It now made sense the few times when the VP had pushed him to sign a couple of things in the middle of a meeting. "I had no knowledge of this. This was not legal. I understand more now, but what I don't understand is why they kidnapped my kids? They thought they had me with the sniper."

Jason, Kevin, and Jack gasped, surprised they had kidnapped his girls. Jason looked at the President. "What? Who took your girls?"

Ben left the hospital with a sling and his wrist in a cast. That Silver Vampire had done this, and he would get his revenge. He would speak on television and make the case to the American public that she was dangerous and had kidnapped the President. All hell would break loose, and this could turn the tide of public opinion against the vampires and her in particular.

Ben spoke to one of his men. "I want to hold a press conference. Can you arrange one as soon as possible?" In no time, there was a crowd of reporters on the granite steps of an office building. Ben walked up to the microphone sitting atop the lectern.

"I am going to make a brief statement and then I will take questions." Ben cleared his throat and began. "Vampires are a threat to the American way of life. Giving them civil rights, rights our forefathers worked for, fought for, and died for, is unacceptable. Vampires did not fight for freedom from the British in the Revolutionary War. They did not die on the fields at Gettysburg. They did not join in the founding of this great country, and they should not share in the fruits of that labor.

"Just this evening, as the President was about to give vampires stronger civil rights and protections under our great Constitution, a silver-clad individual kidnapped the President. It is unclear what her intentions are, but you can bet she wasn't taking him to a garden party. At this point we know that she kidnapped him from the White House and has been seen in the Georgetown area. The police and federal agency personnel are working in a joint force to capture the individual. If you have any information or see the kidnapper, please call your nearest police station.

"Now I will take questions."

The reporters asked fairly predictable questions. Did it really matter what the President was wearing or how many police officers were working on this case?

"Okay, one last question," Ben said at last. "You there in the back."

"Thank you for taking my question. I have heard reports of a second silver-clad person. The man appears to be wearing a silver uniform. Can you give us more information on the second silver person?"

"Not at this time, but that information should be available tomorrow."

Leaning over to one of his agents, Ben tersely ordered him find any reports or pictures of other silver-clad figures. Ben was worried about that last reporter. When a reporter got wind of a story, they could be like bloodhounds. He hopped into his car alone and drove away.

Jack was thoughtful. "Sir, if you don't sign the bill, this can set back all kinds of civil liberties."

"I agree. Look, Kevin, you said you had proof of this conspiracy on my life and my girls' kidnapping. Let's hear it now."

Kevin produced the tape and handed it to him.

# CHAPTER 21

Kaylee returned to Eric's office and immediately rushed to her sister. "Grace, I just came back to give you a progress report and let you know that I am okay."

Grace gave her a big hug as Eric came in to the room. "How long do you think you will be gone on this little project of yours?" he asked.

"I am hoping to be done by tomorrow night," Kaylee said optimistically.

Grace said, "Sweet sister of mine, you have no idea how big this is getting. I just saw on TV that the police are looking for two people in silver wanted for kidnapping the President. I doubt you will be done by tomorrow."

"Just kill Kevin Douglas and be done with this then," Eric said. "I don't want your little field trip to hurt our community or you."

"Kevin is a good man," Kaylee protested. "Even if he is wearing silver, he is still on our side. I know him."

"This is a bad idea, Kaylee. Vampires and humans don't mix."

"Just give me a chance. Kevin is working to get civil rights for vampires. What he's doing will help all of us. And once the President knows about the Silver Agency, he can stop it. Please, just give me a chance to see this through."

Eric was thoughtful for a moment. It would be better for the vampires in his community to have legal protection and to stop people from burning down any more vampire businesses. That bill would be better if it were signed. Could she really help, though? He couldn't bear the thought of something happening to her.

"Okay, you can go back, but be careful. I am not happy about it and I would be less happy if a vampire of mine got hurt or was put in jail. Understand?"

"Perfectly. Thank you!"

Kaylee started to jump when she heard Grace warn, "Get rid of your silver clothes!"

"Thanks!" Kaylee spoke some words of power and was back in regular clothes, with her silver panties well-hidden. She jumped back to the hotel room.

The President wasn't startled when she arrived. "Look, Kevin explained everything to me about the Silver Agency. I had no idea about it, and I want to offer my sincerest apology to you."

Kaylee wasn't entirely sure how to handle this. "Umm, thank you. Honestly sir, I have only been a vampire for a couple of days, so I can't exactly speak for all vampires. But on behalf of my sister and me, thank you. Now for more practical considerations." She looked at Kevin. "Let's get you out of those clothes."

"What?" He wasn't sure what to think about this.

"The TV news is reporting that two people in silver have kidnapped the President. That is you and me, sensei. So we need to change our clothes. I need your size."

Kevin looked a bit sheepish and told her his size. Kaylee disappears in a flash.

"You know, it could really come in handy to be able to flash wherever I want to go," the President chuckled. Then he took a deep breath. "I am worried about my kids. Do you think she will be able to help us find them?"

Suddenly the President's cell phone went off. This was very surprising, as very few people had access to the number. He used it only for his family and a few friends whom he kept in touch with to stay grounded.

"Hello?"

Doug was calling from the boiler room of a dark basement. The call barely got through the layers of concrete and steel. "If you want to get your girls back, meet me at Fort Myer in Virginia tomorrow at 7:00 pm. And come alone. I will call you tomorrow with further instructions. If you show up with someone or if you show up late, your girls are dead. Got it?"

"Don't hurt them! Let me speak to my girls, please?" Everyone in the hotel room held their breath. To their surprise, he was allowed to speak to them. Doug grabbed his eldest daughter by the hair and held the phone to her ear.

"Dad? Help us!" she cried.

His younger daughter started to sob. Doug let go of the older sister's hair and pulled the younger girl toward him.

"Dad!" was all she could get out—everything else was lost in the sobs.

"Okay," Doug said, "you've heard them and they are alive. Keep it that way by following my instructions."

Doug hung up and said, "Your Dad will get you home to heaven tomorrow." Both girls started to cry at this, and the oldest sister wrapped her arms around her younger sister.

Two guards stood outside the door. Doug spoke to the guards as he prepared to leave the hideout. "Watch them and wait until I call you. Once we are sure we won't need them again, we can kill them."

Doug and another guard strode out the door. The remaining two guards looked at each other, they were sure they didn't want to kill children and unsure how to get out of following orders.

Kaylee flew down to a department store that was closed for the night. They should have something for Kevin to put on. She jumped in and began to look around. She really liked the leather clothing they had—it was totally her style. Kevin didn't seem quite like the leather pants kind of guy, though, so she headed to the men's department.

She found some rather nondescript clothing in the sizes he asked for and headed to the shoe department. She had to ask Kevin where he got the silver combat boots; she needed a pair for later. She found some hiking boots in his size and grabbed them. As she was getting ready to go, she saw a pair of silver sunglasses in a case. She had to have them. She made a mental note to send the store some money later and took the glasses.

A police car drove by the store, shining a light in the windows. Kaylee ducked down and picked up a belt. Now she was done, and she jumped back to the hotel room.

"Here you go, Kevin, non-silver clothes. I hope I got what you needed."

"Thanks, this looks great."

"What happened?" Kaylee asked the President. "You all look like you lost your best friend."

The President said, "Someone kidnapped my daughters and I got a call to meet the kidnapper tomorrow at 7:00 pm at Fort Myer."

Jack put a reassuring hand on his shoulder. "I know the base. I was stationed there years ago, and I can help. We have a vehicle here. We should head back to the office and try and run a trace on that call from your cell phone records."

"Where's your wife?" Jason asked the President.

"She is in Paris for few days at a meeting. She should be safe over there." The President stood up and started to pace across the small room.

"Look," the President said, "I know this is crazy, but I am not sure who else to trust. Silver Vampire, can you help me get my girls back? No one else has your unique talents, and I think they will be necessary to get them back."

"I have no training in this. What if something goes wrong?" Kaylee was worried and getting frustrated. How did she get anything done when she was human?

Kevin begged, "Please?"

Kaylee looked at the President. "I will do my best, sir. It was so hard when I lost my dad, I can only imagine that losing a child is just as bad."

The President was appreciative. "Thank you, Silver."

"Save the world; that's my girl."

Jason peered at the clothes she had brought Kevin. "Did you steal these?"

"Yes, I had to. There are no stores open all night in this area. I don't know how regular vampires ever shop for anything, especially in the summer when it is light so late."

That gave the men something to chew on. Kevin carefully saved the tags from the clothes and put them in his wallet. He looked at Kaylee's new silver sunglasses.

"Fine, I will pay for them, *Dad.* I have the tag in my pocket."

The President smiled, "Don't worry, I will pay for it."

Kaylee looked a bit surprised. "Sir, shoplifting isn't my thing. I don't steal things, really. But thank you for your offer. Our house burned down yesterday and I have nothing. Luckily my sister and I were not home at the time."

"What happened?" the President asked her.

"Kevin's Silver Agency burnt it to the ground. And lost my cow."

Jack was incredulous. He looked at Kevin. "One of your people did what?"

"What?" Kevin said. "I didn't have anything to do with burning your house down."

"I know you didn't, but just after you left our house burned down and my cow disappeared."

"Look, I am sorry about your house. I'll look into who ordered the burning and who did the actual work. We will figure it out, but not tonight. You need some sleep. Vampires do that, don't they?"

She sighed, "Yeah they do."

"Then take a rest."

She started to remove the sunglasses. She put them on the stand next to the bed. Jack, who was standing closest to her, was surprised and said, "You have silver eyes too?"

"No, those are contacts," said Kevin as he was taking off some of his silver clothing.

She looked at Kevin, thoughtfully. "No, they are real. I wasn't sure what you would say. I am sorry."

He pursed his lips and glared at her. "What else have you lied to me about?"

Jack wisely took a step back—clearly this was between them. "Nothing, really. Well, my mom was a witch and I inherited some of her powers, but I never lied about that. It just never came up."

"Actually I knew about your father. You forget I've known you since you were a toddler. You didn't inherit any powers from your dad. Exactly how long have you been a vampire?" Some of the venom was leaving his voice. It was hard for him to stay mad at someone he loved so much.

Kaylee looked at her watch. "Umm, almost three days now. And don't start with me about being truthful, Mr. CIA Agent."

She had him there. He was still pissed and it showed. She stood her ground. And he couldn't fault her for doing that, since he had always taught her to stand up for herself and her choices. Damn. She was just the woman he hoped she'd become when he first saw her compete in the karate matches.

Kaylee broke the silence, "Let's get some rest. We'll all have clearer heads after some sleep."

Grace looked at Eric and took a deep breath, steeling herself. She might be the older sister, but Kaylee usually took care of things. "Well, this mess won't be cleaned up in one day, but with Kaylee on the job it will be quick. Let's just be patient. What do you all say we go out and have some fun? Take our minds off of things?" She smiled, showing her fangs.

Joseph frowned. "Do you think it is safe out there now?"

"I have no idea, but I think we really need to get out for awhile anyway. Don't you guys know of a safe bar where we can get a drink? Other than the Longshore, I mean."

All the deputies agreed they needed to get out for a while. Eric relented, "All right, let's go, but watch her." He pointed to Grace.

Grace started to go with everyone else when she remembered, "Oh damn, my motorcycle was lost in the fire."

"Your motorcycle is safe in woods. I will show you where it is," Eric said kindly.

"Really?"

"I moved it with Kaylee," Eric explained.

Grace was so happy she threw her arms around him and gave him a big hug saying, "Thank you!" Eric was at a loss for words at her gesture.

The deputies and Grace walked into another vampire bar in Acton. The TV was on showing a late night report about the President being kidnapped. It showed some blurry pictures of Kaylee flying. No one else could have said who it was, but they knew instantly.

Joseph said stoically, "Live fast."

Eric was a bit more clear in his feelings and used a few expletives that others would not understand as they were in a language long dead.

The TV was showing a special report from a CIA director, Ben Sullivan. "A Silver Vampire kidnapped the President. She is out of control and a grave danger to the human community. America is not safe from vampires like her. When I tried to save the President, she broke my wrist." He held up his bandaged arm for emphasis. "She must be stopped at all costs." The reporter cut to another video showing Kaylee flying, but it could have been a bird for all the clarity it had.

Eric was confused. "Did she kidnap him?"

Grace defended her sister. "No, he is a liar. He did it."

The deputies closed in around Grace. They could hear the crowd, which was mainly but not exclusively vampires, talking about Kaylee. The mood was uncertain but not good. A rogue vampire was not safe given the delicate mood in America right now. Vampire civil rights hung in the balance, and they wanted to be equal citizens.

Harvey Hall, a sheriff from Acton, walked in the bar. He came right over to Eric and Grace.

"ID, miss." He held out his hand.

"Here." She pulled it out of the back pocket of her tight pants. "Happy?"

He looked at it and nodded. "About time, miss." He held his hand out to Eric. "I was real sorry to hear about your bar."

"Thanks. We were getting a bit stir crazy and came here."

They both relaxed and turned to the TV. Harvey asked, "You know anything about this Silver Vampire? Ever heard of anything like this before?"

"Never heard of a Silver Vampire before. I can't touch silver, and I haven't even heard legend of a vampire who could. It is curious," said Eric.

"We need to find out more about this. Any ideas who her master is?" The deputies began to close ranks at this. They weren't sure what Eric wanted to do next. Now Harvey looked at Grace. "Eric, is she in Millbury?"

"Yeah. The silver people burned down her house and she is an orphan. She's under my protection for the moment."

"Miss, perhaps you'd like to go off and get a drink and leave us to talk business?" Harvey shooed her away. She looked at him, raised an eyebrow, and put her hand on her hip. Just as she opened her mouth, Eric raised his eyebrow. She closed her mouth and promptly turned around and walked off to order a drink. He was equally surprised and relieved she'd done as she was told for once.

Just then, Frank Lopez the sheriff from Bolton, walked in. His tall, broad frame barely fit through the door. He ran a hand across his bearded face as he noticed Eric and Harvey talking. He strode directly over to them. A few of his deputies followed behind him. They were all make from the same mold.

"Glad to find you both here. Any idea who she is and where she's from?" he asked, pointing a thumb over his shoulder at the TV.

Ben and David were in the White House. Ben was pacing up and down the well-appointed office. "That Silver Vampire bitch broke my wrist. I need to find out who this other guy is wearing the silver clothes. He is mocking my Silver Agency. What is Plan B, now that A has failed so publically?"

"We have some good news: Tomorrow we can get the feeds from the TV crews. We have technology they don't, so we can clean up the picture and see if we can ID him. Once we have an ID, we can go after them both through other channels."

Ben rubbed his cast. His expression was as dark as a moonless night. He really hated vampires, and the Silver Vampire was at the top of his list.

Kaylee started to float above the bed where she was sleeping. Kevin was startled when he saw this. He'd never heard of vampires or witches floating when they sleep. *Silver eyes and floating—what will Kaylee come up with next*? He wondered.

As the sun just started to peek over the horizon, the first rays shone gold and orange into the hotel room. Kaylee, still sleeping, floated over to the sunbeams, which pulled her like a magnet. The light startled her awake and she landed on the floor. She still had no idea why. *Ugh*, she thought. *When will new strange things stop happening to my body? And why am I attracted to the light*? This whole changing into a vampire thing involved more changes than she expected. Quietly she got up and moved to the bathroom, picking up a pillow as she went. She tossed the pillow into the tub and climbed in. With no windows, this was a completely dark room, so she closed the door. She fell asleep quickly and once again, floated. Without any light, she stayed in place.

Jack's eyes opened suddenly. Something in the room had changed. He looked around and realized Kaylee was missing. He didn't hear her anywhere. He could see Kevin asleep in the chair by the deck. *Hmmm, some sentry*.

He immediately jumped up, waking Jason in the process. "Kaylee is missing."

Jason woke up all the way, "Bathroom?"

"No, it has been completely quiet for the last few moments. I haven't heard her in there."

Both men turned their heads at the same time to the sunlight streaming into the room from the glass doors on the deck.

"Shit. Did she burn up in the sun?" Jack asked. They raced over and woke up Kevin.

“Kaylee is missing and there is sunlight in the room. Could she have…burned up?” At this the President woke up, fully alert in an instant.

Kevin looked around. “No, I don’t see any ash on the floor. She didn’t burn up. Did you check the bathroom? Vampires don’t use the facilities, but maybe she wanted to wash up.”

The President looked puzzled. “Vampires don’t use the bathroom? Where is she?”

Kevin looked a bit sheepish discussing the bathroom habits of vampires. “No sir, they don’t eliminate waste the same way humans do. Becoming a vampire eliminates the need, and they seem to have additional organs and some rituals that help them rid their bodies of anything they don’t need. You don’t see overweight vampires because they won’t eat if they aren’t hungry.”

“I had no idea, and I thought I knew a lot about vampires.”

Jack looked around. “Could she have done her disappearing act and gone somewhere?”

Kevin shrugged, “Sure, it is possible, but she didn’t leave a note and that would be rather surprising. She didn’t say anything to me about leaving.”

The three of them looked a bit deflated at the thought that Kaylee had left them. “Can we even do this without her?” Jason asked the question they had all been thinking.

Kevin stood up. “I need to use the bathroom.” He moved quickly to the bathroom. He turned on the light and pulled up the lid of the toilet, breaking the paper surrounding it. He dropped his pants and began urinating.

Kaylee shouted when she woke up and landed with a thunk in the tub.

Kevin was so startled when he heard Kaylee behind the curtain of tub. She pulled the curtain back. “Why didn’t you knock?”

“A little privacy here!”

She turned her back, and he quickly finished. The others breathed as collective sigh of relief at hearing her voice and then started chuckling when they realized what was going on in the bathroom.

Walking out of the bathroom, carrying the pillow, Kaylee greeted the men. She threw the pillow on the bed and walked over to the glass door to peer out at the traffic. There were a few soldiers on the street, but far fewer than the night before.

Kevin finished in the bathroom and walked out. Astonished, he cried out, "What is going on? I thought you were going to tell me everything?"

"What? I did. I don't have any more secrets."

"Vampires can tolerate indirect sun, but you are standing in the light," observed the President.

They gasped. This seemed impossible, yet here it was.

"Hey, I've been a vampire for all of three days. I have no idea what I can and cannot do. Normally vampires go through some kind of apprenticeship, but I am here instead. As you can see, I am not your average vampire. Sometimes I think you guys know more about being a vampire than I do." She slumped in a chair.

"Just be honest with me, okay? If you figure out something, tell me. No more lies." He signed *I am watching you.* She hadn't seen him do that in a long time.

In the hallway, the maid finished cleaning room #303 and was checking her cart. She was almost out of boxes of tissues. She always expected people to take the shampoos, but the tissue boxes? That was new. Then she paused. She thought she heard voices from #305. She went back to check her list. Just as she remembered, #305 was listed as empty.

She called down from the phone by the elevator. The front desk confirmed her list: #305 had not been booked last night.

Kevin went into the bathroom to change into the clothes that Kaylee had picked out. He'd have to talk to her about her taste—these were a bit more colorful than what he usually wore, and the pants were really tight. He hadn't worn pants this tight since…well, since he was courting his wife! While he was changing, Jason and Jack made the bed and straightened up the room so it looked as if no one had been in there.

"Wow, you gentlemen are hired!" the President chuckled. "I don't think the White House staff is even quite that meticulous."

"I am going pack my clothes in the shopping bag. Is there anything else before we leave? I am starving."

Kevin packed his bag, and they all jumped to the roof. Food had to be the priority.

Down in #305, the manager and the maid peered in to the room. *It looks neater than #303*, she thought.*I must have imagined the voices, or they carried from another room.* She walked in to the bathroom to look behind the curtain. Looking down, she realized the paper wrapper on the toilet was missing.

Ben was sitting in his office. The TV, normally hidden behind expensive cabinet doors, was showing a 24-hour news station. The reporter was interviewing eyewitnesses to the silver people.

Ben flipped off the TV. His phone rang.

"Yeah? Great, hold on for a second. I am downloading it right now." He looked at his laptop, which showed a map of the area. On it was a large pale blue circle. The President's phone had been traced to a cell tower not far from where Ben was sitting. Then a red dot appeared. He had them!

The group exited through the roof access and headed down the stairs of the hotel. Kaylee produced sunglasses for everyone, both for the sun and as a disguise. Kevin was at the rear of the group, then thought better of it.

"Jason, can you take my place here?"

"Sure, what's up?" Jason stood still while the group passed him. "Oh, I see," he smiled and suppressed a laugh. The pants Kaylee had gotten him were beyond tight. They were quite trendy and would have looked hot if Kevin hadn't felt ridiculous.

They stopped at a diner not far from the hotel. The placed looked like one that had many regulars and drew few tourists. Kaylee opened the door. "Order fast and let's get out of here. It feels too out in the open for me."

Kevin moved quickly and took a spot at the rear of the diner. He didn't want people to look at his ass in these pants.

Jack said to the President, who was getting nervous, "Stay cool. No one is going to expect you here."

"Sure, you are right." He took a seat.

They all sat down. Kevin picked up a menu that showed the usual suspects for a diner. "Kaylee, you need to order something or it will be suspicious. No one knows that a vampire can walk in sunlight."

The waitress, who looked like she was a fixture in the place, took their order. Kaylee just ordered coffee, saying she was on a diet.

The food smelled amazing and tasted just as good. "I wouldn't have expected homemade hash in a place like this. This is terrific." Jack complimented every bite and then turned red. "I am sorry. That was rude of me. Do you eat at all?"

"Don't worry about it, Jack. Please enjoy your food. I am enjoying watching you eat, really!"

Breakfast was interrupted when a regular got up and changed the channel on the TV to a news station.

"The Silver Vampire is considered very dangerous. If you sight either of the silver people, you are urged to contact local police or call this tip line: 800-222-2242. New updates will be made every hour. Thank you for staying with Channel 5."

The President felt an itch in his eyes and went to rub them. He started to remove his sunglasses. Kevin placed a hand on his arm. "Don't."

At the next table four young men started to get rowdy. They looked like they had been out all night and were still enjoying the party. One decided to start mess around and make a spitball. He shot it at his friend, but he missed, and it landed in the President's drink.

The President gave the young man a hard stare from behind his sunglasses. At first it looked like the young man was going to apologize, but then his friend sitting next to him blew a spitball at Kevin, who was sitting next to the President. It landed in his plate.

"That's disgusting."

The young men laughed, and a few more sailed across the restaurant, hitting Jason and the President. The young men laughed more. Kevin started to get up.

"Just sit, Kevin. I can take care of this," Kaylee said. She stood up and walked over to their table. She looked at them and politely said, "Guys, don't interrupt us again. Just go back to your own meal and leave us in peace." She turned to walk away.

One of the young men looked at her and asked, "Why do you have glasses on in here, are you blind?" He punctuated this with a spitball to her back. This amused his companions greatly, and they offered childish comments.

She turned and kept her cool. "Do you mind? Leave us alone, please?" A waitress came to young men's table to give them change.

As they left, they stopped at Kaylee's table. One drank out of her glass. She glared at him as he reached his fingers into her drink and flicked the water onto her glasses. The four men laughed, mimicking her movements.

"This is your final warning. If you disrespect my companions or come anywhere near me, I will break your hand. Now go!" Kaylee took off her glasses and wiped them with a napkin.

The young men laughed. Kevin leaned back and warned them, "I wouldn't do that if I were you. I know her well and can tell you it has *bad idea* written all over it."

"What are you, her bitch?" the punk said to Kevin. She reached out and grabbed the young man's hand. The snap of the bones could be heard by everyone at the table. Kaylee's companions were shocked at the speed of her response. The three other young men were stunned into silence, their joking momentarily ceased. Their buddy was kneeling next to the table, his hand still in Kaylee's.

"Don't scream, just leave," she growled. His friends gasped when it was clear that she had broken his hand. He began to wail. One of his friends supported him, and the injured man made his way out of the restaurant.

The commotion caught the attention of police, who were already out in force. Two officers came in through the front door. Kaylee warned her companions, "We must move fast." She stood up and began working her way toward the back of the restaurant. "Back to the kitchen, now move!" she whispered to the table. The restaurant was pretty crowded, so their movement didn't catch anyone's attention, but it took a bit to get though the crowd. A woman stepped back just as the President was passing behind her. She jostled him, and he stumbled. His glasses fell off and hit the floor. As he picked them up, the woman turned to apologize, and her eyes widened in surprise.

She shouted, "Look, it's the President. It's him!"

A waitress now recognized it was the President. She shouted, "The President is here! Call the police!" The crowd looked at him, and somebody tried to grab him.

Kevin grabbed the President and pulled him into the kitchen. Kaylee stood her ground. She pushed a man, and he toppled back onto a few other people in the crowd. They were trying to push forward to get the President. One man grabbed her arm, and Kaylee punched him with her free hand. Another tried to punch her, and she punched him in the stomach. A waiter put a mop through the door of the kitchen so they couldn't get in. Jack and Jason tried to ,protect the President to keep people away from him. Kevin tried to open the door but couldn't kick hard enough. "Help me open this door," Kevin said to Kaylee.

Kaylee kicked the door. The mop broke andthe door flew open. Kaylee was the last to go in.

"Come on, hurry!" Kevin called.

In the kitchen one cook tried to grab Kevin, but he threw up a quick block. Another picked up a heavy frying pan and tried to swing it to hit Kaylee. She blocked the pan, took it out of his hand, and punched him in the blink of an eye.

Kevin shouted, "Come on, this door!"

They ran out the backdoor. As they ran out into the alley, Kaylee shouted to Kevin, "We need to go up!"

Kaylee tried to move the green trash bin in front of the door but there just wasn't time. They ran down the alley and scooted into a doorway. The door was locked, but it gave them some cover. "Take my hand, everyone. Let's hit the roof." They all touched her, and she jumped them to the roof they had been on yesterday.

Police and soldiers were all over the restaurant in minutes. Someone in the crowd said, "The President was here!" They swarmed the entire place and came out to the alley, but all they found was a big green trash bin.

Ben took a drink from a crystal glass and turned to look at his laptop where he was tracking the President's movements through his cell phone. He was confused. The President had seemed to jump two blocks in just seconds. Could this machine be giving him a false reading? "Impossible," he said to himself. He called an officer he trusted and asked for information about the restaurant. When he heard that the President had been spotted there, but wasn't there currently, Ben was thoughtful. The new reading might just be right.

On the roof, Kaylee said, "Gentlemen, we cannot keep this up all day," Kaylee said. "Jumping with other people is tiring, and I am going to need to rest often if we do this a lot."

"Can we just jump to the drop off location in Virginia?" asked Kevin.

"Sorry, but I cannot jump where I have never been."

The President felt stuck. He has no idea how they would get to the base and get his girls. All of the sudden they heard a helicopter come close. They became alert and watched out for the helicopter.

Kaylee pointed to the President and ordered, "You stay. Keep out of sight."

Kaylee flew through the air, trying to stay out of the helicopter's line of sight. The helicopter hovered over the roof, and a lone police officer jumped down. The President came out of hiding, and a rope ladder was dropped out of the helicopter. He was confused and unsure who to trust. He stared to move toward the rope ladder.

Kevin came out of hiding as well. "What are you doing, sir? I don't know if we can trust these men. Don't go with anyone you cannot completely trust."

"I agree with Kevin. This is a mistake. Let's figure out who we can trust before going with them." Jason put a hand on the President's elbow.

Kaylee watched what was happening and was shocked. The President was going with the police? That didn't seem right after all they had been through. She hovered near the edge of a building. "Errgh," she said as she punched the building. A few bricks cracked and broke, which gave her an idea. She took a couple pieces of the building and threw one at the helicopter. The windshield cracked, and the pilot pulled back. The man on the roof got nervous and hopped on the rope ladder just in case. Kaylee flew to the other side of the helicopter and let another piece of debris fly. This also pinged the aircraft and the pilot moved off, swinging the officer below them.

Ben stared at the small red light on his laptop indicating the President was still there. His phone rang. "Yes?" he said as he opened the connection. He balled his hand into a fist. "What?" After a moment, he threw the glass at the door and shouted, "Damn it!" He turned on the television.

A reporter asked a man dressed in white apron, "Did you see the President today?"

"Yeah! Everybody saw the President eating here today. Then this woman wearing all leather beat up a bunch of guys, and now the President is gone."

Ben was pissed off about the TV news. He didn't notice that the red dot was on the move. His phone rang and he looked at the caller ID before answering. "Hello, David. Tell me some good news. I have an interview with the lovely reporter from Channel 5 in an hour. Then we need to head to the base."

While Ben was on the phone, the red light began to move from the roof. Ben, focused on David, didn't notice. When he looked a few moments later, the red dot was nowhere to be seen. Ben realized the tracking was no longer going to work. He banged his fist down on the machine, causing a few keys to pop off.

As Kaylee was flying back to the roof she noticed a small rooftop access door. She brought the men over to it. They kicked in the locked door and went down a few feet by ladder.

They walked into a hallway with apartments on either side. A door was open at one end, and a little face peered out at them. He waved them to him.

The boy had light brown eyes and skin. He was completely bald, not even eyebrows. His big eyes and bony arms suggested that his baldness was the result of cancer treatment. He beckoned them again, "Come on in. My place is safe, they can't keep up with you all day."

They all look at each other, startled.

"He's psychic," Kaylee explained. "It is common among kids with serious illnesses. Not sure if it causes the illness or opens them up to the spirit."

They boy led them through the open door to where he lived with his parents. After they entered the room, the President's phone began to ring.

"Hello?"

His wife asked, "Are you all right? Where are you? How are the girls? I've been in meetings all day."

"Yeah, umm…." He held his hand over the phone. "It's my wife."

The boy looked at the President. "You should get rid of your phone. It is how they are tracking you now. Give her the phone so she can throw it a great distance."

The President gasped in surprise. They all looked at the boy, who was uncanny in his knowledge.

"Sorry, honey, I have to go. I love you."

The President closed the phone and handed it to Kaylee. She opened a window and threw it out over the building next door. His cell phone hit a cop's windshield.

The boy went over to the President. "You are completely safe here right now." They looked around the apartment. It was clean, but the family didn't have much. Kaylee suspected that most of their income went toward his treatments.

Kaylee knelt before the boy so she was eye-level with him. "Who are you? How do you know my strength?" He was happy to see her—he knew she was special. He touched her glasses.

"I am George Cobb. I have great psychic powers and true visions. I can see your fangs even when you have them retracted. I expected you today, and that is why I was at the door when you came in."

"George, please don't say anything about me, all right?"

"I know you aren't ready yet. It's okay."

Jack looked around. "Where are your parents? Are they here?"

"I live with my aunt, and she's gone to get groceries. She should be back soon."

Jack suspected that she might not be too pleased to find five strange adults with George when she returned.

The President was also concerned. "I don't want to get you in any trouble here…"

George cut him off. "Look, if you leave now, they'll bust you in no time. I am taking this chance to save you because of her—she will save you all. I will explain this to my aunt." He looked at Kaylee again. "Can I see them? Would you take off your glasses?"

She looked around at everyone and then at George. She propped her glasses on her head. "Wow, you are special," he said. She smiled in relief and surprise.

Kaylee got right back to business. "Listen, how long should we stay?"

George looked at the clock. "You need to stay until 4:30 or 5:00 pm. That is what I am seeing."

Jason looked perplexed. "That is a rather specific time. It's not 'stay until the blue flower opens' or 'stay until the second bicycle passes,' but 4:30 or 5:00 pm?"

"Once your plan is in motion…" He stopped and looked at the door. "Put on your glasses."

Kevin was surprised. "We haven't even discussed our plan yet."

All of the sudden, they heard a key opening the door. Jack looked at George and asked, "Your aunt?"

George nodded, and his aunt opened the door. She put a grocery bag on the counter and finally noticed the strangers in her house. She gasped and stepped back.

"What are you doing here? George, are you all right?"

The President smiled and said, "We are sorry to startle you, ma'am. We mean you and George here no harm."

George looked at the President and whispered, "Sunglasses."

"Oh, you are right, son." The President removed his sunglasses, and it took her a second to recognize him.

"Aunt Irene, this is President Collins. Sir, this is my Aunt Irene."

"President Collins?"

"In the flesh."

"It is all over the news that you are being held by two silver people and everyone is looking for you. And here you are in my kitchen. Are you being held hostage?"

George looked exasperatedly at his aunt. "No, he isn't being held hostage by them, but they have to stay here for a while."

Jack tried to look sincere. "We won't harm either of you. Please let us stay."

Jason added, "According to your nephew, we need to stay a few hours. I am here to guard the President, not kidnap him."

Irene gripped her keys. She hated to make snap decisions. "George…um, do they know about your talent?"

"They know I am psychic."

"What do you see about this?" She waved her hands around, indicating the people in the room.

"I don't see any trouble. I let them come in because I always wanted to see someone who's special. Remember, I told you? That's her," he said, indicating Kaylee.

"Really?"

"Yes, she is the Silver Vampire I told you about."

Irene was surprised to see a vampire out in the day. She must have misunderstood her nephew. She leaned over to try and talk privately.

"Are you sure she is a vampire? She shouldn't be in the daylight."

"She is special. She can walk in the day."

Irene thought he might be making this more of an adventure and embellishing the truth a bit. She looked over at Kaylee, who was peeking out the window. "Um, my nephew here is convinced you are a day-walking vampire. Can you prove it?"

Kaylee winked at George and popped out her fangs. Irene gasped and fainted.

"Ohh…" said Kevin as he dashed to stop Irene from hitting the ground. He deftly picked up the slender woman and walked to the living room. He carefully deposited her on the threadbare couch and propped up her feet with a pillow.

George smiled, "Guess you are staying!"

Ben called David and told him that he'd lost track of the President. "I am on my way to the base to prepare the weapons. How are the girls doing?"

"They are fine, just fine and dandy."

"Good. I will see you shortly."

The President looked around at the pictures on the bookcase in the living room. One was a nice photo of a black woman and a white man. They bore a striking resemblance to George.

"Are these your parents, George?"

"Yeah. They were killed in a plane crash when I was seven and now I live with Aunt Irene."

Kevin joined the conversation. "I don't want to pry, but are you sick?"

"I have leukemia. Most of the time leukemia is curable, but I have one of the rare kinds that isn't. I will be in Heaven with my parents soon. This last round of chemo didn't help, but we are trying some other treatments."

Irene woke up and was quite embarrassed. "Oh, what time is it?" She looked at the clock on the wall and jumped up. "I have to get George some medication."

She returned a moment later with a pill and a glass of water. He swallowed the pill with the water and handed her the glass back.

"Okay, now that that is done, who are you people? Well, I know you, Mr. President. And the rest of you are…?"

The President spoke for everyone. "This is Kevin Douglas, who is with the CIA, and so is Jason Smith. And this character is Colonel Jack Hopkinton from the US Army. This amazing young woman is the Silver Vampire."

Irene had always known that George was special and that his visions were dead accurate. Too bad they couldn't cure cancer or keep his parents off that plane. He said they didn't always work on the people he was closest to.

"George," Kaylee said, "I need to leave for a bit. Is there a private room I can use?"

"You can use my room. It is the door on the left." He indicated a small alcove. Kaylee opened the door and was surrounded by typical little boy stuff: trains, building blocks of all sorts, action figures, cars, and lots of books. She looked around quickly so she could remember the place and jumped back to see Grace.

"George," Irene asked, "why is this Silver Vampire so important?"

"She has a special gift and will save the world. She got her power as a gift from an angel. I can't explain, but I can see her clearer than anyone else. An angel sent her to save world from a monster."

Kevin asked softly, "Angel? What monster? There are no monsters."

"You will learn of the monster soon. Without The Silver Vampire to fight it there will be no people or vampires. The world will end."

Jack looked at the boy. He was dead serious. He got a chill like his granny used to say came when someone walked on your grave.

His aunt pursed her lips, "I always want to believe you, but this seems…well, impossible."

"Yes, it's real and will happen soon. You'll understand someday."

"Look, I know she doesn't want me to tell you everything, but it is important that you to know about her."

Kevin probed, "What about the angel? Does she know this will happen?"

"Oh, yes. The angel told her not to tell anyone about herself, that it was top secret. So you can't tell who she is."

"I've known her most of her life, how much of a secret could she—"

"You kept your life a secret from her." Kevin went white. "Look, you need to stick with her so she can save the world. She will be the perfect CIA agent. You can help her do this and make travel easier. But you must do it before something bad happens. Something really bad."

Jack crossed his arms. He did not like the sound of George's visions. "I don't like this at all," he said to them.

The President looked at George with hope. "I am worried about my girls. Are they…I need to know if your vision shows…"

"The Silver Vampire will find and save your girls."

"Thank you. Just what I needed to hear." They recognized that they needed to keep Kaylee safe until everything was solved.

"I've had enough. I need rest now." George looked exhausted from talking with them. They walked to his bedroom.

Jason spoke with Jack while they settled George in bed. "He seems smart for his age."

"He has a special gift, but it's sad—his life is short."

As Irene tucked George into bed, she noticed that the Silver Vampire was not in the room. "Where'd she go?"

George said, "With her own people for short time. Wait, can you order pepperoni pizza for supper? Please?"

Money might be tight, but Irene always managed to find a few extra dollars her and there for a treat for George—he got so few. "Of course. You rest now, okay?" She kissed his forehead and they left the room.

They regrouped in the living room and tried to catch up on some news. It was all bad. Story after story told of a Silver Vampire, possibly two, kidnapping the President. Then they cut to a story about the President's girls. One reporter calculated how much the silver people had cost the taxpayers with traffic damage, car accidents, overtime, and more.

Sheepishly, Kevin said, "I hope we aren't in any pictures or anything. These pants are too much and my wife will think I've gone off into the deep end."

The TV was filled with reports of sightings of the silver people and what they might stand for. The First Lady was on screen, tears on her face. She pleaded with the public to give the police any information on the whereabouts of her husband and daughters.

The President was clearly affected by seeing his wife this way. He thought she was still in Paris not knowing anything about this, but she must have called him at the urging of the authorities to check on his location.

A reporter with short dark hair spoke with a woman pushing a baby in a pink stroller. "The Silver Vampire saved us as we were crossing the street. Somebody almost hit us, and I want to thank her for saving my baby and, well, both of us."

The reporter walked through a crowd with her microphone asking what people were thinking about the Silver Vampire.

"Vampires can't save humans. They drink from us; that's all they want."

"I saw her save that baby! She's a hero." A short man turned to the vampire-hater and said, "Not all vampires are bad."

"They are all blood suckers!"

The short man wound up and punched the vampire-hater in the mouth, which stared a fight in the middle of the afternoon on a crowded street. Vampire supporters and vampire haters alike punched and hit, starting what looked like a riot.

Jack said, "Wow, I've never see anything like this before. This could be bad."

The President chimed in, "Bad might be an understatement. Riots like this undermine the freedoms our country was founded on. Without the ability to express ourselves publicly without fear of physical violence or reprisal, no one has any civil rights."

The reporter approached a couple standing by their car after an accident. She pointed her microphone at them and asked them what they had witnessed. The couple was deaf used sign language. Their hands were highly animated—they were having an argument. The reporter turned to the camera, "I don't understand sign language, but they witnessed the Silver Vampire in action."

The woman signed to the reporter, "I am not telling you anything."

Her companion signed back, "Good, because you were texting while you were driving. The Silver Vampire didn't have anything to do with the accident."

The woman was angry with the man and hit him with her purse. The reporter was out of her element and looked unsure what to do next.

Kevin chuckled and Jason asked what was so funny. "Oh, nothing, really. I have a deaf niece so I understand sign language. She hit him because he accused her of texting while driving—it was funny. Never mind."

The reporter continued her search for witnesses and information. Next she found a little girl and her mother. "Did you see the Silver Vampire, young lady?"

"I saw her. The Silver Vampire was flying."

The mom said, "The Silver Vampire is trouble. She's no good."

"I don't care, I like her."

Irene sighed, "George is telling the truth, and that little girl loves her like George does."

The Vice President was on the TV speaking to reporters. "The Silver Vampire took the President hostage. We should, as a nation, hope and pray that the President is still alive. We are continuing to search, and no effort is being spared to find the President. We have additional bad news. The President's daughters have also been kidnapped by the Silver Vampire."

The President stood up and shook his fist at the TV. "I'll fire you when I see you again, you sick bastard!"

Ben spoke again on the TV, and it was nearly identical to his speech from last night.

Kevin panicked for a moment. "Oh jeez, I hope this isn't going to blow my cover with my family."

The newscast continued with a reporter showing drawings of Jason, Jack, and Kevin They were wearing sunglasses, so it was not that easy to see what they looked like.

The reporter continued, "These people are with the President, but this Silver Vampire appears to be in league with another person wearing silver, and they kidnapped the President."

Kevin signed, "Good thing they don't know our names."

Jason observed, "Damn it, they are using this against us. They are making us feel as though it is us against this Silver Vampire."

Jack hit the coffee table, "Oh, this is crap!"

Irene looked sternly at them, "Shhh, George is sleeping."

David was speaking on camera, "The Silver Vampire took his girls too. I worry about the future of America. What is the country coming to if we cannot keep our children safe?"

Kaylee appeared in Eric's office. Michael said to her, "We saw news about you. You are all over the place."

"They are calling you the Silver Vampire. Good thing they don't know your name." Grace gave her sister a hug.

"I need some help tonight," Kaylee said.

Eric looked sternly at her and crossed his arms. "I thought you could handle this? Why do you need us?"

"This is turning out to be more complicated than I thought. I need some help to rescue the President's daughters. They are being held hostage in Virginia"

Kuruk was unsure what to do, but he trusted Grace's visions. "Ask Grace, let's see what her visions say."

"Kaylee's right," Grace said. "If we help her she will be successful."

Eric frowned. "Helping humans is not our tradition. We keep our communities separate." Everyone looked at Eric, he wasn't sure about crossing this line. "I don't know…let me think."

"Are you really thinking about helping humans?" Joseph asked Kaylee.

"Yes, I am. I think this is the right thing to do. The President is trying to help vampires."

"I have lived longer than any of you, and I don't like humans helping vampires. It just isn't our nature to help each other."

Kaylee begged, "I understand that, but just this time, help a human for once?"

Grace spoke up to support her sister. "If you don't, more may die."

"She needs us, let's just get it over with." Michael threw his support behind the sisters.

Eric was thoughtful. He wanted to see Kevin Douglas again, and this may afford him the opportunity to do so without drawing attention. "All right, I'm in. Tell me, what's your plan?"

Kaylee smiled and began to outline her plan. "Remember how I made goggles? You can use them tonight. I will tell you when we are ready. Just wait for me outside the woods near where the Longshore Bar was."

George opened his eyes. He expected Kaylee back any second, and he didn't want to miss her. As predicted, she popped in and saw he was in bed.

"How do you feel?"

"Come sit here," he said. "I want to talk to you without your sunglasses."

Kaylee sat on his bed next him. She put her sunglasses up on her head. George was curious and looked into her eyes. "You still don't know all your powers yet. That's okay. You are a new vampire, and there is no one to show you everything you can do."

She suspected he knew more about how her witch powers might still be accessed. "There's more?"

"Yeah, there are two witch powers. You only need to sleep a little bit each day. Maybe not at all, depending on what you did that day."

"Really? Do I have to sleep now?"

"Yes, do you feel tired now?"

"I am tired."

"I know this sounds weird, but you are not like others."

"Yeah, I figured out that I am not like other vampires." She smiled at him.

"So what's the other power?"

George suddenly started to wheeze and look paler. "Sun…look, I need sleep."

"All right, go sleep." She touched his cheek. She didn't want to force him to tell her what he knew, so she just gave him some time to feel better. George went back to sleep. Kaylee was wondering about the sun and sleep. She looked around his room. Even with the shades drawn there was a bit of light coming in at the edges. She looked at his closet. She opened it up and saw that there was room on the floor. She curled up there and pulled the door closed. In seconds she was asleep like a human.

Eric and Grace were in his office. He was curious about Kaylee. "Did your sister have a boyfriend when she was human?"

"No, most of time she was single. She was always busy with her potions and work."

"She is too beautiful to not have any boyfriends."

Grace suspected she knew why he was asking her these questions and she smiled.

"Do you want her?"

He laughed, "No thanks, not with her silver blood."

The other deputies were checking their equipment and talking. Joseph said, "This is too much for me: monster, angel, silver blood, magic, wizard, and her sister Grace has visions. This is as weird as I have ever seen."

Kuruk added, "Yeah, perhaps she's just a good actress?"

Joseph added, "Does she see a real angel or just imagine one? I remember when I died, I didn't see anything until I got out of the dirty ground."

Kuruk said, "Me too. I don't know, ask Grace."

Joseph was thoughtful for a moment. "Maybe we can learn from them. We can watch them and see what they're up to."

Kuruk smiled. "I hope she doesn't decide to break the law and sneak into my house. She would make a great thief."

Michael decided to support her. "I don't think she would unless she had to…I don't think she is a bad person."

Kuruk smiled, "True, she helped us stop the silver people and she helped save Michael."

Joseph grinned, "Looks like we have a new witch friend, huh?" He left them to go look for Grace in Eric's office. "Grace, can you tell me…"

"No, enough questions. I need to be alone. If I have a vision, I will tell you." Grace took out her book, sat down with her drink of blood, and began to read. Eric and Joseph took the hint and left.

They went back into the main room and met the other deputies. Eric said, "I am not sure how to lead in this situation. I've never dealt with a vampire witch or a vampire with visions before. Do you think we will be in trouble if we help?" The deputies were surprised to hear Eric asking for their opinion.

Michael, who liked the girls a lot, said, "I want to support them, but at the same time interfering with humans is not our way. We can ask Grace. Perhaps her vision could provide some details and tell us if we'll get caught by other vampires."

"You decide, Eric," Joseph said. "If you are in, then I am in."

"Okay, I am in. We pay him a visit tonight."

Michael asked, "Who?"

"That human, Kevin Douglas."

Joseph looked serious and said, "He murders vampires."

"We must be careful about our plans around Grace. She said she could read some of us better than others." Eric looked at Kuruk, who blushed. "So I will share the plans with Joseph now, and the rest of you only at the last moment so she doesn't get wind of what is going to happen."

The human adults were sitting in the living room as the afternoon light stretched across the floor. They all wanted to know more about George and his short but extraordinary life.

"I graduated from Georgetown University and got a job with the government," Irene explained. "I had a boyfriend until I found out that George's parents died in a plane crash. I was his only relative, so I got custody. This was when he was seven. A year later he got cancer. It was all too much for my boyfriend and we parted. I tried to take medical leave from work, but they ended up laying me off. So now I focus on him because he is special…I don't know, but I feel a bond with him. We don't have much, but I still love him like my son."

"You have good heart," Kevin said.

"I can help you find a position in the government—I have some pull," the President winked at her.

"That's nice of you, but not right now. I have to take care of him first."

Grace came out of the office. "Come on, rest everyone. We are going to need our energy tonight." A few of the deputies finished up their blood and put the glasses in the small sink on one wall.

Grace was curious when she saw Eric with H-Blood. "You don't like A-Blood? I've never seen you drink it."

"A-Blood has bad taste to me. It made me sick once and I don't ever want to do that again."

"What about fresh blood from a cow? It is really good."

Eric made a face. "No, I prefer fresh human blood. Cow blood or any animal blood is not for me."

"Whatever."

George woke up from his nap when he smelled the pizza. George headed into the bathroom and then into the kitchen, where he found everyone sitting around the small table.

"There you are." Irene said, putting a piece of pizza in front of him. "How do you feel now?"

"I'm not feeling good, but that smells yummy."

Kevin was curious. "What can you tell me about Kaylee's sister, Grace? Is she human or vampire?"

Between mouthfuls, George responded, "You will see Grace tonight. Silver will wake up soon."

Kevin was surprised that he was going to see Grace tonight. He didn't think George knew their plan, and even he wasn't entirely sure of what might happen.

Irene looked at the mostly uneaten pizza on George's plate. "Please eat a few more bites."

"I've had enough. I still don't feel good."

"All right, I will save this for you."

Silver woke up and came in the kitchen. Irene was a little unsure of how to be hospitable to vampires. She decided to just be gracious. "Do you need to drink anything? I mean, blood? I can get some at the corner bodega, if you like."

Silver smiled, "No, thanks. It is kind of you to offer, but we have to leave soon."

George looked at her. "Can you do me a favor? Can you fly me to the roof before you go?"

"I'd be honored." Kaylee put her goggles on top of her head and pulled her sunglasses out of her pocket. "Is it dangerous if they find us flying together?"

"No, not this time. Start slower than you did yesterday and float if you can. Show me your fangs and your eyes clearly." She popped out her fangs.

"All right…let's fly."

Irene watched from the window. "Oh, it is just like they showed on TV."

Kevin and Irene went out to the roof to get a better view. George looked happier than he had in a long time. He whooped and hollered softly. Kaylee grinned.

"He was so sure she was different, and he was right. She's a special girl," said Kevin.

"George is special too, in his way," Irene replied. "He is extremely intelligent, and his visions are uncanny. Oh, it is wonderful to see him so happy!"

As the floated, George said, "I will guide you around when I am dead."

"Are you scared of dying?"

"Yes and no. The pain will go away, which is good. I can't keep this up much longer." Kaylee hugged him for a minute. "Kevin Douglas will be the one human you will be allowed to see, and you must see him."

Kaylee was curious. "What happens if I don't?"

George smiled, "Nonsense, I can see that you keep track of Kevin. Don't change your path."

"You heard from my angel?"

George chuckled. "No, nobody can hear her but you. It's time for you to leave now."

Kaylee hugged him, and they floated down to land near the others.

Irene said, "Thank you both for everything." She looked at Kevin and the others as they came out of the roof door.

"Let's go! Ready to jump?" Kaylee walked backward to have a room for the jump.

The President shook Irene's hand, saying, "Don't forget to find me when you are ready to go back to work."

Kevin gave George a high five. "Best of luck."

Jack smiled. "Take care and thank you."

Kaylee was watching them say their goodbyes from a distance. They came to where she was standing.

"See ya in the afterlife." George waved his hand at Kaylee. She smiled at him and put her goggles back on. Once again they all touched her, and she jumped them to a different roof above the city.

Ben, Doug, and David were talking in an empty office on the Army base. They were overseeing the preparations for that night.

Doug asked Ben, "Did you find out if that silver man was one of yours?"

"I have nearly a hundred agents on that team. I don't keep such close tabs on all of them. I will call tomorrow to see if anyone is missing."

David looked at the other two. "Forget this, we must focus on tonight for now. We can find out later."

"Do you think he will come?"

"I am sure he will come, he can't hide forever, " Ben reasoned.

"If we screw up, we have to follow Plan C." David was grim as he worked out plans to keep protecting them from trouble.

They climbed down from the roof and looked around. They only had about 90 minutes to get there, and it was too far on foot. They heard a train whistle.

"Can we take the train?" asked Kaylee.

"That train does go the base, but it is for freight only. When I was first in the Army it took passengers too. There really isn't a way to even hop on a car anymore."

They spotted a taxi at a red light a few blocks away. "You stay, wait." She indicated all of them. "And really wait this time," she winked at the President. Kaylee headed down the street and over to the taxi.

Kaylee went up to the cab and looked at the backseat. She flew back and shooed everyone around the corner out of sight. "Okay, you guys sit." They all sat on the ground. "Uh, no, sit like you are sitting on a bench together." They did, and she jumped them to the backseat.

Kevin said, "Ouch!" He had ended up with his rear up against the barrier between the front and back seats.

Taxi driver felt the weight of somebody hop in while he was driving, stared in the rearview mirror, and yelled in surprise, "Whoa, wait a minute! How did you get in? That's impossible! Get your germy ass off my plastic divider right now!"

"Don't look at my ass in the mirror! You pervert!" The President started laughing. "Hey, this is not funny! Come on, you are the President. Have some dignity."

"I can't help it, it's funny."

"What? The President!" said the taxi driver, trying to peer around Kevin.

After much twisting and turning, Kaylee solved some of the problem by squirming through the window of the barrier and sitting in the front seat.

"Hey my rule is that nobody sits in front," said the driver. "I have to pull over and you have to get out."

Kaylee looked serious and moved close to him, saying, "Don't pull over or…." Her fangs popped out as she smiled.

"Uh, okay. Where do you want to go?" he asked, trying to casually hit the call button on his radio to get the police. She noticed, and without taking her eyes off him or moving a hair, she crushed his cell phone and pulled off the fare meter.

"Go around the train tracks and follow that train."

The driver did what he was told, and the passengers in the back seat were knocked around as he took the corners fast. The President looked sheepish and said, "I have to go use the restroom."

Kaylee looked at the driver. "Don't stop. Go!" She turned to the backseat and said, "Sorry, sir, but we can't stop."

"I know, but Jason needs to get off my bladder."

The driver tried to go through a red light in hopes of getting caught, but Kaylee was on to him. "Keep up with the train, but try to use less populated roads, okay?" They passed an old couple on the street.

"Is he mooning us?" the man said to his wife.

"I haven't seen anyone do that in years. Not since we were first dating and you and your friends had too much to drink after the game," she laughed at the memory.

The driver said, "All right, I know where you are going now, and I can get you there."

"Great, keep driving." Kaylee looked at the men in the backseat. "You stay here and wait. I gotta go."

Jason said to Kevin, "You move. I need to sit on the floor."

Kevin said, "All right," but his butt still ended up on the window.

Some officers sat in a cruiser as the taxi drove by them. "Did you see what I think I just saw?" one asked the other.

"Someone with their butt on the window of a taxi?"

"Yep. That means no seatbelt, and I bet there will be whole pile of other violations. Let's go!"

The driver looked in his mirror. "Shit! Cops!"

Kaylee flew back from visiting the train. She knew it would be tricky to jump to a moving target, especially with passengers. She reached through the window, and everyone touched her hand. She noticed the cops chasing the taxi and jumped.

George sat in the living room watching his favorite movie next to Aunt Irene. "You know, I have tried to fight to survive for so long. I was waiting for the Silver Vampire. Now that she's come and gone, I am ready to die tonight."

"What? No, no, don't even say that!"

"I've had enough. I know you love me like a son, but my parents are waiting for me. And you need to get back to your own life. Thank you for giving me my favorite supper for my last meal."

Irene hugged him to her, tears flowing from her eyes.

The vampires and Grace stood in the woods near the Longshore Bar, weapons ready. Kuruk, true to his nature, carried a bow and arrows, while the others had brought guns. Grace stood with them, her hands empty. She propped her goggles on her head. The others wore them over their eyes.

"Grace, put your goggles on and check for any activity," Eric scolded her.

"They already destroyed the bar, why would they be here now?"

"Just check. Humor me."

"Okay." She put on her goggles and looked around. "Nothing. Happy?"

"Giddy," said Eric, crossing his arms.

Michael looked wistfully at the remains. "Oh, I miss that bar."

"Insurance could cover the damage," suggested Joseph.

Kuruk decided to go the practical route and said, "We will just have to go to the bar in the next town for a while."

Grace interrupted, "Where shall I set up her jump site? It will be easy for her to jump here without anyone seeing her."

"Near those big rocks should do it." Eric indicated some large boulders at the edge of the woods. Grace pulled out a few ingredients and set to work making a ward for her sister to jump to.

After riding in the train car for about half an hour, Jack stood up. "We are close. Let's get ready to go."

Kaylee pulled out her long silver staff. She spoke some magic words and said to everyone, "Touch this stick." They touched it, and Kaylee floated straight up like a plane with four people hanging onto the wings. She brought them down just on the other side of a closed train station.

Jack looked around. "Right. We need to travel that way." He pointed into some woods. "It's about two miles."

"Two miles? Will we make it on time?" the President asked, clearly worried.

"We don't have another option, sir. We don't want to meet any traffic."

"We only have one hour and 15 minutes to get my girls."

Jason started walking and said, "We'd best be going, and fast."

Kevin looked at everyone's shoes and said, "Do you think we can get there on time? None of us are dressed for walking it the woods."

Kaylee growled, "Shut up. You talk too much." She glanced at the President. "We need to stay in the woods to keep out of sight. Jack, tell me where they are holding the girls."

Jack pointed and mentioned a few buildings that were good hideouts, but that didn't really help Kaylee. Once everyone was walking, Kaylee sped ahead to find a good place to jump. She went back and jumped them ahead. Now Jack could point out a tall building. She jumped to the roof to get a look and returned a few seconds later.

The President looked anxious. "Did you see them? Are they okay?"

"Yeah, let's go."

She jumped them to the roof, and they looked around.

"My kids must be here, but which building are they in?"

Kevin said, "Ben, David, and Doug should be there too. And Ben prefers to be driven everywhere, so we can look for a limo."

"I will look for your girls, but I have to go alone."

Kaylee used her goggles in a couple of different modes so she could see if any vampires or humans were nearby. There were no other vampires, but there were plenty of humans everywhere. She needed to get a better view.

"Oh," she said aloud. She used the goggles to get a closer look.

"What?" whispered Kevin.

"Shh, be quiet." She looked intently at one spot. "Whoa," she whispered.

"What? Do you see them?"

"Shh, do you mind if I handle this?" She noticed a camera on the roof and over some doors. There was also a skylight on the building and a few trucks parked outside it.

"Tell me what you saw!" Kevin could wait no more.

"Jack, see that building? What is in there?" She indicated a tall building not far away.

"That building was used as an Army training zone and storage for equipment like guns. Sometimes the police used it for training as well."

Kaylee was thoughtful for a moment. "This is getting complicated. I need to bring in some help. Three or four vampires could help this situation."

Kevin went pale. The President said, "Vampires? Are you sure?"

"I thought you could handle this?" Kevin said nervously.

"Sir, you were set to give vampires civil rights. Hopefully that was not just political posturing and you believe in equal rights. Now, I need some special help."

"It is not just posturing. I do believe in equal rights. It's just that you are talking about my daughters in there and I don't want to see them hurt."

"I understand. You stay here, I will be right back." She started to turn. "Really, just stay." The President smiled.

Joseph looked at Grace in the darkness. "Have we waited long enough?"

"She's coming now." Grace hoped he thought it was her visions that let her know it was Kaylee, but really Grace knew her sound. Just before she arrived by jump, Grace could hear a slight noise.

Kuruk looked around. "Where?"

Eric asked, "Do you see her, or are you having a vision?"

"Remember, I told you I can't see her in my visions, but I can see her." Grace pointed to the rocks and Kaylee appeared.

Kaylee gathered the vampires in the jump circle. She was moving a lot of people this way, and the circle made it easier. She looked at Kuruk, "If you don't mind, when we get there, I need you to watch four humans. Just stay with them until I get the girls safely out. Then I'll be right back with you guys."

Kuruk was surprised, "Babysit humans? What's my salary?" He winked at her. It was dark, but she could still see it.

Eric interrupted, "Kaylee, look…"

Grace stopped him. "Hey, don't say her name in front of humans. Remember to call her the Silver Vampire."

Eric shouted at Grace, "I am leader of this community, show some respect!"

"So what? Do you want them find her, huh?"

Kaylee looked at them both. "Enough, no arguing. We need to work as a team on this."

Eric sighed. "Teamwork?"

Kaylee looked at Eric. "Please come with us. Grace stays here."

Michael was surprised. "What?"

"Grace stays because I will bring the young girls to her for safety."

Joseph crossed his arms. "Oh, this gets better all the time. I hate children."

Michael reminded Kaylee, "We aren't allowed near human children. Do you really think Grace is safe here alone?"

Grace spoke up for herself, "Yeah I am definitely safe here. The silver people already burned it down. Why would they come back?"

"Hold on for a second, Grace. Can you tell me where the girls are?"

She closed her eyes and everyone held their breath. "Ah, I don't know, but I can see them in a boiler room. They must be in a basement of some kind."

Eric began pacing, "All right. Let's try not to break any more vampire traditions, okay? Let this end by tonight, no delay." Kaylee nodded.

Jack started to scratch his leg. Then Kevin started scratching his arm. The President looked at both of them and started to chuckle. "Poison ivy?" They both groaned. The President laughed, "This has been the best adventure I've had since college. If it weren't for my girls being kidnapped..."

Jack looked up at Kevin. "Yeah it has been a good adventure. Except for your ass. First the tight pants, then the taxi."

They were all laughing. "Oh great, a reunion over my ass!"

Suddenly a small group of vampires appeared with Kaylee who promptly disappeared again. Kevin turned around and looked panicked. "Look behind us."

Kuruk growled and Michael hissed. Kevin asked them, "Vampires?"

"Ya think?" Michael said, baring his fangs with a menacing grin.

Eric turned to Kevin and walked up to his face. "Did you murder vampires?"

Kevin gasped. He was part of the team that had, but he had never personally carried out the killing. "No, I am not...like that. I was ordered to kill, and that is not an excuse. But, wait a minute, let me explain...."

Eric growled, "Don't bullshit me! How would you feel if I started killing humans *you* cared about?"

Jack looked around and asked, "Where's Silver?"

Eric looked at the humans. "What if I said that Kay— Silver sent us to kill you?" They paled and looked scared but didn't back down.

Kevin stepped forward, "She would never to that. It's impossible."

Jason looked worried and asked, "Did she trick us?"

Kevin crossed his arms over his chest and said to Eric, "No, I know her well, she wouldn't trick us. She really means to help."

The President took charge of the humans. "Please help us rescue my daughters. I will give you anything in my power." His sincerity and humility actually gave Eric pause. Clearly the man was scared, but he loved his children a great deal.

Eric said, "My request? How about 30 of the best looking, sexiest men and women age 18 through 25 years old, alive?"

The President gasped, "What?"

"You asked me for a request."

"I can't give you people. If they volunteered, yes, but I cannot give you people."

Kuruk growled, "Eric, let me scalp them. Relive my old ways and punish them like the white men who stole my people's land."

They gasped. The President stood his ground, "But I am black."

Eric cut the air with his hand, "Enough. Vampires deserve rights in America. We deserve to be equal and not just in name, but in action."

Joseph said to Eric, "Does this mean we can't feed on them? We could eat for a month on these four."

Kaylee landed on the roof and kept silent. A light shone from a basement window. That had to be where the girls were. She floated along the hallways to avoid making any sounds. Looking out for cameras, she sped along so fast that even if she passed a camera, she'd be no more that a blur. She paused before the beginning of the hallway with the boiler room and peered down it.

No one was in the hall, so she floated up to the door. There was a small grimy window and she peered inside. She couldn't see anything at first. Then she noticed a small foot with a sneaker with glittery shoelaces. It had to be the girls.

Then she saw two guards. They were in the outer room, playing cards. Kaylee jumped so she was in front of the girls. She put her hands out to cover their mouths.

"Shh, I am here to get you out," she whispered.

The girls could see she was a vampire, but if she was going to save them, they were going with her.

"I am going to jump with you to a safe place. Ready?"

The girls nodded and she took her hands from their mouths. In a heartbeat, the three of them were with Grace.

"By the goddess, are you all right?" Grace asked the girls.

"This is my sister Grace," Kaylee explained. "She is going to keep you safe for a while, and I will be back. Don't worry."

The younger girl nodded and her big sister took her hand. "Are you a vampire too?" she asked Grace.

"How did you know she is a vampire?"

"Uh, I just looked at her."

Grace shrugged. "Oh. Well, yes, I am a vampire too, but I won't hurt you."

"Where are we anyway?" asked the older girl.

"You are in Millbury, North Carolina. Are you hungry?"

The girls shrugged, still too shaken up to be sure of much of anything.

"Okay girls, I will be back soon." Kaylee jumped back to the woods near the army base.

Eric stepped forward and looked at the four humans. He could mark them now and have control over the President of the United States. The temptation was immense. He focused on Kevin and reached out to grab his throat with his hand.

Kaylee popped back in and pulled out her staff. She put it to Eric's throat. "Don't! Take it easy."

Michael came up behind her and demanded, "Let him go."

Kaylee said, "All right, let's talk. Don't hurt him, please?"

Eric turned with amazing speed and shouted at Kaylee, "Kneel!" Kaylee had no option but to follow his order, so she knelt on the ground and stared at Eric. "Don't use this sliver to touch me ever again! This human owes us for the loss of vampires' lives! He deserves to die!" Eric slapped her face. Kaylee felt stuck between the vampires and humans. She knew that she couldn't do anything because he was her maker and boss. Everyone gasped, not sure if this was part of the plan or not.

Kevin stepped forward and said, "Wait, wait, I was one of them but I didn't kill vampires, I swear to God. I am the assistant director of the Silver Agency. I coordinated attacks, but I never personally killed anyone. I have changed. I realize that was wrong and I am on your side now. The Silver Vampire has shown me the way."

Eric growled at Kevin, "Was it your idea to hunt vampires down?"

Jason spoke up. "It wasn't his idea, it was Ben Sullivan's idea. He is the agency director and he is behind the kidnapping of the President's daughters and the attempt on his life. He doesn't want vampires to have rights. He wants them to be treated like animals and hunted down. If Ben found out Kevin was on our side, he'd kill him too."

"Humans troubles," grumbled Michael.

"I apologize," Kaylee interrupted, standing. "It won't happen again. But can we discuss this later and get back to our plan?"

"What does she need to apologize for?" Kevin said. "She has saved me and the President. She could save the world. I've known her for her whole life. She's my girl, and she will save the world."

Eric growled at Kevin. Kevin gasped. "She is no longer yours, human. She is mine now."

"Okay, okay, she is yours, but we need her help. We must end this."

Eric was quiet for a moment, then nodded, "All right, what's our next plan?"

The President could wait no longer. "Silver, where are my girls?"

"Your girls are safe. I got them out of the boiler room and no one saw us leave."

"Oh thank God. But where are they?"

"Millbury."

"Where?"

"Millbury in North Carolina," clarified Kevin.

"Who's with them?"

"My sister, Grace," Kaylee explained.

Kevin looked surprised and said, "Grace?"

"Yeah, Grace. Look I have to bring the President to his 7:00 pm meeting with the kidnappers."

"Okay, whatever you need to do." Eric gave in about as graciously as he ever did.

"Thank you. Jack, where is the entrance to the base?"

Jack pointed. "There is not just one gate to this base."

"Good. Let's find a good route for the President to walk in."

Kaylee sped toward the woods. Eric called out as she left, "You forgot to take him with you!"

"He can't walk three miles get there on time." Jack looked worried.

"Humans and their limited abilities, " snorted Joseph.

Eric chuckled when he heard Joseph's words. Kaylee found a good spot to jump and went back to get the President. "You need to come with me. Everyone else can stay." They jumped off together to a nearby road next to the woods. "Sorry about the vampires getting angry…"

"Look, I understood how they feel. I pray it's over today."

"All right. Walk down the hill to the road, then go right. Walk as fast as possible and you can go in the gate."

"I'd be lying if I said I wasn't scared about what they will do to me, but it eases my mind to know my girls are safe."

"I will watch over you. Now go."

The President quickly walked down to the road to the gate. Two men were there to greet him. He recognized Doug McDonald.

"Mr. President."

At that moment a car pulled up next to him. The driver rolled down the window and stuck out a gun. "Need a ride?"

The President looked around and got in the back. Doug slid in next to him. "Come on, cuffs on." The President turned so Doug could put cuffs on.

They drove to a non-descript military building with a helipad on top. They parked behind the building. A green military helicopter sat ready.

Kaylee jumped from the woods back to the deputies. "The President is in there now." She knelt before Eric. "Look, don't kill the humans. Just grab their weapons or smash them until they are useless. I am not sure how many people are in there. I just want to be sure we stay safe. First of all, I need destroy those lights or video cameras before you can go in."

"Yeah, avoid getting my naked ass on camera," Kevin said.

Jason and Jack laughed quietly, then Jack said, "I suppose we are supposed to stay here?"

Eric glared at Kaylee. "Are you asking for us to help you but not to kill anyone? How dare you ask me not to kill these silver people who killed vampires? Who burned down your house and my bar!"

"I know, this is much worse…"

"She is right," Kevin said. "Don't kill them, and we will still give you what you requested. I thought you were satisfied."

Kaylee was puzzled. Eric leaned very close to Kevin and growled. Kevin stood his ground.

"What's your request?" Kaylee asked.

Eric didn't want her to know what his request was yet. "Have you lost your mind? Never talk back to the oldest vampire. If you do that again, I will kill you, got it?"

Kevin gasped from fear and the smell of Eric's bad breath.

"How can I trust this guy?" Kuruk said to the other deputies.

"Think they will give us an honest request?" wondered Joseph.

"Ah, I don't know," said Michael thoughtfully.

Kaylee tried to forget about what his request could be because she didn't want to lose any more time. This had to end soon. "Oh come on, stop arguing. It is a waste of time. We have to do something right now."

Eric came close to Kaylee's face and said, "Remember, I am the boss."

"Yeah."

"Yes, sir?"

"Yes, sir."

Eric turned around and faced everyone. "All right, we must keep our promise not to kill anyone unless we have no other choice. You go head, Silver."

Kaylee looked at the vampires. "Get your weapons and goggles ready. Just watch us over there. And when you think it is time, you should go."

"Wait, what's about us?" asked Jason.

"Just stay for awhile and watch. If you feel you are needed, then go. You can try to save him if we don't make it back before sunrise."

Jack and Kevin were concerned about not knowing the whole plan, but they agreed to sit tight until sunrise. They all looked out and saw one of the kidnappers holding the President's arm as they walked to the building. Doug was leading them. They noticed a group of men wearing silver clothing with silver weaponry and a big light.

The President stopped. "What are they doing here? What is this? Why do they wear silver? Is that to hunt vampires?"

The President was surprised that they had created an entire agency, the Silver Agency, without his authority or the authority of federal law. He was witnessing the extent of their subterfuge. Kevin was right, he had the proof right in front of him: silver-clad men with silver weapons. They could only be after one thing.

"Yes, I am afraid you are right," Doug said. "We created an agency to eradicate vampires from the human landscape. Too bad you won't live long enough to do anything about it."

"So you are going to kill me?" He raised an eyebrow. They had intended to kill him all along. That had to be their plan.

"Shut up and move!"

Doug opened the door and went into a room. "Here he comes," he said to Ben.

The President entered.

"About time," David said to the President. "Did you bring the paperwork?" he asked Doug.

"Yes, here it is," Doug said as he handed it over.

"How did you get here? Are you alone?" asked Ben. He had surveillance cameras all over and knew that the President was alone. He just wanted to rub his face in his victory.

"I took a bus, are you happy?" the President said with sarcasm. Ben laughed.

"Yeah." Ben took a photo out of a folder. It had been taken off a surveillance camera at some point during the day. It was of Kaylee. "Where is this bitch, the Silver Vampire?"

"I don't know where she is."

"Tell me who she is and where she is from."

"I have no idea what her name is. Silver Vampire?"

"Look, I know she was with you at some point today. She thwarted my plan. What did she do to you?"

"She treated me nicer than you are."

"Look at my wrist. *She* did this to me."

"That is *your* problem. Perhaps she just doesn't like you very much. You *do* kill vampires, after all. That might have something to do with it."

"My problem? You think it is *my* problem?" Ben turned to David and waved his gun in the President's direction. David slapped the President's face.

"Don't speak to him like that!"

"You sick bastard, where are my girls?"

"I can't wait to be President. I will make a better President and keep vampires out of America," David said to the President. "Here, you need to sign these papers and, when you do, you can have your daughters back."

"Wait, he told me that I wouldn't live, right?" The President pointed his chin at Doug.

"Well, you won't live for long, but it is important that your girls live to grow up," he mocked.

"David, why are you doing this now? In a few years I won't be President anymore, and then you can have your way. Why are you acting like a common thug?"

"You've become a vampire lover. I want nothing to do with you or a second-hand Presidency. Are you willing to sign these papers?"

The President felt frustrated and itchy from the poison ivy earlier. With his cuffs on he couldn't reach his legs to scratch them. "My legs are itchy, can you scratch them?"

Ben waved his gun in the air. "Seriously? The Silver Vampire has no respect for others. Just look at my wrist. Tell me where she is!"

"She isn't with me anymore! Oh, this itches."

Meanwhile, Kaylee sat on the roof and watched. She could see a few soldiers walking around. She took out some silver throwing stars. She took careful aim and threw a star at each of the four skylights, shattering the glass. She was so fast the soldiers couldn't keep up. She floated behind the building so she had less chance of getting caught. The soldiers, for the most part, were checking on other buildings where they would find a single skylight broken.

She looked around and began to take out the cameras. As she was coming upon one camera, the soldier watching the monitors saw her and then saw static as she took out the camera. He sounded the alarm. Speaking into a microphone, he let everyone know what he saw. "Vampire spotted near building six. Repeat, vampire spotted near building six."

Everyone at the base and those outside heard the alarm. Kaylee had been spotted.

She could see a group of the silver-clad agents pulling out their weapons, ready to fight. She looked for the window with the light shining through it.

At last she found the room. She could see the President in handcuffs with Doug, Ben, and David, and a few of their henchmen.

The President heard the alarm and he knew the time had come. Ben shouted at him, "So your Silver Vampire is here, huh?"

"She was here with us all the time," said the President calmly.

David looked at the President, "You lie. We would have known if she was here."

"You keep thinking that."

Eric pulled his sword up. "Charge!"

Michael, Kuruk, Joseph, and Eric ran quickly toward the building with the lights on. There were silver people around the building. The fight had begun.

"Come on, let's go, Kevin urged the others.

"But we have no weapons." Jack held his empty hands open.

"Never mind, come on." Jason began to jog to the base. When the others began to follow him, they picked up the pace and ran the mile or so to the building, hoping that they could help.

The guards playing cards dropped them when the alarm sounded. They grabbed their guns, which were propped against the wall, and went to stand closer to their charges. They opened the door to the room where the President's daughters had been kept and were greeted with silence and a rope lying on the floor.

"Go get the girls now!" David said to Doug. Doug took a soldier with him and they headed down the hall. Just as they got to the room where the girls had been kept, the two guards were coming out.

"Bring the girls," Doug ordered.

"Sir, they are missing."

"Missing?" Doug ran into the room and picked up the empty ropes. He threw them down and pulled out his cell phone to call Ben.

"The girls are gone."

"What do you mean, gone?"

"I mean just what I said, Ben. The girls aren't here, just some rope where we tied them up."

"Damn it." *Time for Plan B*, he thought.

Ben hung up his phone and looked at David and the President. "There's been a change in plan."

"What?"

"The girls are missing. We need to go to Plan C."

David was so pissed that he punched the President. "Where are the girls?"

Doug ran out of the building and found the lead silver agent. "Watch out for vampires, one of them slipped in and took our hostages. If you see any vampires, you have orders to kill them all!"

"Right, sir." The leader turned to his team and gave orders, dispersing the agents.

Looking through night vision goggles, an agent sitting in a tower near the entrance to the base spoke softly into his microphone. "Four vampires spotted coming down the hill toward the gate. They are moving fast and they have weapons drawn."

The agents moved in from many directions to try to surround the vampires. A few ducked into a tunnel that led around the base underground. They figured they might have the element of surprise from the tunnel.

Kaylee noticed them from the rooftop. "Shit," she said softly. She popped up to get a better look at the agents when one spotted her. Kaylee dropped, but it was too late. The agent fired a silver bullet in her direction. It hit the rooftop uncomfortably close to where she stood. She drew out a small knife from her boot. Just as a bullet sang through the air to her left, she threw the knife hitting her target, who dropped to the ground.

She spotted a tower with a sunlight weapon. She flew over to the tower and knocked the operator over. They struggled for a few seconds before her superior strength won out and she tossed him over the side. She disabled the weapon, but she knew there would be more. Looking around, she spotted a radio for making announcements to the base. She grabbed the microphone and held down the button. "Sunlight weapons may be in use! Look out!"

The deputies looked around, alert and watching out for sunlight. "Shit, those things are nasty," said Michael as they ran along.

"Everyone be careful, okay?" Eric turned to make sure everyone was alert and ready.

Just then a beam of sunlight came right over him. He dropped to the ground. His deputies were powerless to help him—if they came near they would be exposed to the sunlight too. His breathing became ragged and he tried not to cry out. Kaylee spotted Eric and went to save him. He was just starting to smoke when she grabbed him and flew off.

"Are you all right?"

"Yes, I am now. Just give me a moment," Eric's panted.

"Look, go get Michael." Eric pointed back to where Michael had tried to hide, but the sunlight weapon found him. She pulled him out of the light and behind a vehicle. Michael groaned, and Kaylee looked at his arm where the light had touched him. It looked like he'd been cut with a knife. Now that he was in the shade, he'd be fine in a few moments.

On the other side of the road, Kuruk and Joseph were pinned down. They could see some of the silver agents looking for them. "We need to find that light and knock it out." Joseph looked around. "Can you see where it is?"

Kuruk nodded. "Ready?"

They moved quickly, avoiding weapons of both silver and sunlight as they headed toward the man wielding the sunlight weapon. Once they were behind the weapon, they easily jumped on top of the man and knocked him out.

Meanwhile, Kaylee looked at Michael. He wasn't healing fast enough. She flew him to the tower so he'd be safe and have a good vantage point when he recovered. "Stay low until all the sunlight weapons are out."

She flew toward the nearest sunlight weapon. She didn't try to do this with stealth, just speed. She was shot at and one agent tried throwing a silver net over her. She landed in front of one weapon and grabbed some rocks from the ground. She threw two rocks, one right after the other, and took out the nearest weapon. The glass shattered and there were shouts from behind the weapon. The flying glass had the agents running. She did the same with the other weapon.

Michael kept low and watched all that was happening. He could see Kaylee taking out the sunlight weapons and Joseph and Kuruk engaging some agents. He couldn't see Eric.

Eric looked up from the shadows. He was feeling much better, but he wouldn't heal completely until he fed again. He could see Michael peering out of the tower. He walked out and caught his eye. Michael could see that he was okay.

Kaylee noticed that some of the weapon fire was coming from underground. How could that be? She looked around and found an entrance to a tunnel. She sped over to the entrance and growled at the person inside. He looked at her for a moment, then ran off. She looked at the weapon he had been holding. She saw a few buttons that she didn't recognize. She looked at the tunnel entrance. She pushed a button that looked it would take her down to the tunnel, and she was right.

She went down into the tunnel and looked around. She met one agent. He gave her a long, slow look from her boots to her glasses. He gave her a big smile, which she returned. She blew him a kiss and he turned tail.

"There's a vampire inside the tunnel!" he shouted as he ran down the silver hallway. He shouted the alert the whole way.

Kaylee ignored him. She noticed that everything, including the walls of the tunnel, were silver. She could see that in the distance there were silver agents running around, and she kept her staff out and ready. She decided to float through the tunnel. She fought a few people along the way. They offered little resistance, and she gathered some of their weapons as she went. She had to try to find where the tunnel led.

Michael felt better and watched the battle from above. He jumped down from the tower and set off to join Eric. Eric noticed and went to meet him part way. "They have large numbers and good weaponry for fighting vampires," reported Michael.

Eric looked around. "We need to separate them from their weapons. Any ideas?"

Michael stared at a number of 55-gallon barrels. One had a pump and a small sign that identified this area as the motor pool. Michael pointed to a sign above the barrels that said "No Smoking, Flammable" and smiled.

They started to move some of the barrels when a few agents showed up. Fists were flying and punches landed. They were able to defeat them easily.

Kuruk looked at Joseph and had an idea. "Let's use the truck as a shield and move it where we want to go."

"Great idea." They moved the truck, flipping it on its side. This provided them protection from the sunlight weapon. An agent ran over to them and Kuruk felled him with one punch. As more joined that agent, the two vampires tried to move more vehicles.

Eric noticed them pushing the truck and realized their plan. He whistled to Michael, and they went over to help. Eric pushed a van over then slid it toward them. Michael moved a truck in place and they were able to box the agents and a few soldiers inside the wall of vehicles. They looked at each other, pleased with their work.

Suddenly a silver arrow hit Kuruk's leg. He groaned and turned. The silver slowed his movements.

Kevin, Jack, and Jason ran, breathing heavily. The silver agents saw them but realized from their heavy breathing that they couldn't be vampires and didn't shoot.

Kevin decided to use his credentials to see if he could stop some of this madness. He walked up to one of the agents. "Stop firing!" he said to the agent and pulled out his ID. "I am Kevin Douglas, assistant director. You need to stand down."

"I am FBI agent Jason Smith. Stop shooting the vampires!" Jason pulled out his ID and held it up. The agents pointed their weapons at the ground. Jason ran toward at Kuruk and he pulled the silver arrow out. Kuruk gritted his teeth and a groan escaped. Then the wound healed on its own.

The lead agent on this mission ran up. "We have orders to take these vampires. What are you doing?" He looked at the agents, then at Kevin. "Sir, I didn't realize it was you." He was confused. "Has the mission changed?"

"Yes, I need you to tell your agents to stand down. We are not fighting the vampires on this one. They are not the bad guys this time. Just stand down and we can take care of the rest."

"I am going to take this tower, you go!" Jack said. He needed to get the soldiers on the field to stand down as well. He looked to the vampires. "Help get me up the tower!" he told the deputies. They heard him and went to help.

Joseph got hit in the arm by a silver arrow. Jason ran toward him and grabbed the arrow, pulling it out quickly. "This is becoming a habit," he grinned. Joseph groaned before it healed on its own.

"Help him get to the tower," Eric shouted to the deputies. Michael ran, grabbed Kevin behind his back, and put him over his shoulder. He climbed up the tower swiftly.

The knocked out agent in the tower started to wake up. Kevin picked up the radio microphone. "Do you mind if I use this?" Then he punched him, knocking him cold again. "That's gonna leave a mark." Michael smiled.

Kevin pressed the button and began to speak. His voice reverberated across the base. "Stop! Stop! Don't kill the vampires! Stand down, on my orders! I am CIA agent Kevin Douglas. Drop your silver weapons now!"

Jack climbed up the last steps to the tower. He looked over at the soldiers and agents. They looked unsure of what to do—they were keeping a close eye on the vampires. He took the microphone from Kevin and said, "This is Colonel Jack Hopkinton, army personnel, stand down and return to quarters. That is an order." He looked at Kevin and Michael and sat down on the floor, saying, "I am too old for this!" They smiled.

The agent started the helicopter with Doug in the copilot seat. They were waiting for Ben and David to join them.

Ben and David were hurrying along the hallway and heard the announcement over the speaker. They had the President with them. "Kevin?" said Ben.

"Was he the silver man with the Silver Vampire?"

"Yes he was," said the President. Some silver people came out of the tunnel from inside the building and were running for their lives. Ben, the President, and David got their attention by opening the door.

"There's a vampire in there," the first man said. They heard more people screaming and the sound of a staff hitting people and occasionally a wall. The President was really glad that Kaylee was on his side.

"Let get to the helicopter now!" Ben shouted to David. He pulled out his gun and a hand-held sunlight weapon that looked like a high-powered flashlight. David pulled his gun out and aimed at the President's head. He pulled back the hammer. Kaylee crashed through the door. She was a powerful sight to see in silver, her hair flying, and a silver staff in her hand. This set Ben and David into a bit of a panic. The President just smiled.

"Let him go," she said to them. Ben pulled out his sunlight weapon. Kaylee saw what he was doing. "Go ahead."

He fired the weapon, but nothing happened to her.

"What are you?" He asked.

"I am the Silver Vampire. What are you waiting for? Come on, kill me." She got her staff ready for a fight.

They heard a helicopter start up and looked to the roof. "Doug!" said David.

"Hurry, shoot them!" ordered Ben.

David pointed the gun at the President again and fired. Kaylee opened her hand to show them the bullet. She had reached out and grabbed it out of the air. She moved toward Ben and took his un-bandaged hand. "How about I give you a matching set?"

"Stop that helicopter!" Kevin ordered the agents and deputies.

Kaylee twisted and broke Ben's other hand. She turned to David and twisted the gun out of his hand, breaking his hand in the process.

"Thank you! Great timing," the President said. He was happy that Silver had gotten here just in time to save him. Ben fell down to the ground, writhing in pain. David reached for the gun with his other hand and pointed it at the two of them . Kaylee held out her hand to the President, who took it. As David pulled the trigger, they jumped back to the woods outside the army base. When they disappeared, David threw the gun at the space they had occupied.

Ben looked up and grimaced. "Where are they?"

"Gone."

Kaylee set the President free and he said, "I don't know how to thank you enough. You are amazing."

Jason shouted and pointed at the roof. "They'll get away. Stop them! Do something!" he said to the vampires. The silver-clad agents stared as Joseph and Kuruk ran over and jumped on the truck's roof. They ran over to the helicopter waiting for Ben and David.

Kuruk grabbed the door and broke it off, growling at the pilot. Joseph took the other door off and growled at Doug. The two humans started to panic.

"Engines off," Kuruk said to the pilot. He obeyed, turning off the engine. The rotors started to slow down.

"Get out," Joseph ordered them.

Ben and David emerged from the building cradling their hands. Ben noticed the agents standing around. "The Silver Vampire is in there! Kill her!"

"Do something! Hurry up!" David shouted.

Kevin's voice came over the loudspeaker, "David Lawrence and Ben Sullivan, you are under arrest for attempted murder and misappropriation of taxpayer funds. This agency was not authorized by law or the President!"

Jason made his way over to the helicopter and took the lead silver agent with him to properly arrest Ben and David.

Kevin spoke again: "Everyone must stay here until the President is safe!"

Michael noticed headlights when he jumped off the tower. He jumped on the roof and dropped down to meet up with Eric, who was speeding around the building at the same time. Eric opened the door and reached in to grab the man. He growled and showed his fangs. Michael started at the other side of the car and did the same. Eric closed the door and crushed it in so there would be no escape. Michael looked at Eric and gave a dry laugh.

Kevin's voice came over the speaker again. Where's Silver?" Everyone looked at each other. She was with the President and safe, but where? They looked around, but no one saw either one of them.

Kevin spoke again: "Check for the President in each building!"

From the woods, the President and Kaylee could hear Kevin on the loud speaker. "Sounds like they are looking for me. It is time to go," said the President.

"Yep, party's over!" Kaylee touched his hand and they flew up to the area near the gate. The silver agents were shocked. The President was with a vampire and not harmed. Kevin saw Kaylee and the President flying together.

Kevin's voice came over the speaker, "Yes! Great, let me get down. Hold on for a minute." A few people chuckled. Kevin hadn't realized the mic was still on. He made his way down the tower and over to the President and Kaylee.

Many of the silver agents were shocked that humans and vampires worked together to save the President. Just as Kevin reached the ground, the President asked Kaylee to fly him up to the microphone. She brought him up and he spoke in the microphone, saying, "Thank you, Silver Vampire. I have something important to announce. I will be making a formal speech tomorrow, but in the meantime, I want to ask the soldiers and agency personnel to put down your weapons and stand down from this mission completely. As Commander-in-Chief, I am telling you that your missions to hunt and kill vampires solely because of their race will end today. Today we will begin a new era of cooperation between all races. I thank you for your service. And God bless America."

A few cheers erupted from the crowd. While generally this change was welcomed, not everyone was so quick to be an enthusiastic supporter.

The local human police chief was called in to take charge of Ben, David, Doug, and their closest allies.

The President climbed down from the tower and walked over the vampires and humans who had helped him so much in the last 24 hours. "I would like to thank you all. I appreciate your help in rescuing my daughters and saving my life. Let's make this a happy ending to our grand adventure. Watch me on TV real soon."

The President put out his hand to Eric. Eric shook his hand and the agreement was set.

"Can you bring my girls, please?"

"Oh, of course." Kaylee jumped to Grace and the girls.

Grace and the girls saw her appear. Grace said, "Look, here she is!"

"I am here to bring you to your dad." Kaylee told the girls. She held out a hand to each of them, which they readily took. Grace decided to go too and grabbed on. They jumped together back to the base.

Both girls cheered, "Dad!" and ran to the President, hugging him.

Kevin said, "Grace?" He noticed that she looked the same age the last time he saw her.

"Yeah, it's me!" Kevin was confused.

"You haven't aged a bit…oh, you're a vampire."

"Yep, I am a vampire."

"Well that explains some things. How long you have been a vampire?"

"About 10 years."

"And you lived with Kaylee all this time?"

"You are her sister?" the President asked Grace.

"Yes, I am."

"Thank you so much for keeping my girls safe."

Eric walked up to the group. "Grace, can you tell me what you see ahead of us?"

"Do you mind if I touch you? Sometimes that helps the visions."

The President nodded and held out his hand.

"I see that the Longshore Bar gets rebuilt and the President signs the bill giving us civil rights. I see the Silver Vampire famous all over the world, and oh…" She looked at the President. "Don't get mad at your girls next week. It was…it will be an accident."

"What a talented family," Kevin said to Grace.

Grace chuckled, "I knew you'd be surprised.... Wait, some TV reporters are coming in soon. We gotta go."

One of the President's daughters reached out and took Kaylee's hand. "Wait. Can I see you again?"

"Well..."

Eric interrupted, "We aren't allowed to see human children, so let us leave now."

The older sister said, "He's mean."

Grace said to the girls, "Please don't tell anyone about Kaylee. Just keep it simple and call her the Silver Vampire. I bet you understand about privacy, right?" They nodded.

The President looked up, unsure. "Wait, I need to know, uh...how many, uh, *items* you need me to send over. I think Eric mentioned, uh...30."

Grace smiled, "Don't worry, we can communicate about the exact details when we don't have young ears around. But you gotta hurry. We only have a minute before the police and media arrive."

"She has Kevin's phone number," Eric said to the President.

Kaylee walked toward to Kevin. "I knew you'd save the world."

"You did too. Thank you." She kissed Kevin on the cheek.

Eric softly growled, "She is mine."

"Come on, the police and some reporters are coming. Let's go!" Grace got all the vampires moving.

George lay with his aunt on the couch. He looked up at her and said, "They are all safe now."

"Good."

"Oh, there are my parents." He pointed to what looked to Irene like empty air. "They are waiting for me. It's time."

He took one last breath, and she kissed him goodbye. She took his wrist to check his pulse, but she knew he was gone.

# CHAPTER 22

The TV captured the President, his daughters, Kevin, Jason, and Jack all smiling. They got into a long limousine with lots of security. Doug was arrested, and Ben and David were sent to the hospital under heavy guard.

A reporter in a yellow tie said to the cameras, "The President has said he will make a statement shortly about this chaotic scene and the startling arrest of the Vice President, a CIA agent, and a member of the treasury."

Kaylee, Grace, and the other vampires were in the woods. "See, I told you she could do it," said Grace.

"Yeah, it was nothing short of a miracle," said Michael.

"Whew…live fast," said Kuruk.

Michael said to Kaylee, "I am glad you are here with us today."

Eric nodded in agreement. "I am impressed with you. You have shown me proof that you are strong, and you worked to be part of our community. I am going to forgive you for making trouble. Thank you to both you and Grace."

"I am so bloodthirsty," said Joseph.

They all grinned and headed back to the office. Everyone but Kaylee drank blood. Eric looked over at Kaylee and Grace and said, "First of all I have to show you where Scott's place is so you can use it until you get a new house. Let's pick up your potions and bring them over there, and then we have an important meeting with Frank and Harvey to discuss the number of vampire deaths associated with all this and the Silver Agency. I will let Kevin know about any human deaths we can confirm. I also want to make sure that they will keep Kaylee's identity secret. I am not sure it's a good idea for people to know you are sisters. It could be used against you."

"What about her last name on her ID?"

"She can keep her last name, but just don't tell anyone you are related. It is possible that you just happen to share a last name. It is a pretty common name in this area."

"I feel like celebrating. Let's go to a bar." Michael was apparently completely recovered from his ordeal and injuries.

The other vampires began to chime in. Grace said to her sister, "Oh, your eyes. I wish you could come."

"Don't worry, I will work on my fake glasses and I will meet you there."

Everyone helped them gather their things and go to Scott's place. They looked around with interest. This was the first vampire house they'd been in besides their own. There was no toilet, of course. Other than that it seemed quite ordinary.

Kaylee picked a space to set up a potions table. "Where's the fire escape? Is there an escape to underground?"

The deputies looked a little uncomfortable. How did she know?

"I don't think we need it," said Grace.

"No, we do. It isn't safe without one. What if there were a fire during the daylight?"

"A fire is pretty rare," said Grace.

"Maybe, but we had one at our old house. You still need to protect yourself."

Grace started to suspect that Kaylee was on to something. She said to Eric, "Is there a fire escape here?"

"Yes, see the rug covers the fire escape."

"I have to get my motorcycle from the woods," Kaylee said. "I hope it is still there. When I find a way to cover my eyes, I will meet you at the bar. I am not sure how long it will take." Kaylee knelt on floor in front of Eric, "Please protect Grace. You know she is important to me."

"From what?" Grace asked. "There are no longer any silver agents out there as of today. What is there to protect me from?"

"We'll protect her," Eric said.

"Thank you."

Grace sighed, "Oh for the love of the goddess."

Grace and the deputies arrived at the vampire's bar in Bolton. Everyone watched a special report on TV. It showed a picture of the President, his daughters, Jack, Kevin with a mask covering his face, and Jason. The reporter said, "Here's an update about the President and his kids. They are safe now. The Silver Vampire saved them. The President returned home with his daughters. Jason will be joining the President's personal security team, and Jack Hopkinton will be taking over Fort Meyers and running the destruction of the silver weapons depot." The reporter also showed a picture of Ben, Doug, and David who were under arrest for unauthorized use of taxpayer funds, kidnapping, and blackmail. The reporter continued, "The President has scheduled a special briefing tomorrow for the signing of the civil rights bill giving vampires equal rights, and we will carry it live on Channel 5."

The vampires in the bar talked excitedly and cheered, "Silver Vampire, Silver Vampire!" Eric noticed that Harvey and Frank were at the bar, and he walked over to them.

Harvey said, "Nice job. Nice and quick."

"I wonder who made those silver agents? Look at Kevin. He wore silver clothes on TV. I wonder what made him change his mind?" Frank asked.

"He is from North Carolina. I wonder if he is from around here?"

"Who cares? At least we are at peace now. I for one am not going to bother to find him anyway." Eric nodded to the bartender to ask for a drink.

"Did you find any information about the Silver Vampire yet?" asked Harvey.

"No, nothing," said Eric.

"I wonder how it is possible that she can fly. I have never heard of a vampire who could fly." Harvey smiled at the thought. "I sure would like to meet her."

"Why don't we get a contract with a private detective to find her?" suggested Frank.

"Good idea. I think there is one in my town who works with vampires."

Eric decided to try and take a different tack in the conversation. "What would you do with her if you found her?"

"Nothing, I am just very curious about her. Do you think she's a sheriff or deputy?" Harvey wondered. "She sure is hot and now she's famous."

Eric and Frank laughed. Eric decided he wouldn't tell them about her, at least not yet. He wanted to keep her all to himself for a while.

Kaylee fixed up a pair of glasses and looked in the mirror. She had blue eyes similar to when she was human. The glasses projected the illusion of color on her eyes. "Bingo," she said to herself. Kaylee tried looking from all angles to see if any silver showed, and one little sliver did. She fixed the glasses and checked again. "Perfect."

She arrived at the bar on her motorcycle with blue eyes. The host stopped her as she walked in. "ID, please."

"I am Kaylee Dailage. Ask Sheriff Eric Longshore. He hasn't made an ID for me yet."

Harvey noticed the host talking with Kaylee longer than usual. He excused himself from Eric and Frank and walked over.

The host turned to him and said, "She doesn't have ID, but she told me to ask Sherriff Eric Longshore."

Harvey sighed, "You stay and wait." He took a few steps toward Eric and Frank, and then motioned Eric to come over. "Who is this woman?"

Eric stared at her blue eyes. "Kaylee Dailage, I am her marker since just four days ago and I haven't made a new ID for her yet."

"She looks so perfect, good job.... Wait, Dailage? Grace's sister?"

"No, they aren't related."

He went back to Kaylee and the host. "Welcome our immortal world, Kaylee. I hear you've only been a vampire a few days?" She nodded.

Frank, who had been watching the whole thing, turned to Eric and said, "She is hot and perfect, but glasses? Vampires don't need glasses."

"She likes to wear them, and they look good on her. So who cares?"

Grace noticed Kaylee come in and went to her. She stared at her blue eyes, saying, "This is unbelievable."

All the deputies looked at each other and decided to come close to her and see her blue eyes. They were all surprised.

"Damn, it actually worked," Eric said to himself. Grace and Kaylee giggled.

"Come on, Kaylee, let me introduce you to a few vampire friends." Grace led her into the crowd.

Harvey shook his head. "She thinks it looks cool, but those glasses are awful. I hope they don't catch on as a fashion trend."

Kaylee and Grace walked off together to talk to people. Grace introduced her to dozens of vampire friends, only about half of whom Kaylee could hope to remember. Eric and his deputies watched their every move. The hostess, Carolyn from Longshore Bar, was there and came up to Kaylee. "Didn't you come to Longshore Bar last week? Before the fire, I mean."

"Yeah I did."

Carolyn was confused. "I thought you were human. I could smell you were human. Wait, you sang at Longshore Bar."

"Yeah, I did." Kaylee was getting nervous.

"How old are you?"

"Four days."

Carolyn knew that Eric had talked with her and suspected it was he who had made her.

"Well, welcome our world."

Eric looked at his companions. "Excuse me." He left them and ordered another H-Blood. The two sheriffs looked at each other.

"Ever see Kaylee before?"

"Nope."

"Grace sure looks like she's known her a while."

When Eric returned to the table, Frank asked, "Where was she from as a human?"

"Waltham. Now she is moving to Millbury."

Harvey nodded at the two girls. "They know each other?"

"Looks like they do. Probably met somewhere before."

Grace brought Kaylee to met Harvey and Frank. "Sirs, this is Kaylee, a new vampire."

Harvey nodded to her, "Hello, baby. We've already met."

"Nice meeting you, child."

"Elders, as vampires age do they lose their memory? I have a name, perhaps you remember it?" Kaylee said.

Harvey growled at her because she was new and talked back. Grace grabbed Kaylee away from them. Grace laughed, "Don't say that. You shouldn't make fun of elder vampires."

Eric hid a smile from Harvey and Frank. "She is a bit childish."

"You have a lot of work to do with her," Harvey said tartly.

"Yeah, I know."

"That baby is going to be a real tough job. Good luck." Frank took a sip of blood.

"We still need to discuss the losses and how to increase our numbers again. How about your office?" he asked Frank. They agreed and headed off.

The next day, all the deputies sat in the living room at Scott's. There were a few boxes and shopping bags in the room. They put on the video that Grace and Kaylee's father had made of them when they were young.

Dave's voice said, "Kaylee flying at three years old in her bedroom." The video showed a cute little toddler floating around her room. A little while later, Dave was videotaping Grace in his workshop. Kaylee flew behind his back, being foolish and making Grace laugh.

Later on a different tape, Kaylee is being filmed by Grace. "Grace is taping me during the night with lights on outside. I am going to fly up and dive into the pool from the second story balcony." Kaylee did just as she said—she flew into the pool from the second story balcony. Grace and Kaylee took turns diving and flying. They cheered each other until the camera was accidently dropped and the tape ended.

The deputies stared at the video of the girls when they were young. Michael asked Grace, "So, your sister was born with these powers?"

"Yeah, don't you see that?"

Kaylee jumped into the living room from the car with an armload of bags. She noticed they were watching the old childhood videos. "Oh, I hate this. I wish you wouldn't show them. Can you come take this?" Kaylee put a box on floor and removed her glasses. She put them on a shelf and showed her silver eyes.

"May I?" asked Kuruk, reaching for her glasses.

"No. Don't mess with my stuff!" He pulled his hand away as she was about to smack it. "Who'd believe you had blue eyes anyway?" She winked at him. "I have to go back and get my stuff. Watch these guys real good, sis."

Kaylee jumped back to her car. Kuruk was still curious, so he put the glasses on. The deputies stared at Kuruk. "Do I have blue eyes now?" They shook their heads. "Silver eyes?"

"Sorry, they are the same color."

Joseph took a turn with the glass. They didn't work any better for him. "Live fast," he said to himself.

"Let me try them on," said Michael.

"Magic glasses," Kuruk said to Eric as he walked in.

"After him, I am next."

"You guys are just big kids!" Grace said. "I know you are curious about her witchcraft, but come on, give her some respect! She makes me babysit her stuff because of you! You make me crazy!"

The deputies noticed that she was really getting frustrated and angry. Eric looked at her and said, "Hold on for a second." He tried the glasses on and then said, "Interesting. Let's go the bar." He carefully handed them back to Grace.

Grace decided to stay to unpack stuff and to pack up some of Scott's stuff. Kaylee decided to bring the whole car and park it in a spot close to the apartment. She scoped out a spot that she thought would be protected and jumped it there.

Grace waved to the guys as they left. "Good riddance!" she said sweetly. They chuckled and left. Grace was already tired of the fact that vampires, lacking any physical defects, chose to make fun of young vampires. Humans make fun of appearance, but the older vampires always picked on new vampires or young vampires. Oh, how she hated that tradition.

As the deputies came out of her apartment they saw Kaylee with her car. Kuruk suspected that this car wasn't here before. "Did you steal this car?"

"No, it was our car." She made a face at him.

"Want to come with me to the bar?" Eric asked.

"No, I am busy. See ya later." Kaylee carried some boxes into the apartment.

At the vampire bar in Bolton, Harvey watched a special news update. Kevin, wearing a silver mask, was pictured. A reporter's voice said, "This special agent doesn't allow his face or name to be identified on TV, but he is responsible for helping to destroy the secret Silver Agency and sabotage the plot against the President. He is now working to close the agency and clean up the corruption."

Frank came in and joined Harvey. Jack was now on the screen saying, "I am going to help rebuild the Army and remove the silver weapons. They will be safely decommissioned and researched halted. Special thanks go to the Silver Vampire and her four vampire friends who saved us all and saved America."

Eric and his deputies joined Harvey and Frank. They were getting ready for the special report from the President. The TV showed a life-sized cardboard cutout of the Silver Vampire.

The President appeared on screen and said, "There are those in government who sought to undermine the very foundations of America. They were greedy for personal power and curtailed the freedoms of us all by creating a false agency within the government and funneling taxpayer dollars to fund their own hidden agendas.

"That is not what America is all about. As a nation, we should come together, vampire and human. We should make this country better by treating all races equal. We should stand united under one flag, as one nation. I am asking all Americans to help our nation move forward, to work together, to lend a hand when needed, to help our neighbors. This America should be about freedom, honesty, and equal rights for all races—human and vampire. To support this, today I signed into law a new amendment to the Constitution giving vampires equal rights in America.

"Thank you, and God bless America."

The vampires in the bar cheered and shouted. Glasses were raised in toast to the Silver Vampire and the President.

Harvey smiled, "That Silver Vampire is quite impressive."

"I wonder who the hell her four vampire friends were?" Frank asked.

"I don't give damn about them...maybe someone from Washington."

Harvey wished that he could find the four so could track down the Silver Vampire. "We will probably never find them or uncover the Silver Vampire's real identity."

At Scott's place, Kaylee and Grace were home alone. Kaylee slapped her forehead, "I forgot to remove my wards for jumping. I have to go back to DC."

"Oh, you have to go. What if another witch finds them?"

Kaylee looked hopeful. "Wait, what if Eric requested I go?"

"You may not like this, but Eric requested humans be brought to him alive."

"What? Oh, that's an old fashioned vampire tradition."

"Old fashioned?"

"The oldest vampire actually needs human or animal blood for survival, not like now. Now younger vampires can buy blood from a store or never kill anyone."

"Eww, lucky me, I am not from their centuries; I wouldn't have the guts."

"Yeah I know."

Kaylee jumped from at Scott's apartment to back Washington, DC. She went to George's roof and then to his bedroom. It was empty, and she knew why. Irene was sleeping so she didn't disturb her. She was sorry and she missed George. He'd never told her what her second secret power was.

Next she jumped to the White House. The President was there, sitting at his desk reading. He noticed that she had her fangs out, but he wasn't worried. He came out from behind his desk to greet her.

"Hi, Silver! What's with the blue eyes? Colored contacts?" Kaylee moved her glasses up and showed her silver eyes. "Magic trick?"

"My eyes will always be silver, but the blue is magic. I'm sorry, I don't mean to trespass here, but I have to clean my ward for jumping."

"I would like to give you a reward for your service to America."

"I don't need a reward. All I wanted was peace."

He could see that she had a good heart, but he was surprised that she didn't want any reward.

"All right. Would you mind if I woke up my girls? They are anxious to see you. You could take them for a short flight around the White House perhaps?"

Kaylee sighed, "You know I am not allowed to see human children!"

"Who's to know? It isn't likely they will call me a liar."

"All right." Still thinking about human children, she said, "I went to see George."

"He passed away just as our adventure came to an end," The President said. "His aunt is moving. I hired her and her new job starts in two weeks." He looked at Kaylee. "Retract your fangs." Kaylee smiled and retracted her fangs.

The President led her to the girls' bedroom. The first bodyguard looked startled and said, "Wait a minute! How did she get in?"

"I invited her in."

The second bodyguard walked over from his patrol. "Where did she come from? I didn't see anyone come in."

"I didn't see her either," Said the other guard, "but Mr. President invited her in."

The younger sister woke up and said, "Hi, Silver Vampire!"

The older sister yawned, "Wow, what happened to your beautiful silver eyes? The blue is pretty too."

"Yeah, thank you." She removed her glasses and put them in her pocket. "Your dad asked me to take you for a short flight. What do you think?"

The girls were very excited. She jumped the three of them to the roof and took the girls flying. Kaylee seemed to be enjoying it as well. They returned to the girls' room and Kaylee jumped. The President kissed the girls and told them to go to sleep. As he left their room, one of the bodyguards said, "Wait! Where is that woman? Is she still in there?"

"Oh, she already left. You must have just missed her."

"No, I didn't see her come out. Let me check."

Both bodyguards went in the girls' room while they pretended to be asleep. The guards looked around and checked under both beds. Nothing.

The door opened to the judge's chambers. A security agent came in and looked around. "The President would like to see you," he said to the judge.

"Sure, let me check when I can get over there."

"No, the President wants to talk with you now."

"Oh, well then. Send him in." The President walked in and offered his hand.

"I would like to check on the date of an upcoming trial."

The judge was very curious about why he wanted to know about a trial date and why he didn't just call. "Certainly, what can I help you with?"

"Here's an envelope for you. Inside is an itinerary for a trial next week. There will be no delays and it cannot be postponed for any reason. They aren't going to prison. You must sentence them to death. Given the serious nature of their crimes and the laws of our country, that will be your sentence."

"You cannot tell a judge how to rule, even if you are the President."

"When you read the details of their crimes, you will come that conclusion. I am not telling you to rule that way. I am saying that after you read these documents, you will come to the same conclusion.

Agent Kevin Douglas will take custody of them. He will wait outside of his plain white truck at the back of the court building."

"Where will he take them?"

"To see an old friend. A vampire is our lethal weapon."

The judge gasped. "Jesus H. Christ. What?"

"Their crimes were not only against humans, but against vampires. Since they occurred before the signing of the bill, the vampires have the right to punish them. It's only once. Let them learn that what they did to vampires is wrong. Now thank you for your time. Good day."

"What should I tell the court?"

"Lies."

Kevin was working hard to find the humans that Eric had requested. There was a mountain of paperwork to transfer control of male and female prisoners who were the worst of the worst. Most were on death row in one state or another. The rest faced a lifetime in jail. They were loaded onto a truck with Kevin driving.

In the courthouse, the judge banged his gavel, and that was that. All three men were sentenced to death. Many people were shocked not only by the decision, but by the speed of the decision.

One of the lawyers continued his protest, "This is wrong. I don't have enough proof! I need some more time! I want to make sure everything is cleared up. What about an appeal?"

"Take them out now!" the judge ordered his bailiff. He walked back to his office and closed the door. He put his head in his hands.

At the appointed time, Kevin stood outside in an unmarked white truck. Three prisoners with chains on their legs and handcuffs on their wrists were delivered to him. Kevin drove with another agent. He watched as the bailiff secured the prisoners in the truck. He got in and looked at the men in the mirror. The bailiff came around and let him know that all was secure. Kevin started the engines and left Washington, DC.

Kevin pulled out his cell phone and called Kaylee. "They are all set here. We'll be there in about four hours. Where do you want me to meet you?"

All the deputies and the two sisters were at Scott's apartment. It was close to dawn. Eric told Kaylee to tell Kevin to meet them in the woods near the Longshore Bar. Kaylee relayed the information to Kevin, who agreed and hung up.

Ben suspected he knew why there were men and women on the truck. They were all beautiful, young, and healthy. "Our Plan C failed."

David looked at him. "The Silver Vampire ruined our lives."

Doug swore, "Damn it."

True to his word, the President had found Irene a job. She worked hard and had even gone on a few dates. She missed George and had a picture of him on her desk. She looked at it as she picked up her purse and turned out the light. She was headed home for the day.

The President's two daughters wore silver clothes for Halloween costumes in TV spots about the First Family. The older girl said, "I love you, Silver Vampire!"

The two had everything Silver Vampire: Dolls, books, pens, tee-shirts, lunch boxes, fake fangs, and more. She had single-handedly boosted the economy. Everyone wanted to have a bit of her spirit and save America.

The President's wife even joined the new fashion inspired by the Silver Vampire. Most were elegant pieces of silver clothing and tasteful leather clothing. She decided she would also try some of the less elegant Silver Vampire-wear and surprise her husband. She wore sexy clothing and a pair of fake fangs and walked into the bedroom. The President was surprised that his wife was acting so flirtatious. She growled and kissed him passionately, biting his neck with the fangs.

A billboard next to the highway showed the Silver Vampire against the backdrop of an American flag. The writing across the top read: "We Want You!" Across the bottom it read: "Save Our World."

The young man whose hand Kaylee had broken walked into the diner again. He had just gotten the cast off. He paused when he noticed that there was a stranger wearing leathers similar to hers. The stranger stood to leave and stopped. "Move your car now. I need to get out."

The young man gasped, "Don't hurt me, please. I will move my car."

"Hurry up."

The stranger's friend shook his head and said, "What's he afraid of? Is he mental?"

The strange man and his friend walked outside. "That was very quick. I am impressed."

His friend laughed, "He'd make a good slave."

The young man looked down and mumbled, "Thank you." Then he rushed back to his apartment, closed the door, and locked it.

Kevin was asleep in the truck, his CIA partner driving. He pulled off and said, "Come on, wake up."

Kevin woke up. "Okay, let's get their masks on."

He opened the back door of the truck. The prisoners watched.

Ben shouted, "Kevin? You ruined my life!"

David said, "Was he the silver man?"

"Yeah he was," said Ben.

"You asshole."

Kevin smiled at him. "Go to hell."

Kevin and his partner proceeded to put a hood over the prisoners. They closed the rear door and locked it. His partner said good night and headed over to his own vehicle. He drove away as Kevin hopped into the cab of the truck. Kevin drove alone for six miles. He drove into woods and met the deputies, Grace, and Kaylee next to the Longshore Bar. The new foundation was in and building had started.

Kevin hopped down from the truck and hugged Kaylee and Grace. "Hi, I haven't see you for a while. I've been very busy running around with this project. Hey, wait a minute. You have blue eyes? Contact lenses? I thought you had silver eyes permanently."

Kaylee chuckled, "I do have silver eyes. These are my magic glasses. Do you like them?"Kaylee removed her glasses so he could see her silver eyes.

"Wow, great magic trick." Kevin pulled out a clipboard with lists of names. "All right, look here are the three lists you asked me for with their names and identification. Do you want to double check it before we take them out?" He handed the list to Eric.

"No, I trust you. Let's proceed."

Kevin opened the gate at the rear of the truck. Then he explained. "There are three groups, each with a separate identifier of who they are and where they are to go. I have them set up so there is a right, left, and middle row. I am not sure which one is yours though."

When Ben heard Kevin's voice, he shouted, "I will kill you, Kevin!"

Kevin whispered in Eric's ear, "That's Ben. He's on the left row, if you want him." Kevin indicated that row on the clipboard.

Eric looked at list. "That helps a lot. Thank you. I will be back when it's empty." Eric got out of the truck and waved to his deputies. "Michael, take these prisoners out from the left row." He gave the list of names to Michael.

"Sounds good, boss."

"Don't start without me. I will be back in about a half hour or so. Just wait for me." He watched at the deputies lead the line of hooded prisoners out of the truck. Michael and Kevin closed the truck. Eric hopped into the plain white truck that was previously used by the silver agency. This seemed like sweet justice.

Kevin shouted, "Clear." Eric drove away, and he made a delivery to Harvey and Frank in their respective towns.

Ben shouted, "Where are you taking me?"

"Somewhere special. Somewhere very special," Kevin answered.

Ben started to panic at the sound of Kevin's voice. "David? Doug? Are you there?" He heard no response. They must be in a different group. He heard the engines of the truck fade.

"Attention prisoners," Michael announced. "Follow me now. Just listen for the sound of my voice." They followed him as much as they were lead by the chains around their ankles. They could hear that they were in the woods: leaves crackling, birds singing, insects buzzing. All the deputies were with them. They watched them to make sure nobody escaped or got hurt. Grace, Kaylee, and Kevin sat on logs in the woods next to the ruins of the Longshore Bar. They looked at the new skeleton and the half-started wood building that was going to be the bar.

"Oh, guess what?" Kevin said. "I am going to be a director. I got a promotion and I will lead my own group in the CIA agency. I am going to pass on the karate lesson business to my son now. Uhh, Kaylee, I was wondering if you would let me volunteer to help you if something big comes up?"

Kaylee suspected that she knew how he knew that she still had big jobs coming up. She looked at Grace. "What do you mean, big?"

"Wait, I forgot to tell you that he already knew about the strange creatures."

Kaylee was puzzled now. "Did George tell you that?"

"Yeah, strange creatures. I can bring you over there for a visit with the authorities, but you need an ID to work with the CIA. This doesn't mean you work for the CIA daily—I know you don't want that. This is just in case something big comes along. Strange creatures or whatever. Tell me you'll accept my offer? I just want to help you."

"Yeah, I believe George told him," said Grace, "but I can see that he really wants to help us destroy the strange creatures. I think that would be good idea. We need him because he can find out fast if there are national or international connections. It would be good to have his credentials backing us, especially if we needed to travel quickly or get into trouble. Not that we'd get into trouble, but just in case."

"Do I earn money for working with the CIA?" asked Kaylee, ever practical.

"Yeah you would earn money. I would bring you on as a special consultant. And it would only be on important cases when I need you to save the world." Grace and Kaylee looked at each other and smiled. They thought it was a great idea.

Eric drove to Acton and headed into the woods to meet Frank and his deputies. He was to drop off one row of prisoners, which included Doug. Then he drove to Bolton to met Harvey and his deputies in the woods. Once again, he dropped off a row of prisoners, this one included David.

In Bolton, the men and women prisoners were in a line with their hoods still covering their faces. Frank looked at his list and noticed the name of Doug McDonald.

"Would Doug McDonald please step forward?" Doug stepped forward. Frank ordered his deputies to remove the hoods from all the prisoners. Once this was done, the prisoners saw that vampires surrounded them with their fangs out. The panic and fear could be felt in the air.

Frank gave a short welcome speech to the humans. "Humans, you are here because you were on death row or going to spend your life in prison. Here today, your sentence will be carried out. We are the perfect weapon for your death." The prisoners gasped. Could the justice system really do this?

"I don't want to die! Please no!" Doug begged Frank.

"Humans, some of you are being punished for being silver people who killed vampires, others for killing other humans. Regardless, my deputies and I will drink all your blood, including you, Doug."

Doug gasped, scared. Frank looked at Doug. Some of the other prisoners might become marked humans and regular feeders for vampires, but not today. "Kill them all, now."

The vampires attacked the humans and made quick work of killing them. Frank saved Doug for himself. He wanted to be sure he was completely and totally dead when he finished.

In Acton, it was much the same story for David Lawrence and the other prisoners. Harvey ordered his deputies to remove the masks from all the women and men, including David. The prisoners gasped in fear and panic when they saw the fangs. Harvey gave the order and the prisoners were put to death quickly.

In all the towns it was the same—some particularly sexy humans were made into vampires and the remainder were put to death and their blood used to feed vampires.

Kevin was sitting in the driver's seat of the truck. "Thank you. See you all soon when the Longshore Bar opens."

Grace and Kaylee waved to him as he drove away.

"The deputies and I are waiting for our large meal," Eric said. "Come on, let's go. Would you both like to join us?"

"Uhh, I am not interested," Grace replied. "Whatever deputies want to do is fine with me. You go ahead, but me, I am too squeamish."

"Kaylee?"

"Remember I am a baby. In this instance I am happy to keep it that way. Do what you need to do, kill what you need to kill. We need time to get together alone later, okay?"

Eric knew that new vampires are often scared of trying to kill humans. The fear diminished with age and experience.

Eric chuckled. "All right," he said as he headed out to join the others, but Grace stopped him.

"Wait. Can you save some blood for me but not bring me their body, please?"

Eric chuckled, "Sure." Grace was beginning to grow up. He left them and sped into the woods.

Eric, his deputies, and some other vampires who lost their marked stood in line in Millbury. Eric called out, "Please step forward, Ben Sullivan?"

Ben stepped forward. Eric ordered the deputies to remove the hoods from the prisoners. "Welcome. You have all broken human or vampire law and are here today for your punishment. You are being put to death, and we are the weapons."

Ben shouted, "Noooo! Don't kill me! I have two sons who need me, wait! Am I to become a vampire like you?"

"Vampire? Hell no. Your boys are already over 18, they don't need you anymore. You are to die today and stay dead."

"Oh God. Wait, isn't it illegal for a vampire to attack a human for blood?"

"You murdered vampires. How is this different? You have all been sentenced to death, what should it matter how you die?"

Ben gasped and yelled, "Nooo!"

"Kill them now!" The vampires attacked the prisoners, and Eric saved Ben for himself. After a short time, the prisoners were dead or dying.

Eric looked around and said, "Go ahead, deputies, drink them until they are empty. I will honor you with his body. You can hang it as decoration. Here we will remember that he murdered vampires for the first time in our history. His body is yours, but I want his head. I want it for my office in the rebuilt Longshore."

"Sure, boss," said Joseph as he wiped his mouth.

"Great idea. You need a new skull since the other one burned," said Michael.

Kuruk and all the other deputies took a small drink of Ben's blood.

Kaylee and Grace knew what was happening and were pacing in the living room. They knew the basics but didn't want to know the exact details.

Kevin arrived home, worn out by his long trip. Kevin's wife was in a good mood. She handed him some clothing and said, "Wear this and come to bed. I want to see you in it."

Kevin sighed, "I am very worn out. I've had a very busy day driving all over." She interrupted him with a passionate kiss. "All right, give me a minute to change," he said. He took the clothes into the bathroom to change. His wife changed into her Silver Vampire sexy clothes. She watched him walk out of the bathroom.

"Whoa, that's really sexy! Dance for me."

Kevin started to flirt with his wife then saw what she was wearing. She was dressed up like the Silver Vampire. "You can't do this," he said. "You can't dress up like that. It is just too…I just can't."

"Really? I like it." She put a few sexy moves on him. He fell forward on the bed. "Come on, sweetie." He started to snore. His wife stared at his ass in the leather pants and grabbed his butt with both her hands.

Kaylee and Grace sat on a blanket in the yard of their old house. The looked up at the sky and Grace drank some blood.

"Thanks for giving me Mom's visions. I only wish I could play the lottery!"

"You deserve half the power. I only wish I could give you more. You are the best big sister ever!"

"You have such a good heart. I can't believe you are a vampire now. I never thought it would happen like this. I'm kinda sad that I will never get to see your grandchildren and great-grandchildren. This is the end of our family tree. It's dead right here."

Kaylee chuckled, "Yeah, this all surprised me too. Oh, wait. Speaking of children, kids can see my silver eyes even with glasses on and they know I am a vampire even without me showing fangs."

"Really? Well, vampires aren't allowed near any human children. If any are out now, they are in bigger trouble than we would be since it is way past their bedtime!"

Kaylee laughed, "Right."

"Did your angel tell you about any of this?"

"No, nothing at all until George bought up this issue."

Grace chuckled, "What a crazy adventure. Oh, smell the honeysuckle!"

Kaylee sniffed. "Oh man. I can't smell. I can't smell humans or animals or any foods or or even bathrooms."

Grace chuckled. "Really? Oh good. I need that power because I hate smelly bathrooms! It's probably because you have no prey. What else is new? Do you have any new powers or abilities? Did your angel give you any hints?"

"My angel told me to figure out what I am and learn some new things about my powers on my own."

"So what have you got so far? The silver magnet thing? Children under 12 can see through your disguises? You can't smell at all? Any others?"

"George told me I am supposed to sleep like a human being daily. It will depend on how much energy I use. My angel didn't tell me this at all."

"Sounds like he had true visions," Kaylee said.

"Also, my body likes to float in the sun when I rest. It is like a magnet."

"Yes, I've seen you do that."

"He said something else about the sun, but he didn't finish. I wish he'd said more."

"I have questions too," Grace reflected. "I need to figure out why I can't see visions of you or Eric. Sometimes I see Joseph. Maybe I need to train myself more or maybe they are blocking me? That's what I need to work on."

"That's weird…Eric feels you?"

"Yeah, Eric can feel me, and the other deputies, well—" Grace stopped talking when she heard a moo coming out of the woods. They looked in that direction and saw a cow walking. They cheered and laughed. Their cow had returned.

Eric wore his formal white wig and blue jacket in his role as judge. He spoke to a vampire couple. "Here's your dead marked vampire. You need to sign here. I hope you are satisfied with him. You are responsible for him, and you need to explain vampire law and traditions to him. That can be a tough job, especially until he is about six months old. In about a week, you and your marked have to come back and sign for him so he can get a new ID issued. Do you understand all of that? Good luck to all three of you." The couple departed, the man carrying the dead body over his shoulder.

Michael knocked at the door to Scott's place. He knew both sisters were home. Kaylee opened the door.

"Hi, come on in!" Michael walked in, smiling.

"Hi, Eric wants you to wear clothes from when you were last human. We need you to meet at the office. He has a surprise for you."

"Do I have to wear the silver clothes that I wore as a human?"

"Correct. Wait, you knew this all along?"

"Yep. See you there!"

Grace stood up and walked over to the foyer. "Hello, Michael. What are you guys talking about?"

"Never mind. I will see you there," he said to Grace.

"Wait, I don't have anything to wear from when I was last human."

Kaylee smiled, "I already took care of that. You don't know that I saved the clothes you last wore as a human."

"What? Let me see them."

Michael made a face because Kaylee already knew about vampire tradition, even before she became a vampire. "Don't show me," he said. "I want to be surprised. Just meet me at the office in 30 minutes." He took off.

Kaylee closed the door. Grace made a face and said, "I can't believe you kept those clothes for me for all these years."

Kaylee searched the few boxes they had left after the fire and found a box that she had saved for Grace. She opened the box. "Remember this?"

"Holy shit! Well, screw this. I hate these clothes. They are out of style."

"Come on, you have to wear what you were wearing the year of your death."

Grace really didn't want to wear the clothes, but she accepted Kaylee's word that this was vampire tradition.

At the office, they found Kuruk wearing very old leather clothes with feathers, beads, and shells carefully sewn on. He had animal skin boots and a bow in hand. Joseph wore a knight's helmet and chainmail. He had leather boots that showed the wear of someone like a solider who used them daily. Michael wore poor clothes that were nearly colorless and threadbare from his days as slave on a farm. Eric wore what looked like a mixture of knight's armor and a uniform. "This is a rather confusing outfit," he explained. "I was a spy working for my king and a soldier."

Grace still looked confused, but she kept silent. The sisters stared at the vampires. Their antique clothing suggested they had been vampires a long time.

"Wow…interesting. You guys have been around a long time."

Kaylee was curious and asked, "Does it overwhelm you to see such change and have to learn so much new information every day?"

"Yeah, it did at first," said Michael.

Kuruk agreed, "There have been big changes in my vampire lifetime."

Eric smiled, "That's what we call Live Fast. The language that I spoke as a human has died away. It died before you were even born as a human. Vampires live a long time."

Kaylee was wondering if she could get a picture of them in their clothing. It would be quite spectacular to get such a clear timeline.

Grace looked at her sister and asked, "How did you find out about their clothes and all of this?"

Kaylee could see that Grace was getting really upset. "You will learn this too."

"Wait a minute. You knew this all along?"

"The antique clothing display is for deputies only. It is a way of showing that they are the oldest members of our community. It is symbolic of them being the wisest as well."

Grace was a little indignant, "Thanks a lot. If you knew about this tradition, why didn't you tell me?"

"Look, I love you. It is nothing serious, all right? Now you know too."

Grace was still a little mad, but she was willing forgive her. "All right."

Michael already knew that Kaylee understood vampire traditions, but this was a surprise to the other deputies. Kaylee was just like an old sheriff because she always knew things.

"What we wear honors our life as a human as well. We take that wisdom with us into our vampire life. Grace and Kaylee, will you do me the honor of becoming deputies with us?"

"Seriously?" Grace said. "I thought that only the oldest vampires could do that. Isn't that what Kaylee just said?"

"Yes, normally, but you both have helped to bring us a great peace from silver people and helped us gain equality. It would be an honor. Would you accept this offer?"

“Hold on for a moment.” Grace pulled her sister with her over to a corner. The deputies watched them whisper in private.

Grace and Kaylee came back to them. Kaylee said, “We have one question before we make a decision. Will you all help us defeat the four creatures and allow me to see the human Kevin Douglas?”

“I don’t think so…”

“Listen, we aren’t going to share our lives with him. We just want to work with him and go on these four quests with him. That’s all.”

“Do we have to?” Michael crossed his arms over his chest.

“Would it really be just the one human, Kevin?” Kuruk asked.

“Wouldn’t this require us to change or make new laws?” Joseph asked Eric.

“No, we cannot change our laws and I am reluctant to make a new law without some precedent.” Eric paced a bit. “What if we don’t agree? What are you going to do?”

“Well then,” Kaylee said, “I can’t accept the offer to become a deputy. I want you to want me to be a deputy. This is a good bargain. I have a lot of skills and I am gaining a national reputation. These could be assets to our community. I am also able to work during the day and with humans. That could really help build up a shared economy. And I haven’t even started on Grace’s skills. Just think of her visions and how useful that could be.”

Eric was not sure what to do. There had never been a negotiation for a deputy before. It has always been the eldest vampires in a community. No questions, no bargaining. He paced some more.

“All right. I accept your offer, but understand that when it ends, you must stop seeing Kevin. Deal?”

“Sure, but what’s the point? He’s human, his life is short.” The deputies chuckled. She was fitting in very well in the vampire world.

Eric chuckled and agreed, “Deal. Welcome, young sheriff Kaylee and sheriff Grace. You are the first young deputies in this century. I will teach you our ways. We will come up with a plan to deal with these four creatures. And remember that Kevin is the only human whom you are allowed to see, and I am boss of this group—obey me. You cannot tell other vampires that you are our new deputies. I am not ready to tell them yet. It's too complicated. Now kneel on floor." The girls knelt and Eric's sword touched their shoulders. "Here's the oath: On your honor, do you pledge to never betray your community, your integrity, your character, or the community's trust? You must agree to always have the courage to hold yourself accountable for your actions and serve your community and country." They both nodded. "On behalf of the vampire community of Millbury, congratulations," he said to them.

Kuruk brought five glasses over. In four of them he poured H-Blood and he left one empty for Kaylee. They clinked glasses, toasting each other. Kaylee used the empty glass and cheered along with the others.

"Congratulations, young deputies!" Kuruk bestowed a rare smile upon them.

"How about a picture together?" Michael offered, knowing they had many pictures in their home before the fire.

"Deputy Kaylee, change your clothes." Kaylee was happy to hear those words and changed into her leather clothes with a wave of her hand and a few words. "Oh, and can you explain why there is a cow in the backyard? Is it truly yours? Or did you steal it?"

She was so happy now. She was not only a deputy but also she and her sister could live together out in the open. And they had their cow back.

# CHAPTER 23

Joseph and Kuruk shared an apartment. Joseph sat in the kitchen and was talking on the phone.

"Can you believe she could fly? How is it possible that she is such a baby vampire and became the youngest deputy ever? Eric broke the law and let her become a vampire instead of killing her. She was a human living with her sister who was vampire." Joseph listened for a moment. "Yes, I am working on it, sir."

A month later the Longshore Bar had a grand re-opening. The bar was open to everyone—vampires and humans. Kevin walked into the Longshore Bar alone with two long tubes and sat down at a table. The bar had been open for about three hours.

Grace noticed Kevin when he walked in and she joined him at his table. "Hi, how you doing?"

"Hi, I am good."

"Don't you love the bar?"

"Yeah, it looks good in here."

Eric noticed them and came over, but he didn't sit down. "Hi Kevin, how's everything going?"

"I've been quite busy with all the new civil rights for vampires and governmental changes. I am glad the uproar is over though and we can get down to the business of real life again. I am truly pleased to see you again."

"That's good. Can we talk? Please, come to my office."

"All right, if you don't mind?" he said to Grace as he stood up.

"Yes, sure, go ahead."

Eric led Kevin to his office, where Kevin noticed that door had a sign barring humans. Eric looked a little sheepish. "That doesn't apply to you," said Eric as they entered the office.

Kevin looked around and saw the skull penholder on his desk. He pointed to it and asked, "Is it real?"

"Yeah it's real. That was Ben Sullivan."

Kevin took a step back and said, "Wow. I am not sure what to say to that."

"I had one in my office before the fire. I am happy to have a replacement."

"I am glad he's dead, though I am not sure I would need that kind of souvenir."

Eric chuckled. "Right. What is in this tube?"

"Oh, this is for you. For the bar."

"A gift for me?"

Kevin handed the tube to him. "Yeah."

Eric opened the plastic tube and pulled out two papers. They were posters of the Silver Vampire. "Thank you. That was kind of you." He had just the spot for them in the bar.

"You're welcome."

"Hold on for a minute." Eric picked up the phone and said, "Kevin is here in my office." Then he hung up. Eric walked out of the door with his poster. He called over to Joseph. "Joseph, put this poster over there in the frame, and keep the other for me."

"Sure, boss."

"Thank you," said Eric as he headed back to his office. He closed the door and looked at Kevin. "Kaylee will be here in a second. Move a little to the right—that is where she jumps in. You can see the ring on the floor."

"Oh okay," Kevin said as he moved his chair a little to the right. A moment later, Kaylee appeared in Eric's office.

"Hi Kevin, how are you doing?" she asked as she hugged him. She was dressed to sing with her hair up, make-up on, and even high-heels. She still wore her glasses.

"I am good and very busy. You look fabulous, my girl." Eric's mild growling reminded Kevin that Eric didn't like it when he called her his girl. "Sorry," Kevin said, winking at Kaylee.

"Ignore him. So should we discuss the four creatures?"

"Now that I am director of my agency and have more control over missions, I can help you."

At the bar, Joseph, Kuruk, and Michael looked at the Silver Vampire poster.

"She looks sexy," said Michael.

"She could be a model," commented Joseph.

"She's the most famous vampire in the 21$^{th}$ century, possibly ever in history."

In the bar, Grace could hear some of the other patrons talking about the poster. The vampires kept talking about her sister. She'd have to get used to her being famous.

"Where can I find her?" one dark-haired vampire said to his blond companion.

"She's hot."

"I wish I could see her face."

"I wonder what her real name is."

Grace looked over at the poster. It was really good. The deputies walked over and she joined them at the bar. "Oh, the poster is fabulous."

They agreed. They overheard the vampire next to Grace say, "The Silver Vampire is hot. Wish I knew where she lived."

The deputies all looked at each other and smiled. "Maybe she lives in a cave or is homeless?" said Grace.

They all laughed, and Joseph said, "She thinks she's so funny."

Kaylee walked onto the stage. Eric stood by the stage and Kevin went and sat alone at a good table. Kaylee talked with the band for a moment.

"Hi everyone, I am Kaylee and welcome to the new bar. Let's celebrate!" She picked up the microphone and began a song with the band.

Grace noticed that Kevin was sitting alone and decided to join him. "I am so excited. It has been a long time since I've heard her sing."

Carolyn, the hostess, came over and asked if they wanted a drink.

"A-Blood," said Grace.

"Uh, ginger ale, that's all."

Carolyn left the table as Kaylee started singing. Everybody in the bar stopped to watch her. Harvey, Frank, and their deputies came in just then. They wanted to check out the bar. They nodded in approval, and most of them headed over to the bar.

The crowd was a mix of humans and vampires, but they were all enjoying Kaylee's singing. Eric stood by the end of the bar and couldn't keep his eyes off her. Frank and Harvey joined him.

"Kaylee?" said Frank. "I am impressed with her talent." Looking around, he could tell that the crowd agreed.

Kevin looked at the stage and took a sip from his drink. "She has the voice of an angel."

"Yes she does," smiled Grace.

*The End*

Made in the USA
Lexington, KY
31 July 2015